Clean Sweep

KATIE CROSS

KCW

To Cindy-Mom.

Thanks for giving me your son.

Chapter One

LESLIE

Something fuzzy lived in the dish at the bottom of my fridge and it had been there for over a week now.

The old ceramic dish had a glass top so I could peer inside. At best, the contents appeared mushy and gray, with a slight green tint around the edges. Mold, for certain.

Never mind that my divorce had been final for over a year now, Mrs. Cortez still brought dinners for me and my son like we actively mourned my first marriage.

No, that thing *needed* to die. In fact, that marriage had died long before the divorce drove a wooden stake in its soul-sucking, vampiric heart.

Not for the first time, I regarded the moldy dish, shuddered, and closed the door.

"Not right now," I whispered, then crept away, like it would grow across the floor after me.

Coffee almost sloshed out of my mug as I set it on the table and called out, "Blake! You have five minutes before you have to leave. If you're tardy, you'll get detention and I am not saving you again."

An unintelligible, teenage grunt followed. I fought not to roll my eyes, but at least the thudding music quieted a little. I passed by a load of clothes that Blake still hadn't taken upstairs even though I'd graciously folded them in piles on the table. Most of the time these days, he dressed himself from the dining room.

Beneath the table lay carpet that needed a good vacuum a few weeks ago. Various parts of my kitchen and entryway boasted floorboards that weren't gray, but *appeared* to be from gathered dust. One wall collected cobwebs at the seam like an old lady would cats. Behind me, the dishwasher let out a groan as it attempted to clean an overly-full load I'd forgotten to start last night.

"Hello, Monday in the middle of November," I muttered, then sighed.

My phone chimed with a text from my oldest of four sons, Landon. At twenty-three and *almost* accepted into medical school, he currently finished up his last semester of his under-grad in Jackson City. It was a bigger—but still not big—mountain city forty-five minutes up the canyon from here in Pineville. He'd saved up all his online classes for his final semesters so he could move to Jackson City, work, get a hold of debt, and still graduate on time.

Sensible, this kid.

Landon soothed my Mama nerves every time I saw his name. Easy going. Hard working, but wasn't obnoxious about it. His latest girlfriend of four weeks showed real promise this time.

Not like all the others, anyway.

Landon: Can I come home Saturday for food?

Leslie: Sure. Your favorites?

Landon: You're the best. We'll be there at noon.

I paused.

Although he'd been idly mentioning a woman named Starla every now and then, there had never been a *we* attached to anything.

In fact, he'd almost disappeared since they started to officially date. Not only had I not met Starla yet, but I knew nothing else about her except her name and a vague mention of a *super awesome first date, Mom. Tell you about it later.*

Leslie: We?

Landon: Yeah, I'm bringing Starla. I proposed to her last night, thought you'd want to meet her. This seemed like a good time.

I blinked.
Wait, what?

Leslie: I'm sorry, you did what?

Landon: It's a conversation better to have in person, but didn't want to spring too much on you at once.

Leslie: Is this a joke?

Landon: No. It's a long story. Could we have BBQ instead of pasta?

"No," I murmured. "This . . . this has to be a joke."

Landon is not the son that would casually mention a proposal or break life-changing news to me over a text message without any contextual basis at all.

Certainly not after dating for four weeks!

This was something my second-oldest son Max would do, because he fell in and out of love every twenty seconds.

Not Landon.

Furious, I tapped the phone icon and listened to it ring in my ear. He denied the call, then texted back.

Landon: Can't talk now. At work. Later.

"You did not just decline me," I growled.

Blake descended the stairs, thudding like he stomped out cockroaches on his way down. He zoomed by, a blur that managed to snatch his car keys before disappearing out the kitchen door with a "Bye, Mom!" tossed over his shoulder.

I sent a vague wave in response.

With all my control, I stopped myself from calling Landon again. I settled on the most threatening I-brought-you-into-this-life-I-can-take-you-out-of-it message I could conjure with so little brain capacity left.

Leslie: We WILL talk later, young man.

Landon: Thanks, Mom!

Sensing that he must be nervous about this—or he would have told me about it already—I schooled my inner Mama Bear and gave a calm reply.

Leslie: We'll eat at six. See you then.

Then I set my phone down and screamed like a wild banshee.

* * *

After a few deep, calming breaths, I paced across my kitchen.

My fourth read-through of the conversation allowed the truth to gain full hold in my mind. With it came a flush of cold as brittle as the winter mountain wind.

My brilliant, would-be-a-cardiothoracic-surgeon-and-always-followed-through-responsibly son had just proposed to a woman he'd been dating all of four weeks.

Four.

Weeks.

My heart did a double whomp for a tenth time. Pretty soon, it wouldn't restart. I leaned back against the wall and stared at the floor. Shock made me almost entirely mute. My mouth opened, then closed while my brain looped around that single line.

I proposed to her last night.

I proposed to her last night.

I proposed to her last night.

Unable to stay still, I began to pace again.

The tile floor squeaked under my shoes every time I turned. Something in the weird noise calmed me. It gave me a thing to wait for. Something that wasn't the crash and demise of my only child that didn't think like a caveman. The only one who *called* on a regular schedule, for cripes sake.

I stopped, turned to the fridge, and grabbed a permanent marker. Now that Landon was bringing home a fiancée, there was so much to do.

List time.

My thoughts moved faster than my hands could write as I scrawled tasks across my favorite bright green sticky notes. A sense of relief followed as I peeled each note off and slapped it onto the counter.

By the time I'd emptied my brain of the populating tasks, a pile of green awaited me.

One at a time, I placed the sticky notes on the wall under different headers. **Food** went next to **Work** which sat next to **Non-Alcoholic Divorce Recovery.** Leading the battle for tasks-I-couldn't-care-less-about was **Cleaning**.

Laundry, dishes, floors, dusting?

"No thanks," I sang under my breath.

Then I sucked on my teeth as I studied a pattern of notes that, to my delight, resembled a Christmas tree.

Thanksgiving was next week, which had its own to-do list. Merging the two of them just asked for disaster.

My gaze lingered on the far column again.

Cleaning.

Blerg.

After raising four boys—five if you included my ex-husband, which I did for at least the first fifteen years—then I'd been doing house management and housekeeping for the last twenty five years. Ethan and I had married young. He was twenty two, I was barely twenty, and I had Landon before my twenty-second birthday. Which put me at forty-five. Two-point-five decades and a still-messy house to show for it.

Why had I even bothered?

While there was some satisfaction and joy to be found in the process and journey of raising my boys, that ship had long since sunk. These days, the last thing I wanted to do was mop. I'd earned my time off.

Now that I had daily work duties at the local Frolicking Moose coffee shop, home took a backseat for the first time in . . . ever. Also, it wouldn't kill me to get a new pair of shoes since these had holes in them.

The status of my house, my utter lack of conviction about cleaning it, and the fact that Landon would be bringing a woman—no, a fiancée—home on Saturday, meant it was time to do something I'd never done before.

Something drastic.

Something supposedly selfish, but probably not really. Something that I'd wanted to do for the last two decades but I had never let myself do.

Hire a maid service.

I grabbed my phone, searched for Dahlia, and tapped on the icon. Once I set it on speakerphone, I put the phone on the counter while it rang. Moments later, a bright voice called, "Aloha, boss lady!"

"Aloha, amiga."

Dahlia, barista at The Frolicking Moose, blew a light raspberry. "You're mixing your languages again."

"I know!" I straightened up. "Listen, do me a favor?"

"Always."

"On the cork board near the door is a list of papers offering local services, right?"

"Right," she drawled.

"Is there one that Celeste just put up a few days ago about a cleaning service? She said that she and her father were taking new clients in the area, or something."

Dahlia tutted under her breath, then let out an exclamation of success. "Yes! Right here. T&C's Cleaning Services. You want their number? You finally hiring out some help already?"

"You know it."

Dahlia cheered. "The Frolicking Moose is a big enough mess for you to clean up, you shouldn't have to take care of your house too. I'm with you, boss lady. I'll text you the info."

"Thank you!"

The phone cut off. Seconds later, a notification popped up with a contact page. Before I could talk myself out of it, I clicked on the number.

While it rang, I attempted not to think about my unhinged son. About the implications of a wedding in my life right now. No, there were enough celebrations for other people to plan, I didn't need another.

This whole thing was probably a big mistake. A phase. An I-did-something-stupid-and-I-feel-stuck kind deal.

Stuck.

Uh oh.

My stomach clenched. Sweet baby pineapple, as Lizbeth would say. What if the girl was pregnant?

All the blood rushed out of my head at once. I wasn't ready to be a grandma! Responsible or not, Landon *definitely* wasn't ready to be a father. He had medical school! A cardio-thoracic internship and . . . medical stuff to do.

A firm voice in my ear brought me out of my spiraling terror.

"Hello?"

The feeling of ice water flooding my veins sent me reeling, and I scrambled to get my voice back under control.

"Hey. Hi. Sorry. I just . . . I was . . . anyway—"

My mind became a snowy, blank canvas. I attempted to conjure up who I called and why, but all presence in the moment had disappeared under the terrifying thought that my son might have gotten someone pregnant.

I blinked.

Did I call someone, or did they call me?

"This is T&C Cleaning Services," the male voice said. A note of amusement lingered in his silky tone. His voice, while not as resonant as Maverick's, had a touch of smoothness to it, like ripples on a lake.

Singer, maybe?

Wait, what was I supposed to be thinking about?

My silence stretched too long. Cleaning services? Why would a cleaning service call me? Did Mav—

He cleared his throat. "Hello?"

Memory served.

Landon. Fiancée. Disastrous house.

"Right!" I cried, dragging a hand through my hair. "Sorry. Rough morning. Right. I called you."

"Can I help you with something?"

Aggravated now, I shoved away from the wall and resumed pacing. When had I become this scatterbrained? Oh, with the first pregnancy. There was no true recovery from that. At least I found myself back on the original path of my thoughts.

"Yes, thank you for your patience. I was calling to see if you could send someone to clean my house. Like . . . today. Or, at the latest, tomorrow."

A rummaging sound issued in the background, as if he sorted through paperwork. Beyond that, the distant sound of a truck backing up. T&C Cleaning Services meant I must be speaking with the owner, Tanner. His daughter, Celeste, went to school with Blake. Both of them were seniors in high school. I'd seen Tanner around Pineville now and then, but not often.

"Today?" he asked.

"It's a long shot, I know."

"Let me see."

While Tanner countered with a few basic questions about my house, I sank into a kitchen chair and gazed around with new eyes. The mess that I'd been ignoring for—oh, who needed to count the days?—suddenly looked a lot . . .

. . . worse.

"Today is pretty open," he murmured. "We had a last-minute cancellation. In fact, Yessica could be there around 9:30. Would that work?"

My gaze lifted to the clock over the table. Almost 8:00 now. I could be out of here before Yessica arrived and stay away all day at work. Someone else cleaned my house while I made money doing what I loved?

Yes, please!

"Should be perfect."

"What specifically are you needing help with?" he asked.

"Can you just come and take it all and I can start over new?"

My quip had been mostly joking, although I'd take the offer if he responded in the affirmative. Getting rid of all the old furniture and stuff left behind when Ethan left? Another easy hallelujah.

Instead, Tanner fumbled over his response for a moment. Out of experiential pity, I saved him.

"Just kidding. You don't have to take all my stuff." I tucked some hair behind my ear and leaned forward. "Look, on Saturday my son is bringing a woman home that he just proposed to after only knowing her for four weeks. I'm super busy at work and don't have time to clean. Scratch that, I could make time, but I just . . . I really don't *want* to clean."

"Okay."

"Frankly, I've done the whole stay-at-home-mom-clean-up-after-everyone thing for the last two decades and I'm over it. I couldn't care less about my floors if you *paid* me to care less about my floors. No one gave a damn then, and no one seems to care now. So sayonara suckers! I'm out of the cleaning game."

I gave a flippant salute to the ceiling, but had no idea who I meant. Of course my sons hadn't cared about the house, and Ethan hadn't been awake enough on a good day to consider something like, oh, laundry.

These were the thoughts the divorce stirred up in me the most. The ones I should have shared sooner.

On a roll now, I kept going.

"Still, I want to make a good impression on this woman. Also, I'm not a disgusting person, so this isn't a hovel, okay? It's . . . lived in. All right, it's chaos. Even with just me and Blake living here. I need help."

The other three words I should have said sooner.

I need help.

The end of my much-needed diatribe halted so quickly it left dead space. I paused. Had I overshared again? I had a thing about doing that. Apparently, honest details made other people uncomfortable.

"Well," Tanner cleared his throat, "we can help you out with that. A deep cleaning, maybe? We do floors, windows, dusting, counters, general clean up, that sort of stuff. We can go as heavy into details or as light as you'd like."

I closed my eyes and tilted my head back against the chair. "Deep cleaning would be great."

"I can't give you a quote until I stop by to look at it."

Over $1,000 had been burning a hole in my underwear drawer ever since the divorce finalized. Once I let Ethan officially go, my great aunt—who was somewhere between ancient and Moses's wife—sent me $1,000 with a card that simply said, *About damn time. Now go do something crazy.*

This was just the level of crazy that I needed.

"I don't care how much it costs."

"We . . . I'm sorry?"

"I don't need a quote. I want a clean house." I cut a hand through the air, even though he couldn't see me. "I want to walk out of this mess, then come back into something that sparkles and smells just a little bit like lemon. Organization would be great too. Also, the dishwasher struggles and my disposal sounds like something is dying inside, if Yessica is handy like that. No obligation on those two."

"Lemon," he repeated flatly.

"You got it. What else do you need from me to make this magic happen?"

He stumbled for a minute before he said, "Uh, I . . . well . . . just a credit card for a deposit to hold your spot."

"Done. Let my grab my card." Once we finished swapping details, I asked, "Do you need my address?"

"No, Mrs. Miller. I know where you live."

My cheeks heated, though I didn't know why. Tanner and I had never directly spoken before. Clearly, we knew of each other. Yet, the fact that he knew something as intimate as where I lived caught me by surprise.

Then again, Pineville was a *very* small town.

The use of my married name jolted me even more than the thought of him knowing my house. Yes, I'd been Mrs. Miller for years, but hearing it after the divorce still felt strange. Tendrils of my soul instantly called, "Foul! Foul!"

I wasn't, technically, Mrs. Miller anymore. I'd already changed my name back to my maiden name, Hill, as a way to accept my new reality. Leslie Hill felt strange next to Leslie Miller, like two women attempting to be the same person.

"Great," I said, and didn't bother to correct him.

"I think we're set."

Something stopped me, but I couldn't tell what it was. Witty repartee had been a usual strength of mine, but I had locked it up like a clam after the divorce. Now, it felt good to let the truth out.

This easy flow of conversation was a breath of fresh air. Tanner had been more tolerant to my conversation than responsive, but even *that* felt good compared to Ethan's heavy eye rolls and impatient breaths.

Also, I didn't want to hang up because of Tanner's smooth voice. The way he spoke reminded me of a silk ribbon in a breeze, particularly the rolling between words. It had a melodic tint to it.

"Thanks," I finally said. "I appreciate the help."

"No problem."

The call ended abruptly the next moment. I stared at my phone, perplexed, before I set it aside. A quick glance around the house confirmed my worst fears. Oh yeah. This place would take Yessica hours to get to the bottom of.

With a slap of my hands, I stood up.

Welp.

Not my problem anymore.

Chapter Two

TANNER

Yessica's phone rang for a fourth time.

Aggravated, I shoved a hand through my hair and leaned my head back against the headrest again. Where was she? We had a cancellation about twenty minutes before Leslie Miller —was it still Miller?—called with her desperate rant and hope for help. Yessica should already be halfway to our usual meeting point.

For a fourth time, her voicemail picked up.

"You've called Yessica!" she said brightly on the recording. "Sorry, I'm not—"

Her young voice disappeared when I clicked the phone off again. I'd already left two messages, a third wouldn't help. I growled. Yessica, my best cleaner, had never shown up late to an assignment. She kept everything in order, finished her houses on time, and made friends with everyone she spoke to. Her radio silence while I tried to confirm her pop-up appointment at Leslie's house meant nothing good. I had a feeling I knew *exactly* what this meant.

Determined to confirm my suspicion, I called one more time. The phone rang again in my ear. This time, a garbled voice picked up. Hearing someone else speak startled me so much that I nearly dropped my cell.

"Hello?" I said.

"Tannnerrrrrr," drawled a languid voice. "Hey, man. How are ya?"

I gritted my teeth at the sound. Yessica's only weakness and flaw had been the idiot she'd been dating for the last two years. Idiot was, perhaps, a strong word for Wesley. Fool might fit better, or complete-waste-of-flesh would be another.

"Wesley, is Yessica with you?"

"Yessica!" Wesley called, the phone held slightly away from his face. "Your boss is calling. Did you forget something?"

His irritating tone set my teeth on edge. A squeak followed. Seconds later, a breathless voice came onto the phone.

"Tanner? Oh, Tanner, I'm so sorry. I totally forgot."

"Forgot?"

"To call and let you know. Wesley and I eloped last night!"

The *clunk* of my jaw hitting the floor was my only response. For five seconds straight, I fumbled to form a reply. Yessica and Wesley had been engaged for two years now. She was in a constant state of wedding planning, because the date had been squirrely. Twice we'd passed the day she was *supposed* to get married. In hindsight, elopement wasn't a massive stretch.

But it still shocked me.

Wesley sang something in the background in a tone horribly off key. Knowing him, he did it on purpose. Then he laughed in a loose, half-drunk kind of way.

"Eloped?" I managed.

"Yes, I'm sorry." Regret stained her tone, at least. "I thought I'd covered everything that would need to be taken care of as we packed, but I forgot to request the time off. Please don't be mad."

"When will you be back?"

"Next week?"

My nostrils flared. "Next week? Yessica! We have eight houses booked in the seven days you'll be gone. What am I supposed to do?"

"I'm sorry!" she cried again. "Wesley found these red-eye tickets for a steal and then a Groupon for a resort place. I couldn't turn the offer down!"

A cheap flight and a Groupon for a resort. Next thing I knew, she'd be telling me their wedding dinner had a buffet.

"And the food here is wild," she continued. "Wesley can't stay away from the buffet."

I metaphorically threw my hands in the air. Sometimes, my fifty years of wisdom was almost obnoxious.

"Fine. Is this a resignation or just a huge mistake on your part? Because this is a big deal, Yessica."

"I know, Tanner, and I'm sorry. *Really* sorry. Just take it as a resignation, because I really don't know when we'll be back. Maybe we can talk when I get there, but I gotta go! The ice cream truck is swinging back by and we just scrounged enough coins from the sidewalk to share one. All the cleaning stuff is in the truck, organized the way you like it. Good luck!"

The call ended.

I set the phone down in my console and stared out the window, jaw tight. Is this what utter shock felt like? I'd lost my only rockstar employee over a cheap buffet and a kiddie ice cream cone bought with money found in the sidewalk cracks.

With a muttered swear word, I shoved my phone into my pocket and cranked the work truck back on.

Looks like I had a house to clean.

* * *

The physical release I would experience while cleaning Leslie Miller's house all by myself didn't ease the frustration of losing Yessica. I wanted to punch something, but I'd make do with rampant organization.

While my mind spun through how I'd get a job advertisement out, I navigated through Pineville. Pineville had something like 200 residents in the town proper. More were in the outskirts, but they hardly counted.

It was easy to know exactly where everyone lived, even though I didn't live here. Ten years as an assistant basketball coach and algebra teacher at the high school had given me intimate knowledge of the area. I'd left that job five years ago to start the cleaning company, but relationships lingered in the meantime.

Every school day, Celeste and I got ready early in the morning, drove down the canyon, and I dropped her off at the high school. We lived too far into the mountains for a bus to come far enough anyway. If she did hook up with a closer school bus, she'd be riding for almost two hours. In the spring when there wasn't snow and ice on the ground, I let Celeste drive herself.

A bit too protective, maybe, but I accepted that fault.

My trucks had a lot of miles on them, but it didn't matter. Celeste would graduate next spring and all of this weird routine would disappear forever. The time I had her in the car with me, one-on-one, made all of it worth it.

While Celeste went to school, I stayed in Pineville to work on odd jobs the company received, make phone calls, prospect clients, or to help Yessica.

Sometimes, I drove back to Jackson City to work from our home office there. We had a sister cleaning company in Jackson City that I also owned. If I didn't make it back to Pineville to pick up Celeste right after school, she hung out at the Frolicking Moose coffee shop to wait. Which is exactly why I knew Leslie Miller.

Because Celeste was *obsessed* with her.

A few lazy snowflakes twisted out of the sky as I pulled up to Leslie's house and pushed my truck into park. I stared at the exterior for a full minute.

A waist-high fence had a few boards that could be knocked back into place with a hammer. No gate either. No hinges even, like it had been ripped off. She had the snowy lawn of every house here. A pair of sneakers had been discarded on a porch filled with ice. A hose that had been detached, but not yet put away, lay on the ground.

"Should be great," I muttered as I climbed out of the truck. Tired appearance aside, Leslie's house was well-enough maintained. It was a far cry from dilapidated, but pride of ownership wasn't apparent.

I knocked on the door and called out, but no one answered. The door knob twisted, then squealed as it slowly swung open. Needed some oil, for sure. Like most Pineville residents, Leslie kept her door unlocked.

"Hello?"

When no one responded, I stepped further inside. All the lights had been turned off. The distant crackle of a dying fire kept the place from being still as a tomb. I shut the front door behind me and let my gaze travel around.

Automatic tallies populated the cost of cleaning in my head. After five years of business, that came as instinct now.

The other half of my brain began to wonder over Leslie's real story.

Celeste had given me tidbits here and there. Leslie had four sons. Blake, the youngest, attended high school with Celeste as a senior. I had coached or taught the other three various years ago. Leslie had divorced after twenty-some-odd years over a year ago, but they'd been planning it longer than that. She ran the Frolicking Moose as a manager and loved organizing parties.

The house was normal enough. Old, but upgraded with wooden floors, a thick oak mantel over a brick fireplace and a sad Christmas tree.

Had Blake chopped it out of the backyard? Limp garland stuck up over top of a piano with yellowing ivory. The tips of my fingers ran across the keys as I walked past, little blips of sound following like rain on a puddle.

The living room gave way to a small hallway that split into two bedrooms and a bathroom. Drawn curtains and a closed door on the far side, and a partially open door right in front of me.

I stepped closer to it and pushed the door open to a room with a queen sleigh bed and feminine clothes everywhere, like a dresser had exploded. Discarded jewelry hung off a mirror. I pushed the door farther, but met resistance. Shoes cluttered the ground behind the door, making it almost impassable.

Leslie's words came back to me.

I've done the whole stay-at-home-mom-clean-up-after-everyone thing for the last two decades and I'm over it. I couldn't care less about my floors if you paid me to care less about my floors. No one gave a damn then, and no one seems to care now. So sayonara suckers! I'm out of the cleaning game.

Interesting.

Mid-life mom burnout?

A very real part of me could relate. Although Celeste had a strong relationship with her Mom and saw her several times a month, Celeste had largely fallen to me to take care of for most of her life.

Some days, the thanklessness of parenting could suck the soul out the best of us. Besides, Leslie's boys had been bright, intelligent, and determined. Harnessing that kind of power for good must have been exhausting.

Celeste had told me more about Leslie before she headed off to school that morning. Over a cup of coffee she said, "Leslie is, like, so cool Dad. She's understands high schoolers without suffocating."

Whatever that meant.

While Leslie's name was a common word around town, I couldn't picture her in my mind. Interaction with parents as an assistant basketball coach had been minimal, but I could remember her husband, Ethan.

I backed out of her room and headed down the hall, then stopped near a crooked photo in the hallway. I straightened it without thinking, then tilted my head to study it.

Four youngish boys attempted to throw a woman into the reservoir. They were easy to pick out. Landon, the oldest. A star basketball athlete bound for big things in the medical field. Max, the second oldest. He'd lived, breathed, and died football, then went on to get a scholarship for college football back east. Then Nicholas, who had aced my advanced algebra class but focused more on wrestling. The youngest, Blake, was outside my time at the school.

In the picture, Leslie's sunglasses were skewed. She laughed, a bright, white-toothed smile almost obscured by dark blonde hair falling out of a hat. The four boys seemed to be laughing as they attempted to shove her off a pier.

I grinned. Yeah, this house that hadn't seen a deep clean in awhile made a lot more sense.

Vestiges of my own divorce lingered on my mind. For a year after, I didn't want to talk to anyone. Part of me had wished I could just erase all those lost years in a failing marriage and then move on, but that would erase Celeste. I wouldn't do that for anything.

No, the divorce had taught me how to swallow my pride, admit mistakes, and use time to get past it. Did Leslie have the same experience?

Divorcées, particularly ones as attractive and compelling as Leslie, were rare in these parts of the mountains. The mix of reality and humor in Leslie's voice when she'd ranted about cleaning her house for decades remained with me.

Why? Maybe because her honesty had been refreshing, to say the least.

Women probably processed divorces differently than men, but I couldn't even fathom how.

Didn't want to, either.

Instead, I continued my quick tour. More of the usual. General disarray. Dust in the corners, on the baseboards. Everywhere. A vacuum had clearly been run now and then, but only in the general living areas. She'd kept her living room normal enough, but the rest of the house had been left to its own devices.

But why?

Bills fluttered as I strode past the table. With a quick glance I saw something from the local attorney, a pay stub, papers from a bank—probably a mortgage statement—and receipts from the grocery store. Her divorce was, clearly, still apparent enough that it hadn't entirely subsided.

Questions lingered in the back of my mind, burning there.

Why did Leslie stop caring?

What finally pushed her to call my company for help?

Why did she divorce Ethan?

The questions plagued me as I headed back to my truck. There were cleaning supplies to gather now, and a whole house to scrub all by myself. It had been awhile since Yessica hadn't been able to take a basic job like this, and I looked forward to the feeling of setting things right.

Chapter Three

LESLIE

The back corner of the Frolicking Moose had become my world-domination home base.

I didn't love working in the middle of the coffee shop all the time. Too much noise, bustle, and distraction. If I had to accomplish a pile of sticky notes, I required silence and aloneness.

Thankfully, Bethany had included a decent-sized office into the renovation plans of the Frolicking Moose years ago, but I sometimes sat in the shop area just to remember what I really did here.

The Frolicking Moose was more than just a coffee shop. It was a community center. A place of refuge for many, particularly during the fire last summer. Pineville residents and tourists had slept in the parking lot and congregated in the store. Fire officials had eaten meals here and given quick updates during the mandatory evacuation of the north hills of Pineville.

People came to the shop for more than just nourishment, but connection. Mountain residents, starved for human interaction, craved the ability to see and talk to other people. Now, with the loft rented out as a HomeBnB, the Frolicking Moose also provided shelter and a safe place to sleep.

Caring for others was something I took very seriously.

While at work, I tuned out all the years of being a Mom, a wife, a homebody, a person that oriented herself around the lives of others, and stepped into my favorite role in the whole world: party organizer.

When it came right down to details, that's all my job entailed. I coordinated every aspect of an ongoing party that rolled from one day to the next.

That afternoon, I sat in the corner booth with my back to the shop and let the world unfurl behind me. Most people didn't talk to me when I sat like this, but it allowed me to keep a thumb on the general ambience.

Too busy? Okay schedule for the baristas? Check-ins for the loft at the right time?

As usual, Dahlia and the new barista, Katelyn, flowed through the long line of customers as easily as a gentle mountain stream.

In between inventory calls and texting Maverick details for his upcoming family reunion, my brain idly comprehended the fact that a girl named Yessica was cleaning my house. I'd be able to go home, take off my shoes, finish up the cornbread recipe I'd started, and have a glass of wine.

Why hadn't I hired a housekeeper sooner?

A bright voice caught my ear.

"You're here!"

I lifted my head as a ray of sunshine slid into the chair across from me. Celeste, a bright-eyed teenager with ultra-blonde hair, big braces, and an even bigger smile. She wore a subdued olive shirt with a pair of black pants. Her sprawling purse—she'd kill it as a mom with a bag like that already—dropped to the bench next to her.

"Hey," I said with a smile. "How was school?"

Celeste gave a flippant wave of her hand, her wrist popping. "Fine. I can't wait to be done. Senior year kind of sucks. But I submitted another college application yesterday, so that's exciting."

"Very exciting."

Her perfectly sculpted brows lifted. Celeste clearly had a mother who knew her way around a fashion magazine. Not only were Celeste's eyebrows expertly plucked all the time, but her manicures were usually on point. Someone had guided this girl into a natural state of flair.

"What about you?" she asked.

Her eager inquiry didn't surprise me. For all her teenage-naive-to-the-world happiness, Celeste had always been drawn to me. Why? I couldn't fathom, but she helped me stay connected to Blake's world so I kept tabs on things from a different perspective.

The urge to ask more about her parents had always followed me, but held back. They'd never come up naturally in conversation, and I didn't want to halt what we spoke about to pull it forward. I wasn't sure why. Something told me she might spook, and I liked that she felt like we could talk.

"More work stuff." I spared her the gory details of my son's phone call. "But Landon will be here on Saturday, so that's exciting."

"You love having your kids back."

I smiled. "I do."

Celeste leaned back in the seat. "Dad's picking me up soon. Said he was running a little late on a job and told me just to come here. Mind if I do some homework?"

I waved a hand toward the table. "Please, feel free."

"Thanks."

"Hey, boss lady," Dahlia called from the other side of the room. "Take a look at the espresso machine. The error message is coming up again and I can't get it reset."

I pulled in a sharp breath. That stupid machine would, one day, be on the receiving end of a bat wielded by me.

"On it," I called.

For the next ten minutes, Celeste poured over her homework while I fought with the machine. By the time I wrangled it back into submission, Celeste was gathering her books up.

A truck pulled up in front of the Frolicking Moose that I didn't recognize with a T&C sticker on the passenger door. Inside, I could just make out the silhouette of a man with darker hair. He appeared to be on his phone.

"That your Dad's truck?" I asked as I returned to my booth. Celeste collected all her paperwork and shoved it into her book.

"Yeah."

Celeste stood up, looping her bag over her shoulder. Somehow, she still looked chic, even with her hair a bit flat from a long day at school and a glazed look in her eye.

"His employee ran off with her crappy boyfriend this morning. He texted me during lunch and said he had to go clean a house all by himself today."

Something cold slipped through my veins. *Clean a house all by himself?*

Was it possible that . . .

No.

I barely managed to keep my voice this side of strangled. "A house?"

She motioned toward his truck with another flap of her hand. "T&C Cleaning. It's supposed to be Tanner and Celeste, but I don't want anything to do with the company after high school, to be honest. He'll probably sell it."

"Oh."

She shrugged. "He doesn't really care. He's just doing it until I graduate college, then he plans to retire somewhere. I mean, he's got the money so why hang around here?"

I swallowed hard. T&C Cleaners was a relatively new company to the Pineville area. While I didn't know the particulars, Celeste talked about living in the deep mountains outside Jackson City. Her father drove them forty-five minutes down a mountain canyon every day to come to school in Pineville.

Another lingering question about Celeste.

And her father.

"Your father cleaned the house by himself?" I asked, just to make sure I'd heard correctly.

"Yeah."

"Did he say anything about it?"

Her brow wrinkled. "No. Why would he?"

Relief flooded me. I didn't want him commenting to other people about the state of my house. Also, what did she mean he did it himself?

Huh.

I . . . supposed I was okay with him cleaning my house, but . . . I mentally fidgeted. Something didn't sit right with the idea of Celeste's father scrubbing my toilets, I just couldn't put a finger on what.

Celeste wrapped her thin arms around me in a quick hug, then disappeared out the door with a wave to Dahlia. I watched her go. Tanner remained a vague face in the driver's side of the car. He seemed to look up and right into my eyes, but I couldn't be sure with the falling shadows.

Just in case, I turned away.

"Tanner Beck is suuuuper hunky," Dahlia sang from behind the counter. "A veritable silver fox, if you will."

I scowled. Trust Dahlia to read my mind. Her use of his last name caught my attention. Beck. Why did Beck sound familiar? Celeste had been coming in here almost daily ever since this school year started, but I couldn't remember a time when she'd told me her last name.

"Silver fox," Katelyn agreed.

Katelyn, a thin girl with a quiet mein, light hair, and a different pair of designer glasses everyday always backed Dahlia up. Without Dahlia, Katelyn had been quiet as a mouse. With Dahlia, she found her courage.

"What are you talking about?" I asked them. "What's a silver fox?"

Tanner's headlights pulled out of the parking lot and into the main flow of traffic. They disappeared seconds later and I finally relaxed. Dahlia straightened, her glossy black hair shining around her shoulders.

"You know," she said, laughing. "A silver fox is a guy that's really attractive and middle-aged. Grayish hair. Handsome in that wise-to-the-world kind of way." She made a clucking sound. "That's Tanner. Hasn't reading romance novels with Lizbeth taught you anything?"

I glared at her.

She held up two hands in surrender.

"I wasn't thinking about romance," I said.

Yet, I had been thinking about *him*.

Though, there was no reason for her to know that. Even with concerted effort, I couldn't pull a mental image of Tanner into my mind. At best, I had a niggling instinct that he was *very attractive* and to *avoid him because of said attractiveness.*

Also, I'd been burying my head in the sand regarding men for years now.

"Look boss lady, I'm just saying that Tanner Beck is a really attractive, post-divorce, middle-aged man with a really sweet teenager that adores you and . . . he doesn't have a girlfriend or other female attachment right now." Dahlia's eyes widened. "I'm just sayin'."

I lowered back into my booth and desperately tried not to take the bait.

Too late.

Bait was gone.

My mind already spun out questions over what she'd just said. Mostly *should I be totally embarrassed that he cleaned my disaster of a house?* and *what kind of woman would let that kind of man go?*

"Fine." I threw my hands in the air. "I give up. I'll bite. How do you know so much?"

Dahlia squealed, rushed around the corner of the counter, and threw herself into the seat across from me, long locks flying. Katelyn remained behind the counter with a subdued, amused smile.

Dahlia's eyes widened. "Let me tell you *aaaall* the deets," she murmured, a wicked glint in her eye. She put Serafina to shame when it came to gossip about Pineville.

"Please no." I held up both hands. "Just tell me how you know so much about Tanner and Celeste."

Dahlia put a hand on her chest. "I run this town, please. I know everything that happens here."

Well, I couldn't argue that.

"Tanner divorced years ago, when Celeste was young. At least, that's what she told me," Dahlia said in her usual hushed tone, like a librarian had just scolded her, but she still wanted to be heard. "He's raised her, but she still sees her mother."

"Huh."

"No girlfriend for Tanner," Dahlia said. She folded her hands in front of her and peered into my soul. "No. Girlfriend."

"For cripes sake, Dahlia. I haven't even met the man."

"Maybe you should work on your priorities!"

I groaned. "My priorities are fine. They begin with this ridiculous fiancée dinner, involve something like Thanksgiving in between, and end with Maverick's family reunion over the Christmas holiday. A man? It'll just . . . that would mess up everything. Besides, I promised myself I wouldn't date until Blake was out of the house."

"You're a crazy *palangi,* boss lady." Dahlia sighed. "What if someone else snatches him up? He's beautiful and funny and still looks like a gym teacher, or something."

The idea of Mr. Beck spun through my head, but I forced it aside. No matter what he looked like, figuring him out would never be greater than my desire to see my ultra-clean house. If Tanner had just left, that meant he'd been there for the whole day. What would eight hours of cleaning look like on an invoice?

Didn't matter.

Auntie had my back.

"Fine, I won't go into any more than that." Dahlia leaned back against the seat. "I can see you're distracted. I'll just say that I think you should go out with Tanner."

"The last thing I need is another guy to take care of." I closed my laptop and gathered a few scattered invoices. "I just got rid of the one that hung around my neck for two decades."

"Tanner is not a guy," Dahlia said with a perfectly straight face. "He's a man."

With that, she slipped out of the booth and sauntered away. Katelyn pointed to Dahlia and mouthed, *what she said.*

I rolled my eyes, but couldn't get the ring of her words out of my brain for the rest of the day.

* * *

Maverick: Hey Les, got a minute to chat about the Mercedy family reunion?

Leslie: Tomorrow morning?

Maverick: Talk then. The rest of my siblings confirmed the lodge you recommended. All of us will be there on December 24th, kids included.

Leslie: I'll contact the lodge owner in the morning to finalize the reservation. He'll want the deposit. Shall I put it on the credit card?

Maverick: Please do.

With that taken care of, I shoved my phone into my purse and slipped out of my car.

Thudding music upstairs meant that Blake was already home. A rush of anticipation met me at the door as I threw it open, then my jaw dropped.

"Ah!" I cried. "Whose house is this?"

A gleaming tile floor awaited me as I stepped into the laundry room through the back door connected to the garage. *Gleaming* tile floor. I'd totally forgotten that the tiles had a sheen.

Lovely.

"Oooooh." I set my purse on a wiped-free-of-crumbs counter, next to a glimmering sink. Below, the no-grime floor continued to amaze me with yet more tiles. He'd even wiped down the front of the fridge and—gasp—did he organize my *magnets*?

Nice touch.

As requested, lemon lay heavy on the air.

Slowly, I walked through each room. I hadn't even cleaned up the stuff on the counters to make it easier for him, but Tanner had figured it out. No, he'd more than figured it out.

He'd *organized*.

The cereal boxes were closed, lined up, and alphabetized in the small pantry off the kitchen. Fridge had been wiped clean, veggies organized into various trays, and the lunch meat separated from the cheese and bologna that Blake loved so much.

Oh . . . this was a step beyond the pale. The man had removed the moldy dish on the bottom shelf. A quick glance over my shoulder confirmed that it didn't even wait in the sink.

No. The dishwasher purred. He'd *fixed* it. No more ugly cranking sounds.

Cripes.

This man hadn't just cleaned—he'd made a statement.

"Hey!" I called up the vacuumed stairs. "Blakester! Take a look at all of this. Isn't it wild? Like, we have white walls. Did you know that?"

Blake replied with something unintelligible, but I wasn't listening anyway. I'd already moved on to my room. The bed was made, the corners mitered, and the windows gleamed. The man had cleaned my *windows*.

Whaaaat?

Dazed, I wandered through the rest of my swept, mopped, and vacuumed floors. Dusted knickknacks, streak-free windows, no errant shoes laying around. For a while, I didn't want to sit down and mar anything. Then I noticed a piece of paper out of place on the table.

A note waited there.

Hope the lemon smell is strong enough.

—T

I blinked.

"Well," I murmured as I lowered into a kitchen chair, still a bit dazed. "Now I *have* to meet Tanner Beck."

* * *

My children had never made me nervous.

Okay, maybe the time I found one of them on top of the roof, ready to jump into a pile of leaves. Or when eight-year-old Max tried to write and sing a song of true love to the fifteen-year-old neighbor girl. Or any assortment of the medical procedures and surgeries that we had to go through. Seeing my boys had almost always brought me true joy and excitement.

Except for the next day, Saturday, when dread lived like a low burn deep in my stomach.

With my house miraculously still clean and BBQ chicken shredded in the slow cooker, my hands fluttered around to find something to do. Landon and Starla would show up any moment now. Blake played a game in his room while he talked to a girl on his headset, and I didn't even have work tasks to occupy me. Maverick had stopped sending incessant text messages about his upcoming family reunion because, for now, everything was on track.

Lizbeth popped into my mind, but I dismissed her. She'd sent me some new books to read by an author named Jess, but I didn't have the mental bandwidth for romance right now.

Or . . . ever, really.

The books remained unread in the dresser drawer of my nightstand, where they'd stay until Lizbeth descended on me with threats and fire. At which point we'd debate about romance again, her incessant optimism would drive me to roll my eyes, and we'd agree to disagree after I waved my just-had-a-divorce flag in front of her face.

She usually backed down at that point.

From romance, I turned my thoughts. Unbidden, they found their way back to Tanner. The weirdness of having a total stranger like Tanner not only clean my house—but also organize it—made me walk around and stare at everything as if I'd never seen it before.

What did he think of me now? Did he see me as harried? Inept? Desperate?

A bad Mom?

I shook my head. Wait. No. My house was no reflection on my parenting, thank you very much.

The upcoming Thanksgiving holiday didn't spur a large desire in me to decorate, but I'd pulled out a few of the long-time favorites. A cornucopia overspilling with different colors of pumpkins. Burnt orange and red leafed wreaths on the door. Mellow yellow lights draped behind some ivy outside, giving a gently-decorated glow. The autumn leaves scented candle did the rest of the work.

At least my house *felt* like fall.

When I stepped into the laundry room to shove a load in the washer just to have something to do, I stopped. A vacuum and a bucket filled with an assortment of cleaning supplies sat on the floor. I frowned. Tanner must have left this behind yesterday.

For a man as thorough and detailed as he'd been in cleaning, such a massive oversight seemed out of touch. Then again, hadn't Celeste mentioned he'd been here all day? Maybe he rushed to get to the shop to pick her up because he didn't want her to wait.

For almost a full minute, I chewed on my bottom lip in indecision. Should I call him?

No, that seemed weird too. What would I say? *Hey, great job cleaning up my disaster of a home.* That would be a little too on-the-nose about the situation. In general, I didn't like to acknowledge my messy house, even though everyone could see it. Denial made a cozy place to curl up for a while. Acknowl-edging a disaster just . . . made things a little too real.

Besides, if the number I'd called was a work phone, it might not even take text messages. I dismissed that thought almost as soon as it came. Who doesn't have cell phones these days? When I'd called before, he'd sounded out and about, not stuck in an office.

Besides, I didn't know where his office technically lived. The postage-stamp sized town of Pineville meant I could recite all the stores and their owners by heart, and T&C Cleaning wasn't one of them. He probably stored all the supplies in that massive truck he picked Celeste up in.

Deciding there was nothing for it, I sent the same number a text message.

Leslie: Hey! This is Leslie Miller. Actually, it's Leslie Hill now. Anyway, the house looks great. Thanks so much for the help. A vacuum and bucket of cleaning supplies was left behind. Can I bring it to you somewhere?

Was that too passive-aggressive of a way to let him know I'd changed my name? No. That was the least weird way to do it at this point.

Could I actually meet him somewhere? My gaze darted to the clock. Landon and his supposed fiancée would be here any moment now. Technically, I could take the vacuum to Tanner if it was somewhere local. Would prefer to, in fact. The thought of Tanner coming here and seeing me face-to-face in my house seemed mortifying.

But why?

Anyone else? I wouldn't have cared. I blamed Dahlia and Katelyn. They'd built him up, now his reputation preceded him and made me nervous. I couldn't deny my curiosity about him being a *silver fox*.

He's not a guy, Dahlia had said. *He's a man.*

"Of course he's a man," I muttered to myself. "What's the difference anyway?"

The difference was probably something significant that I

didn't want to face, so I snuggled deeper into my denial and pulled the blanket over my shoulder.

My phone buzzed with a new message.

Tanner: Ah, my bad. Can I drop by to pick them up in ten? Celeste and I are on our way to our first job of the day.

Dread pooled inside me. If it had been only him, I could have left the bucket and vacuum on the front porch and never had to face him. With Celeste, however, I wanted to see her. *Should* see her.

When it came to teenagers, everyone in the village had a responsibility to be present.

Leslie: Of course.

The vacuum and bucket waited for their owners in the living room, next to the front door, while I pulled plates out of the cupboards and arranged silver utensils.

My thoughts flittered around like deranged butterflies, going from Landon and his girlfriend-I-wouldn't-call-a-fiancée-just-yet, to Blake and homework, and back to Tanner and the note he left behind.

That blasted note about the lemon scent. Had it been an attempt to be witty? Had he been serious?

Why couldn't I get him out of my head?

The fact that a male had come to my house, organized it, straightened it, and cleaned it better than anything I had ever done didn't startle me. If he held that skillset, that was fine. But the fact that . . . what?

That someone *else* had done it? Someone else who was reputedly attractive, potentially available, and could be judging me for the state of my house?

That bothered me.

How old was I? Twelve?

I growled and shook my head. Fresh cornbread browned in the oven, only momentarily drawing my attention away.

The Tanner Situation bothered me mostly because he didn't have to help as much as he did. He didn't need to organize my cupboards, for one. Or wipe down my dust boards for another. Fix my disposal, my dishwasher, and a squeaky window.

Sure, I'd said deep clean, but he'd taken it a step farther than that.

Why?

Getting to the heart of my agitation set my teeth on edge, because then I knew exactly why I was upset about Tanner and my perfectly immaculate house.

He'd done it out of pity.

The residents of Pineville had been wonderful to me for the past twelve months. Like my aunt, they congratulated our decision to divorce because, for the last several years, we hadn't been all that happy anyway. Maybe longer, if I were frank with myself, but getting caught up in children and life and the flow of things meant we hadn't really noticed the drifting apart.

Until we did.

After Ethan moved out, friends had dropped off chocolates, flowers, dinners, offered to help drive Blake around before he had his official license, and any number of things. The help was heartwarming and lifesaving and I appreciated every act that came my way.

But now?

Now I had this. It had been a year since the official divorce, and two since the separation and discussion of it. What mourning that needed to happen had already happened. Pineville could let me take back control of our life now, thanks.

Tanner Beck included.

This idea percolated in my mind while I stewed around the kitchen, searching for utensils and items that I didn't really need. When a knock came on my door, I'd worked myself up into a gentle tizzy that already had a tone of scolding. So when I ripped open the door, I knew exactly what I'd say.

And everything died on my lips.

Celeste stood on the porch next to, presumably, her father. Startled, I quickly glanced at him from feet to head, and my heart gave an irritating little patter that felt like betrayal.

Holy cripes.

Dahlia wasn't kidding.

Tanner Beck was a man *and* a silver fox. He wore a pair of work boots and well-worn jeans that fit the way they were made to be worn—just right. He had an old black t-shirt underneath an unbuttoned flannel shirt the color of the deepest forest.

A sculpted face had silver stubble, just present, as if he forgot to shave that morning. He kept his hair cut short, particularly around the ears and the sides, but slightly longer on top where it carried a dark color with flecks of running gray. His eyes were a gentle, yet deep, hazel.

Such a striking gaze gave me pause once it met mine.

This silver fox had just scrubbed my really-gross-I-have-a-teenage-boy toilets. Before I could make an utter fool of myself, which I felt on my immediate horizon, Celeste threw herself into my arms with a squeal.

"Leslie! Hi. This is your place? It's adorable!"

I returned her hug, grateful to have an excuse to look away and gather my thoughts. My throat felt a little too tight for my own comfort.

"Thanks! I've lived here forever so I think it's a bit frumpy."

She shook her head as she laughed. "Anything you touch being frumpy? No way. It's perfect."

Did Tanner chortle inside at that? She hadn't seen my perfectly frumpy, disastrous house before he got his capable hands on it.

I pulled away to smile at her. As usual, she looked adorable in an outfit that had the markings of a professional designer, but had likely been scrounged together from discount store steals and serious dedication to flash sale sites.

A pair of distressed jeans, an oversized sweatshirt, and old sneakers completed her ensemble. The way she'd pulled her hair into a messy bun and kept it back with a headband had me totally impressed.

Celeste pushed a stray lock of hair back into her bun as she peered inside around me.

"Where's Blake?"

"Want to come in?" I rallied my courage and flashed Tanner a quick look to include him in the invite. He hesitated, but Celeste rushed in ahead of him.

"I'd love to!" she cried.

"Sorry," he murmured. "She's a bit of a rocketship."

"She's a wonder," I replied without quite meeting his eyes. "Come on in."

Celeste already studied photos on the opposite wall. The very ones that I'd almost scratched my ex's face off of after the divorce. Even when amicable, divorce totally sucked. It brought out new parts of someone that you thought you knew, even if it was the *go quietly into the night* side of them.

Seeing that new side of them is when you realized you'd been secretly holding your breath, hoping they would fight for you at the very end, when it really mattered the most. Most of the time, it turns out, the fight had already been taken out of both of you and no one tried to save anything.

That's when the pain really started.

I felt Tanner following behind us. Knowing he lingered

back there distracted me from my weird-divorce musings that had become more of the background as time passed by.

"We've lived here for twenty-six years now," I said, not sure if I spoke to Celeste or Tanner. Why would Celeste care?

I placed a hand in my back pocket as I gazed around. The place almost looked brand new after Tanner had finished cleaning it.

"We've redecorated and updated a few times but it might need another round soon."

"Looks great," Celeste said.

"Thanks."

The sound of the vacuum wheels turning caused me to spin. Tanner bent over to grab the bucket and I had to force myself to look away from a beautiful backside in that perfectly-fitting pair of jeans. Ogling Tanner in front of his daughter would be the height of weirdness.

Not to mention that that backside had just scrubbed my tile grout.

Still couldn't wrap my mind around it.

"Is Blake home?" Celeste asked.

"He's playing a game with someone upstairs. A girl across the country, I think? I don't know, they meet up online every Saturday morning for a few hours to play."

Her expression fell. "He sounds busy. I won't bother him, just wanted to say hi. Tell him I stopped by?"

"Of course."

Celeste smiled again, then headed back to the door. Tanner easily carted the basket and the vacuum to the truck that rumbled around town. A woman had driven it a few times, if I remembered correctly. Yessica, I would imagine?

I purposefully stayed back on the porch while they returned to their truck, as far away as reality could put me from Tanner Beck.

"Good to see you!" I called to Celeste, then to Tanner as

he closed the tailgate. "And thank you again. The house looks fantastic."

Tanner waved, but vaguely seemed to avoid looking my way. Which should have given me relief, but instead I felt a twinge of annoyance. Why couldn't hunky men be adorably awkward like in the movies? Instead, he was downright dismissive.

Maybe a touch . . . cool.

Or maybe I wanted a reason to not crush like a fourteen-year-old on him. Celeste walked backwards as she waved. "Good to see you again, Les!"

Before she made it to the sidewalk, and just as Tanner headed toward the driver's door, a familiar car pulled into my driveway. As soon as the wheels rolled to a stop and it parked, a lean body unfolded from the driver's seat. Landon shot out.

"Hey, coach!" he cried.

Tanner's head snapped up. A moment of confusion registered before a huge grin split his face. That ridiculous, white-toothed smile sent my heart into a mad whirl.

Hold the phone.

Coach?

"Landon Miller," Tanner cried, looking like a totally different person now. "My, my, look how you've grown."

The two of them collided in a man hug that would have sent shockwaves through lesser humans. While Landon thudded Tanner on the back and they exclaimed in surprise, Celeste pointed to them and mouthed, "Did you know about this?"

I shrugged, equally stupefied.

The title "coach" meant this could be a tricky story to unravel. Landon had always been humming in and out of sports. Basketball, soccer, frisbee golf, ultimate frisbee, you name it, he played it. Ethan had dealt with the coach side of things while our boys participated in different leagues through school or summer camps.

Ethan had always taken sports a little too seriously, and Max carried that flag now. Landon enjoyed the structure and achievement of different sports, while Max thrived on the pressure and competition. Nicholas had some interest, but he stayed solely focused on wrestling. Only Blake showed no interest in competition or sports and there was considerable distance between him and Ethan because of it.

While I'd attended as many games as possible, bought more jockstraps than I'd ever care to admit, and dealt with the laundry and medical fall-outs of all those sports, I hadn't met the coaches one-on-one much.

The mystery of Tanner Beck's familiar name?

Solved.

From the corner of my eye, movement registered in the front seat of Landon's car, which drew my brain away from attempting to remember Tanner. This time, my heart did another whomp for a totally different reason.

The fiancée.

Landon had a strong head on his shoulders and would go places after he finished medical school. He wouldn't wallow around this small town, accruing bitterness, debt, and a dependency on too much TV to get through the day.

Like his father.

This girl needed to carry that same torch, and it was a big pair of shoes to fill.

I straightened up. Through the windshield, I could see the girl in the front seat close her eyes, draw in a deep breath, then hurry out the door, as if she had to propel herself out. Once out, she slammed the door shut, then spun around.

Within moments she faced me. Her globe-like eyes widened, terrified, and filled with something I'd call hope.

I'd expected a diva with an agenda, to be frank. A controlling woman that snapped her fingers and received her magical wish. Maybe someone investing in Landon with the hope for a lot of money on the other side of medical school. Landon wanted to specialize as a cardiothoracic surgeon. Any woman would want the sort of prestige and stability that came with a life like that, even if it undoubtedly meant a long college life before he was good at what he did, and then lonely days while he worked too much.

A diva would be easy to release my stress over. Their fling would fade before the wedding. I could talk him out of a terrible decision and he'd come to his senses soon enough.

But this girl?

This was a down-home girl with full cheeks, freckles, and a bright expression. She wore a long shirt made out of checkered flannel that reminded me of a local ranch store. Her dark jeans flowed into knock-off boots that were sensible, but not ugly. The terror in her eyes told me all I'd needed to know.

My son had proposed to a girl.

And he would absolutely marry her.

Chapter Four

TANNER

Landon's firm grip on my shoulder, his bright eyes, and the general happiness about him sent a thrill through me. It wasn't often that I ran into my old basketball students anymore, but when I did, I remembered all the good times that came with coaching.

"Life is so good right now, coach."

Landon's eyes held a special energy as he said it. Without releasing me, he turned, canted his body, and revealed a girl with strawberry-blonde hair.

She stood just outside the car door and stared at the porch, where Leslie looked equally attentive to her. Both of them seemed a bit wary, maybe startled by the other.

Based on Leslie's furrowed brow and an expression of mild confusion, it was immediately apparent that *something* was going on here.

"Coach," Landon said with a final slap of my shoulder. "This is my fiancée, Starla. I'd love for you to meet her."

The sound of her name drew Starla's gaze away from Leslie. She turned to face us, a hesitant smile lingering there.

I motioned to Celeste to give me a moment. She had a

nose for drama, and I could tell her senses were on alert. She waved for me to go, and I had a feeling she wanted to see this unfold.

Celeste hadn't mentioned a fiancée or a wedding in her recent review of Leslie's life. If there had been one, Celeste would have mentioned it. Celeste leaned back against the truck, wide eyes glued to Leslie.

Landon led me over to his car.

"Starla, babe, this is my former assistant basketball coach, Coach Beck."

A quick smile illuminated her face as I held out a hand. "Please, call me Tanner. Coach makes me feel old."

"Good to meet you," she said.

Her voice had a quick, quiet, melodic tint to it. Her hands were clammy when I accepted the offered shake.

Right away, her subdued, easy personality was apparent. Perhaps a good match to Landon's intensity. On or off the court, this kid had always been moving, thinking, trying. It had been harder to get him to scale back than to move forward. Rumors around Pineville spoke about medical school, a scholarship based on merit, and several recognitions for high honors.

None of it surprised me.

"A pleasure to meet you," I said.

Landon tucked Starla into his side as he spun to face Leslie. The befuddled expression had cleared from Leslie's face, replaced with something like mild curiosity. I sensed a mask. Knew a mask.

"Can coach stay for lunch, Mom?" Landon called.

Shocked, I turned to stare at him. What did he just ask? Leslie opened her mouth, seeming equally shocked. I stepped forward, a hand held out.

"That's not necessary, Ms. Hill."

Celeste bounced to life. "Say yes, please! It smells so good."

I gritted my teeth and set a mental reminder to talk to Celeste about manners—and avoiding awkward situations at all costs.

Leslie's gaze darted to Celeste, then back to me. I thought they flickered to Starla for a moment, but couldn't be sure. Leslie's hands clenched at her side.

"Of course. It's fine. We have plenty of food. Please, come inside."

Well, what did that mean?

With a squeal, Celeste darted past me, rushed inside behind Leslie, and disappeared into the house. My thoughts broke apart.

Once Leslie left, Starla's shoulders dropped almost to her knees. Landon held her more tightly around the shoulder.

"You got this." Landon leaned down to whisper in her ear. "Everything is going to be just fine. I know she's going to love you."

"I'm fine," she said firmly. "Really. She didn't kick me out so . . . maybe we should just . . . I don't know. Break the air or something? Let's just tell her one thing. Don't mention—"

Landon cut her off with a finger to her lips.

I tried to step around them to give them a moment, but they seemed to have forgotten I lingered back here.

"No," Landon said, "let me handle this. I know my Mom. Let's just tell her everything and get it over with. We'll give her time to think about it and then talk later. We can do this."

"But—"

Landon put a hand on her shoulder as I attempted to dodge to the right, unsuccessfully. I could push them aside and get by, but that would only make things more awkward.

Finally giving up, I held back and pretended to study the eaves. Signs of Christmas lights from previous years lingered in the chipped paint along the edges. Would Leslie need help putting them up this year?

"It will be fine," Landon said in a soothing voice. "Trust me. My mom raised four boys. Nothing surprises her anymore."

"A four week fiancée clearly has!" Starla cried under her breath. "She didn't say anything to me. We just . . . stared at each other."

I closed my eyes.

Four-week fiancée? No wonder Leslie wanted a deep clean and called someone else. The thought of Celeste popping home with someone I didn't know and a ring on her finger after four weeks sent a shiver of something rather angry through me.

Nope.

This was the worst possible scenario. How had I forgotten the stupid vacuum? Did I curse God? Was this punishment for something?

"I've got this," Landon said. "We'll tell her the news about medical school and this won't seem so bad."

"Landon," Starla cried, her face in her hands. "This is the worst idea ever. I just don't think your plan is—"

"It's fine. I've got this. I'll take care of you now. We're in this together. We need to just break the ice and then talk to her about it later, okay?"

He cupped her face in his hands. I turned my back and wished myself on Mars. Maybe Jupiter? Someplace that didn't have air so I could focus on the panic of death instead. I'd take that.

Anything but this.

Starla let out a long breath. "Okay. I'll trust you."

After a 5,000 year eternity stretched in front of us, they clasped hands and turned to enter the house together. I sucked in a sharp breath when Celeste let out a peal of laughter and confirmed there was no getting out of this now.

Reluctantly, I followed behind the happy couple.

Stirred up drama that had nothing to do with me sounded like a miserable time, but the woman behind the mess had me intrigued.

At least I knew the house was clean.

* * *

Once inside, I peeled my boots off and glanced around.

Not a knickknack or frame had been nudged out of place. She'd clearly taken pains to keep everything together in the twenty-four hours that had passed.

A lot of years went behind my hidden superpower of cleaning, organizing, and then making online videos on how to get the stains out of carpet. My more comedic ones, like how to organize a junk drawer by dumping it into the trash can and starting over, had even gained our business a lot of clients. Sure, it all looked fun behind the scenes.

Mostly, it was.

But most people didn't know that I hated cleaning. Hated the grungy work in other people's houses, breathing their fumes, inhaling their dust. I loved the feeling afterward, though, and that made it worth it.

There had been times in my life when I couldn't sort all my problems out. Or any of them, really. Instead of the chaos of a small child and an immature wife, I found refuge in controlling what I could.

Namely, my house.

Eventually, I made a temporary career out of it. One day, I'd sell the business. For now, it taught Celeste how to work hard, provided a means for her to save for college, and got me out of the teacher-grind that had burned me out.

Lines of strain had appeared around Leslie's warm smile as we shuffled into the kitchen. The air lay thick with the meaty scent of BBQ. A golden pan of cornbread sat on the table, near a bowl of coleslaw and buttered corn.

Leslie covered her tension with happy small talk and puttered around, grabbing plates and giving instructions on dishing up food. Another kid—probably Blake, whom Celeste spoke about often—descended the stairs. He spoke with Starla, giving her a shy smile, then nodded to me.

Meanwhile, Leslie and Celeste made little whirls in the kitchen.

I stood back and took it in. Hopefully, cleaning her house gave Leslie the same sense of control I often craved. I didn't know Leslie, but I felt for her. Perhaps I'd gone a bit too far with the organizing and fixing, but I'd been on a roll. It had felt good to get back into it and one divorcée to another—it was needed.

Besides, the invoice would be nice.

Landon hadn't let go of Starla as they walked inside and he held onto her now. He had always been a good kid. Intelligent to a fault. A little bit impetuous, but focused when he needed to be. Had he fostered those traits, or had life after high school eaten him whole and spit him back out as a mess who attached to a girl who wasn't good for him? I knew that story with personal experience.

Could go either way.

Celeste still chattered happily with Leslie, and I couldn't help but wonder if *she* was why Leslie invited us in. If Celeste had any superpower, words were it. She could talk her way out of almost any situation. I had the scars to prove it. If nothing else, Celeste filled the awkward void that threatened to descend. It seemed to hover above the house, like a lead weight about to plummet.

Maybe Leslie was more strategic than I'd thought.

"Come on in," Leslie called, waving a hand without

looking back as I crossed the threshold inside. "Lunch is ready to go."

Landon turned away from Blake, arm still firmly around Starla, and put his free hand on his stomach with a dramatic groan.

"Smells so good, Mom!"

Indeed, he had that right. If I had to be put in this terrible situation, a little bit of delicious-smelling food would have a redemptive factor.

When I ventured into the dining room, which was an open space attached to the kitchen area separated only by a bar that jutted out from the wall, Celeste stood in the kitchen. She stirred something on the stovetop with steam billowing out, her voice moving almost as fast.

Leslie moved in between the fridge, the sink, and the counter, but her movements didn't have a lot of purpose.

Mostly misdirection.

Landon's words *we'll tell her the news about medical school* rang through my head again. I had a dark feeling Leslie was about to get sucker punched twice. No parent deserved that. Particularly not one surviving a divorce, four boys, and the resulting hailstorm of change that ensued.

Despite myself, I couldn't help but feel a touch protective toward her.

Not to mention attracted.

Her blonde hair was lighter toward the tips, but darker at the roots. It rested on her shoulders in lazy curls that looked too good to be accidental. She had a quick—if not currently twitchy—smile and intelligent gaze.

Were those blue eyes, or gray? She cut a cozy figure in a simple pair of jeans and a black shirt that flowed around her pockets and halfway down her arms.

Despite what had to be an inner core of steel after raising Landon and three others, I sensed a softness about her that had been missing in my life for a while. Leslie Miller—no, Hill —was a tangled mess indeed.

Maybe I didn't hate all messes.

Landon stopped at the counter, fingers still tangled in his fiancée's. "Ready to eat?"

"Dig in," Leslie said with a tip of her head. "Let your guests eat first."

I waved Leslie off when she glanced my way, so she ushered Celeste into line first. Starla followed, then Blake. Landon reluctantly let go of Starla, but he kept a keen eye on his Mom the whole time.

I leaned against the wall to wait for the teenage surge to pass through. Leslie appeared busy enough that any expected, initial small talk with Starla could be explained away. But not entirely.

So when would Leslie *really* acknowledge Starla?

The question lay in the air. Celeste, not entirely oblivious to the tension in the room, settled at the table. While Blake picked a spot next to her, she snuck a glance at Landon, then Starla.

Leslie handed me a plate, a not-so-subtle hint to move already, and I accepted. Only a few minutes passed with Landon and Celeste maintaining an easy chatter before all of us congregated around the table.

When Leslie finally set her plate down, Landon opened his mouth, then closed it again. If possible, Starla seemed to shrink back further. Rampaging Mother in-Law situation, perhaps? Leslie didn't remind me of the type.

Leslie drew in a deep breath, then looked up. Her eyes immediately caught Starla's. A beat later, she smiled with real warmth.

"Starla?" she asked. "Is that right?"

"Yes, ma'am."

Leslie's nose wrinkled as she set aside her napkin.. "Ugh, please. Not that. Never that. Just call me Leslie."

Leslie walked around the table and collected Starla in a long hug. Landon sent Blake a look of visible relief. Fascinated, I watched Leslie tuck away whatever angst had been in her mind and pull back, hands on Starla's shoulders. Starla beamed.

"Thank you. Leslie, then."

"Much better."

Everyone at the table seemed to share a metaphorical breath as Leslie returned to her seat. Somehow, she'd caught the exact moment *before* not acknowledging Starla would have become too awkward to salvage.

Impressive.

She sat next to me and I caught a hint of brown sugar in the air. Having her at my side would be easier. I wouldn't have to stop myself from looking at her every other moment.

"Well, thank you everyone for coming to our little place," Leslie said with a quick smile. "I've been looking forward to meeting you very much. Everyone?" She held up two hands, all traces of stress gone. "Let's eat!"

Relief made Starla a ball of goo as a steady, rambunctious chatter replaced the uncertain quiet. Celeste and Blake joked with Leslie about surviving their teachers, and Starla begged for more embarrassing stories about Landon during high school. Only too happy to oblige, I provided several.

By the time conversation wound down, only the inevitable questions remained. As before, they lingered in the air.

Would Leslie call out their engagement right now?

Or let it slide?

"So, Landon tells me you're engaged?" she said to Starla. "Can I see the ring?"

I blew out a breath. Right for the kill. Damn, she didn't hold back. Then again, what mother would?

Starla blinked, then covered her surprise with a smile. "Of course." Her hand glittered as she lifted it over the table for Leslie to study. Small diamond in the middle of a silver band. Modest was a word for it.

Fake could be another one.

"He proposed a few days ago." Starla swallowed. Her nostrils flared a bit. Although she seemed to try to keep it steady, her voice wavered a touch. "At an ice skating rink."

Leslie blinked, as if the confirmation had startled her. The smooth way she bowled over whatever the engagement story brought up was almost seamless.

Almost.

"It's fast," Leslie sang with a little smile and a touch of tightness around the edges, "but I can't wait to hear the story. Will you—"

"First, Mom," Landon said, "I have some other news."

Starla sucked in a deep breath as he spoke. My entire body tensed, waiting for a punch that wouldn't land on me. Leslie tilted her head to one side, eyes narrowed. Oh, a wily woman all right. She already knew something was up. Landon sat across from his mother, right in her cross hairs. He'd put a hand on Starla's arm and fidgeted with the edge of her sleeve.

"Other news?" Leslie asked.

"It's about medical school."

"Oh!" Leslie brightened. "Wonderful. Did you get your acceptance? I don't see how you couldn't with—"

Landon let out a shaky breath. "Yes, but . . . I dropped out."

I closed my eyes.

Idiot, I wanted to say. *Never give your Mother a double-whammy.*

Over several seconds, Leslie paled. When his words appeared to have sunk in, she opened her mouth, then closed it again. I grimaced. Celeste froze. Starla held her breath, face twisted in an expression that indicated she expected Leslie to self-combust. Blake pretended none of it was happening and plowed into a piece of cornbread.

"What do you mean?" Leslie asked carefully.

Landon's throat bobbed. He spoke slowly, as if he knew he'd been given an extension on his life for one more minute, and he'd better make the best of it.

"It just . . . it wasn't right. I know that I had big plans and I've wanted to be a surgeon forever," he said quickly, "but the thought of that much school? I just couldn't do it, Mom. I'm burned out. The expectations, training, and time away? I want more of a life than that."

Leslie blinked, only slightly mollified. At this point, I imagined Landon had just about crammed all the shock into his mother he could manage, and I hoped he had nothing left to drop.

"I'm looking at something else." Landon leaned back in the chair. "I'm not 100% sure what it is yet, but . . . I have a feeling I'll stumble on it. Maybe a park ranger or an auto mechanic or something simple."

Leslie's gaze dropped to the table top. Her eyes widened. "Okay," she murmured.

Her modulated tone struck more fear in my heart on Landon's behalf than the flared nostrils and tensed neck. Based on the puzzlement in her voice, she worked this out with each word she spoke.

"Okay." She nodded once, lips pressed again. "I . . . okay. I guess there's a lot to talk about, isn't there?"

"This has nothing to do with me!" Starla blurted out, then slapped a hand over her mouth. Landon's mouth tightened at the lips. His grip on her wrist seemed a little firmer. Blake looked up at this, crumbs from the cornbread on his lips. Celeste's mouth hung half open.

As if she couldn't hold it in, Starla cried, "I'm sorry, I just .

. . I didn't want you to think that our engagement had anything to do with his decision to leave medical school. I'm not pregnant, he wanted to stop medical school before I met him, and I love him so much."

An eternity followed.

This lunch would hit the record books.

To my shock, Leslie softened. She reached out and put a hand on Starla's arm. With a gaze full of long-suffering she said, "I understand, Starla, and I don't blame you. Landon is his own man and always has been."

Landon's tight jaw loosened ever-so-slightly, but he watched his mom like he anticipated an attack. He should. If she didn't, I might. Leslie glanced at him, and a flash of murderous rage caught me by surprise. It disappeared, but Landon hadn't missed it. I bit back a laugh when he paled.

Oh, he was in for it.

A saccharine sweetness coated her voice when she spoke next. One that was subtle enough to pass by Starla's terror unrecognized, but obvious for the rest of us.

"Let's talk about this more in-depth after lunch," Leslie said. She gazed around, looking at empty plates and dishes. "Landon, would you and Starla mind being on dish duty? Celeste and Blake, you can package up all the food that's left-over, please. We'll send it back to Jackson City with you tonight if anyone wants some."

Then Leslie's gaze slammed right into mine, sending a shockwave ripple all the way through my body.

"Tanner? May I please speak with you outside?"

Chapter Five

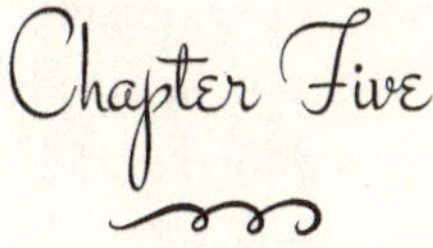

LESLIE

My mind looped around itself, zooming like a race car.

I can't do this.

I can't do this.

I can't do this.

The only thing that kept me from absolutely exploding was knowing that I had to step outside and talk to Tanner. Tanner, the impossibly handsome, had-to-be-here-at-the-exact-wrong-moment father of Celeste. Tanner, who stood back like an awkward shadow and tried to look everywhere *but* at me.

Why had I invited them in?

Why had I said yes to this lunch without talking to Landon in private first?

Why was my son such an idiot?

Tanner disappeared out the front door as soon he'd nodded to my request, as if he couldn't get out fast enough.

Not that I could blame him.

I didn't even know what I was going to say, I just knew I needed air. That the room around me thickened and wavered.

If I had to maintain this facade for one more second, I would explode.

The kids had zipped right to their assigned chores, and a friendly banter filled the air. Banishing the panicked thoughts, I yanked on a jacket and stepped outside.

Tanner stood on the porch, hands in his pockets. He stared out as I shut the door behind me and joined him. Neither of us looked at each other. I gazed on the empty neighborhood, the mountains in the distance, and the dirty rims of his truck. How often did he wash it?

His calm voice broke my stupor. "That was a big bomb or two he just dropped."

I blinked out of the piling thoughts. Somehow, that was the exact right thing for him to say.

"Agreed," I said.

He turned to study my profile, but I made no move to meet his gaze. I didn't have the mental ability to look at him right now. He was far too attractive. Too . . . with it. One compassionate word and I'd . . . I didn't know.

The crisp air made it easier to breathe. I closed my eyes and focused on the silence. A calming sensation followed, rippling through my muscles like a cup of warm tea. I'd bought myself at least a few minutes before I had to go back in, somehow separate Landon from Starla, and drag the truth out of him.

Tanner didn't ask if I needed anything, for which I was grateful. I didn't know what I'd say. Asking him to step out with me came from sheer desperation to get away and not have anyone follow. Meanwhile, my sluggish brain began to catch up to what had just happened inside.

Engaged after four weeks.

Almost-hysterical soon-to-be bride.

Dropped out of medical school and his years-long career pursuit.

No idea what he'd do next.

In the end, I came to the same conclusion that I had yesterday morning when Landon texted me the news—this had to be a joke. Max could have pulled this kind of stunt and I wouldn't have doubted its veracity. Landon, however, had never been the troublemaker.

Medical school. The thought gave me a pang. If my son didn't want to do that, I wouldn't force it on him. For years, however, he'd had a single-path goal. Get to medical school, save lives in surgery. His focus had been absolute. I'd done everything I could feasibly do to support the dream. Now that he let it dissolve away, I had to restructure the life I'd pictured for him.

That was harder than I'd thought.

All the years of parenting Landon stacked up behind me, helping me know exactly what I needed to do. I just didn't want to do it.

Landon would come to me with more details . . . eventually. At least, he always had in the past. We'd get rid of the basics, think it over, and come back together later. Didn't matter that I wanted to hash it out now.

I needed to wait, even just a few hours.

The courage I needed to step back into the house and say nothing lay somewhere in all my decades of time as a mom.

Tonight, before he left, I'd pull him aside. We could chat more then, with the air cleared and everyone relaxed. To prepare myself for returning, I gathered bravery like a desperate woman. I pictured it like glitter and piled it into my arms, then shifted to go inside again. When someone shifted next to me, I froze.

Oh yeah.

Tanner.

I'd completely forgotten about him. How could I explain?

What should I say about the fathoms of dysfunction that I saw in the decisions Landon recently made? How could I say that I had only needed to breathe for a few minutes, and he'd been little more than a convenient distraction?

I couldn't.

Tanner cleared his throat. "Yesterday, I noticed the dryer vent had some issues. Glad we came out here to fix it before you had a fire. Thanks for letting me show it to you."

Confusion clouded my mind. Dryer vent? What was he— the thoughts cleared. Oh. He'd just given me an excuse for coming out here. If anyone asked why we went inside, I'd have something to tell them.

Tanner turned and gestured inside with a tilt of his head. I forced myself to look at him, awash with relief and gratitude. He'd just given me the best gift I could ever ask for.

Support.

No judgment.

Not a word of advice.

My mouth closed before I could summon a single word. I nodded and managed a croaky, "Thank you."

Tanner shuffled to the side and opened the door. Why did I have the feeling that he felt as *let off the hook* as I did? I stepped back in the house ahead of him and Tanner closed the door behind us.

* * *

That night, the air turned frigid.

Standing on my back porch felt more like shivering in a refrigerator than enjoying my garden, but I stayed anyway. Somehow, the cold held me together and helped my thoughts slide easily.

I sat on my swing on the deck, surrounded by bare,

wooden structures. In the spring, they'd host teeming green vines and fragrant flowers and *life*. For now, the ghosts of my old plants remained behind, but their ghosts were enough to give me unequivocal comfort.

A reassurance of something better to come.

Through the years, the garden had been the one thing I'd maintained. The only *me* space I'd allowed mentally, emotionally, and physically. A structure away from my husband and kids, a place for me to go. It often helped me recover from the draw on my time and energy. Gave me something to adore and own.

The garden often required more physical energy than I had to give with four boys, and definitely required more time. In the end, however, it had always been worth it. During the babies and lean times and school plays and medical disasters and teenage-dating heartbreak, the garden had always been mine.

Now as Landon and Starla snuggled up on the couch to watch a movie, and Blake pretended to do his homework but really kept talking to Landon about their mutually favorite band, I sat in the cool air and stared at the stars.

My mind wandered all over the place, and I let it go. Text messages buzzed in my pocket, but I ignored those.

The time after lunch with Starla, Landon, Celeste, and Tanner became a get-to-know-Starla fest. Tanner maneuvered a few treacherous parts of the conversation that led toward territories I didn't want to discuss with a crowd—namely Landon's massive life decisions. When the topic threatened close, Tanner saved me by telling humiliating stories about Max or Nicholas, enough to make everyone laugh.

Tanner slipped through my thoughts again, liquid as silk ribbon. The thought of him didn't suck. He was more attractive than I'd expected, and I'd expected a lot. Beyond that, however? He'd been frighteningly perceptive. With only a few words, he'd imparted courage, support, and strength.

Perhaps I should have focused my open attention on Landon and the next steps in his life. Starla, her family that she breezed over, and how she and Landon came to the conclusion that four weeks was enough time to get engaged.

Instead, I kept thinking of Tanner, and the thoughts were far more pleasant.

When my phone buzzed and a local number popped up, I frowned. Who would be calling me now?

I answered it with a quick, "Hello?"

"It's Tanner."

My heart dropped all the way into my stomach with a juicy crash. I straightened, swallowing past my shock.

"Oh. Hey."

"Sorry to call unannounced."

"No problem."

"I think we have a problem with leaving our stuff over there. Celeste says she left her jacket on the chair in the family room. It's gray and pink. Can you send it to school with Blake on Monday?"

"Of course."

"Thanks."

"No problem."

He paused and my flopping heart almost stalled in the meantime. Was he going to bring up my abject humiliation from the past few hours? I sincerely hoped we could end this call and never see each other again. No, wait. I still wanted to see him. Ogling from a distance would be preferred.

Interaction? No thanks.

"Did you want me to come back next week?" he asked. "I forgot to ask you today."

My brain stalled. "For lunch?" I asked, my voice an octave too high.

He laughed. "No, to clean. But I'd take lunch too."

Mortification crept through me in a hot wave. Okay. I needed to just die right now. Of course he meant to clean.

"Oh, right." I cleared my throat. "Uh . . . yes. Definitely. What's my invoice for this time? Great Aunt Martha isn't going to die anytime soon so I'm not sure I have the cash."

"You have a great Aunt Martha?"

"Yes."

"Me too."

"Weird."

"Is it?"

His quick question gave me pause. No, it really wasn't that weird. Martha was a fairly common name, but it *felt* weird, particularly encased in this conversation, which I still couldn't fathom. In the background, the sound of rustling papers ensued.

"Invoice," he murmured. "Oh, right. $300."

"That's it?"

"You want me to charge more?"

"Well . . . weren't you here all day? There's no way you accomplished this in four or five hours."

"It was six. That's fifty an hour. I'm fine with increasing it, if that's what you want. It would probably just be $150 next week, a basic clean."

"Oh, that's doable and I'm happy to pay the $300. You earned it and more."

"Great. I'll go ahead and charge the card we have on file, if that works."

"It does."

"Okay. Well, next week sounds great."

"Does the day before Thanksgiving work for you?" I asked. "That would be a huge help."

"It does. You did great, by the way."

"I'm sorry?" I asked.

"Today. Landon dropped a few too many bombs on you, with strangers around, and when you weren't expecting it. I'm sorry he did that. There were better ways to break the news."

"Oh . . . thanks. I agree."

I relaxed against the seat, gratified to have another parent's opinion. I hadn't asked Landon if his father knew what he revealed tonight. Ethan cared more than I did about medical school and had a bitter streak toward young marriage a mile wide. A niggling suspicion in the back of my mind wondered if Landon did this to get back at his Dad.

I shoved that away.

"It's hard, isn't it?" I asked. "Being a parent. You want your kids to take care of themselves but you don't want them to be idiots doing it."

"Oh, I feel you. Of course, I have one teenager still at home. I haven't broached the whole sending-them-into-the-world thing."

"It sucks."

"Can't be worse than puberty."

I tilted my head back and laughed. "It's so much worse! Just in a different way. I guess as a man parenting a daughter, it may not feel that way."

A low chuckle followed my response, and I was grateful for the easy flow of conversation after a rough day. I shifted.

"Thanks for your help out on the porch today," I said, my cheeks warming again.

The demise of my marriage revealed to me that I didn't do *vulnerable, open conversations* very well. Maybe if I had, I wouldn't be single in my garden, wondering if I messed my son up beyond repair.

"Not just with the whole awkward lunch that you were wrangled into, but for cleaning the house. You organized it too, which . . . wow. Means so much."

"My pleasure."

His clear tone held no platitude—he really meant it. Sensing the end of the conversation, I said, "Well, I'll send Celeste's jacket with Blake on Monday morning. Thanks again."

He spoke a quick farewell, then hung up the phone. I clicked it off then let it sink back to my lap, my head tilted back, and closed my eyes against the velvety backdrop of the stars.

Before I sank into a gentle doze, ready to get rid of the day, Landon's head popped out the back door.

"Bye, Mom! Call ya later."

I startled back to life with a half snort. "What?"

The door shut before I could get a response out of him. I mouthed his words twice before they sank in.

"Wait!" I cried. "Are you leaving?"

By the time I untangled my legs from the blanket and got my mind working again, the front door closed. Half-swearing under my breath, I managed to get back into the house without tripping.

Blake sat at the table, head bent to his homework. The couch lay empty, nothing but two folded blankets on one end. Had to be Starla's touch, because golden child or not, Landon had never folded a blanket in his life.

"Where is he?" I asked.

Blake motioned to the front door with a jerk of his head. "Gone."

"What?" I screeched and waved a hand in the air. "We haven't talked about all of this yet."

"Yep," Blake said with a little *pop* of the p. "He knows that."

My gaze tapered. "Is he avoiding me?"

"Yep."

In a mad dash, I made it to the front door in seconds. Landon was ahead of me, though. Headlights pulled away from the sidewalk with a high-pitched squeal before I could make it down the driveway.

In the receding brake lights, I thought I saw a vague wave of a hand saying goodbye.

Chapter Six

TANNER

The truck purred beneath me the next week as I sat in the parking lot of the Frolicking Moose and waited for Celeste.

It was Wednesday night, just before Thanksgiving, and chalk turkeys decorated the chalkboards on the interior of the store. I snorted at the turkey with a waddle that looked like a croissant.

Naturally, my thoughts streamed back to Leslie Hill.

Our call on Saturday night had been easy. At first, I hadn't been sure if she'd take it. So many people didn't answer their phones now, and I doubted she had the company number programmed into her contact list. The gentle surprise I'd heard in her voice when she answered meant she hadn't known it was me.

Would she have still answered?

Jury was out.

Calling her had been a gamble. Her embarrassment from lunch had been smoothly enough covered during the meal. A grateful, but a little uncertain, goodbye had followed.

Could I blame her? Not for a second. I'd given Celeste a ten minute lecture on the way home from Leslie's house and made her promise on her life that she'd never do the same thing to me.

Although a bit impetuous, I felt better after the phone call. I wanted to check in on Leslie . . . without actually checking in on her. She was undeniably savvy and would have seen through it in a moment. Pride held that woman together at this moment, and I wouldn't be the one to shatter it.

Here I sat days later, *still* thinking about her.

With a quick beep of the horn, a thin, blonde figure arose from a chair and headed outside. Celeste looped her backpack over one shoulder, a coffee in hand, and headed for the passenger side. I blamed her mother for the coffee addiction. From inside, a vague wave followed from Leslie.

Celeste beamed her usual chipper smile. "Hey, Dad."

"Hey sport. How was school?"

She shrugged and shoved the backpack to the floor between her feet.

"Fine. The usual. Aced a test. Same old."

"Sweet."

Our companionable silence continued while I headed out of Pineville and up the canyon, toward our home south of Jackson City. The thirty minute drive up the canyon and to our rather remote home had always felt like a pain, but on days like today, I liked the space it gave me to think.

"How did you become such good friends with Leslie?" I asked.

Celeste glanced at me, then back to her phone. Her fingers flew over the screen, probably in a text message.

"Oh, while waiting for you to pick me up at the coffee shop every day we chat. She's there every now and then. I talk to Dahlia and Katelyn a lot too. I want to work there." She perked up. "Would you let me work there?"

"If you find someone to replace you and you make better money than at our company, then yes."

Her lips formed a duck face as she thought about it, then shook her head. "Definitely not as good of money."

"What do you like about Leslie?"

Celeste shrugged. "I don't know. She listens to me. She takes me seriously. Dahlia is really fun too, but we're more like . . . friends. Leslie reminds me of a mentor. She gives great advice and even better hugs."

"What advice do you need?"

"Her favorite tampons. Best cramping medication. Cups instead of pads," she shot back with a witty smile.

I shuddered. "All right, all right. Point made."

Celeste laughed. "Just kidding, Dad. I call Mom for that stuff, although I'm sure Leslie would help me too. I talk to her about guys at school."

The blinker clicked as I flipped it on, glancing her way for a moment. "Don't you talk to your Mom about that stuff?"

"Yeah, but . . . it's different. Leslie is here almost every day and I only see Mom every other weekend."

"Fair."

The thought that I didn't hug Celeste enough occurred to me. We'd never been all that touchy . . . but maybe it's because *I* wasn't that touchy. I'd never asked Celeste if she wanted more physical affection, but had always assumed she was happy enough.

"Do you want more hugs?" I asked.

Her nose wrinkled. "Uh, no. Thanks. I'm good."

Ah, that was why I didn't give more hugs.

"Got it."

"Why are you curious about Leslie?" she asked, flipping her hair over her shoulder. She wore a faded denim jacket that looked like someone had driven over it, tumbled it in a washer full of bleach, then tried to resurrect it with bad dyes. She loved that thing, and I heard from a reliable source that her mother had paid a couple hundred dollars for it.

Ridiculous.

"Not sure," I murmured, "but I keep thinking about the lunch on Saturday. Was that *super* weird, or is that just me?"

Celeste giggled. "No, that was totally awkward and awesome and I'll never ever forget it."

"Same."

"Leslie held herself together like a rockstar," Celeste said, eyes tapered in thought. "I think Mom would have freaked out on me if I had done that. Can you imagine? She'd throw a plate at the wall."

She would do that because she had at some point in our marriage. Some fuzzy, distant point that I strove to keep at the back of my mind and not ruminate over too much. Down that path lay a lot of regret which was better to leave tucked away. Brooke and I had long made peace over what failed between us. Thankfully, I lucked out and received most of Celeste in the breaking apart.

I cleared my throat.

"Weird lunch aside, I'm thinking about asking Leslie out."

Celeste's smile widened. "Really?"

"Yeah." The truck built up speed as we headed into the mountains. "What do you think about that?"

"It's awesome! I love Leslie. I think you'd be a great fit. I mean, she just got divorced. You could break her in and stuff."

The phrase made me want to vomit. *Break her in*?

"What the hell does that mean?" I asked.

"Just that she hasn't had a date after the divorce, which means the last time she went on a first date was with her husband. How many years is that? Like twenty?"

If her oldest son was twenty three, then even longer, but I didn't want to press the point. It certainly didn't rosy up the details. Besides, if that were true, it made me internally blanch a little.

Well, maybe I didn't want to ask her out. Would there be baggage there? Would Leslie even say yes?

I dismissed those thoughts. First, the report that Leslie needed to be *broken in* came from a seventeen-year-old that lived on assumptions. Second, Leslie was a strong woman that could clearly take care of herself. Third, I didn't fear rejection. After years of being single and dating occasionally, the last thing I needed to worry about was the opinion of someone that probably wouldn't impact my life in a massive way.

Besides, baggage was something I carried plenty of myself.

"What if you took her to a really nice restaurant in Jackson City?" Celeste asked. "The new one that opened up recently. French, something?"

My nose wrinkled.

"Upscale is fine," I said. "French? Not so much."

"Italian?"

"Better, but feels trite."

She immediately tapped into her phone. "Something romantic," Celeste continued. "Leslie needs to be taken care of. Lizbeth has told me about her ex-husband. He doesn't sound like a bad guy, but he also doesn't sound all that . . ."

"Romantic?"

"In tune."

Screens populated on her phone as she swiped around, mumbling to herself. The internet would cut out here soon enough.

Hey, wait a minute.

"What does in tune mean?" I asked and nudged her with my elbow. "What's that supposed to mean? How is a man in tune?"

Celeste didn't hide her eye roll very well.

"I guess romantic is a word, but I mean someone that's . . . paying attention. You see her, you know? You get what she wants, what she doesn't want, and when she wants it. That kind of thing."

"Oh, right. I've heard of this. It's called *mind reading.*"

"Daaaad." She tilted her head back and groaned. "No, don't get all . . . fatherly . . . on this subject. It's more about knowing them well enough that you get them. For example, you don't know Leslie well enough to know what restaurant she'd want, but I do. I'm in tune with her. Don't have to read her mind. I just pay attention."

My mind churned over that for a while. Having a teenager daughter was more enlightening than I'd expected. Also, I still thought she meant mind reading, but whatever.

"Fine," I said. "Find the perfect place for Leslie, romantic and all that ridiculous stuff, but good enough we can still talk and I can get to know her. I haven't committed to this yet, you know. I'm just thinking about it."

"Whatever. You'll do it. Once you set your mind on something, you make it happen. I'll help, but this is your only pass," Celeste muttered. "Next time? You have to know her well enough to pick the place."

"I accept."

"By the way, Thanksgiving is tomorrow," Celeste drawled. "You ready?"

My lips twitched with a grin. In the back of the truck, an assortment of grocery bags awaited. Pie crusts, pie filling, heavy whipping cream, a turkey, and various assortments of all our favorite foods. Christmas was an okay day in our house. But Thanksgiving? The holy grail of holidays in our world.

"Ready to eat pie and gain twenty pounds," I said.

Celeste reached over and we high-fived. I grinned. Felt good to have the coolest daughter in the world.

And so much pie in my future.

Chapter Seven

LESLIE

The coo of a baby drew me out of my office the week after Thanksgiving.

I slipped into the coffee shop to find Stella standing at the counter, a bouncing baby boy held in her right arm. His bright eyes and strong head gazed around. Spit bubbles formed at his mouth. Like his father Mark, he had a bright smile and so much thick hair on top of his head that I wanted to run my fingers through it.

"There's my handsome guy," I cried.

Stella turned to me with a bleary smile, then gratefully passed Mark Jr. into my outstretched hands. He stared at me, a bit dazed, but made no protest as I bounced him in place. I glanced at Stella. Dark marks lingered under her eyes, no doubt from sleep loss, but her smile seemed genuine. Her hair had been fixed, she had a hint of lip gloss on, and she wore real clothes instead of sweatpants.

For a new mom of a four-month-old?

She was killing it.

"How are you, Stell?" I asked with a hand on her shoulder.

She let out a long sigh as Dahlia bustled behind the counter, fast at work with a coffee pot.

"Tired."

"It gets better."

Hope filled her eyes. "When?"

"Realistically? When they leave for college, but even then they're stressful. Sleep, however, comes in longer snatches closer to six months."

She sighed. "I can do that."

"How was Thanksgiving?" I asked.

"We ate sliced turkey sandwiches with cranberry sauce, avocado, and fake mashed potatoes. Mark was in charge," she added, as if we needed to understand why such a thing would happen.

"You didn't have JJ cater?" Dahlia asked with a dramatic gasp. "Are you crazy?"

Stella smiled. "No, he and Lizbeth were at Maverick and Bethany's and I didn't want to leave home. I'm just . . . not really up for lots of people for a long time while Mark Jr. is still so little. Maverick and Bethany were really cool about it."

"Sounds like the perfect holiday," I said with a sigh. "Landon stayed in Jackson City with his new fiancée—said something about being busy up there. The other boys are coming home for Christmas, so it was just me and Blake. We kept it simple too."

"Wait," Stella cried, "Landon is engaged?"

"What?" Dahlia said at the same time.

I patted Stella's arm. "I'll tell you about it later, when I know more myself. In the meantime, have a seat." I nudged her into a nearby chair. "I need some baby time while you chat with Dahlia. She has all the gossip for you."

Dahlia's eyes gleamed with excitement.

While I swept Mark Jr. around the shop with me, Stella sank into a chair. The longing for real-life connections outside of spit up and breastfeeding was all too fresh in my mind, despite my youngest being on his way to graduate from high school. I was only too happy to take Mark Jr. for a while.

Sometimes, I missed the early years. Not the tantrums or exhaustion or sense of helpless I-don't-know-what-I'm-doing. But the feeling of having them close, within touch. Knowing that I could make their day better with a bandaid and a smile. This whole sending-them-into-the-world-to-make-big-mistakes could go rot.

Suddenly, I understood the appeal of grandbabies.

Dahlia and Stella provided soothing background chatter while I mentally puzzled together pieces of Maverick's family reunion. Catering on certain days. Pizza on others. Hotel rentals, car coordination, a blow-up bouncy house for the little kids. The Mercedy family didn't mess around.

Mark Jr. remained in my arms, contemplative as I carted him around while I did inventory one handed, made a few phone calls, and kept my ear attuned to the conversation in the shop.

"The forest around Adventura was spared from the fire," Stella murmured in the background. "There are a few spots that tried to take off and burn up the mountainside, but the hot shot crew thankfully put them out. Adventura is good to open up in the spring with campers, thank heavens."

"Sione called me last night," Dahlia said. "Said he landed safely in Tonga to see our grandparents. He's not coming back until right before Adventura opens."

Their conversation continued to flow, and took my mind with it. Right back to where it had been going every hour ever since the disaster of yesterday.

Tanner Beck.

After Landon's hasty departure—which clearly indicated a guilty conscience and a lacking desire to talk to me about his life decisions, the twerp—I'd spun my mind back through the afternoon. Had I done something wrong? Should I have said something different?

Inevitably, my brain landed right back to the phone call that came from Tanner and into the words he'd casually said.

You did great, by the way.

They had a not-so-casual effect on me. His compliment had, several times, settled the rattled part of me that blamed myself for my son's behavior. At twenty-three, Landon was more than old enough to take responsibility for himself. Most of the time, I did a great job of giving him said responsibility. The rest of the time?

Well, being a mom wasn't easy.

After thirty minutes had passed like a moment, Stella glanced at the clock and cried, "Oh, I'm so sorry! I didn't mean to take up so much of your time!"

I emerged from my office with a reassuring smile. "Please, take more of it anytime. Mark Jr. and I are going to be close!"

Dahlia snorted. "Are you kidding? I loved this. And I'm paid for it!"

Mark Jr., on seeing his mama, let out a little gurgle and a quick smile. His wiggly legs flailed when Stella gave him a warm grin and reached for him. Reluctantly, I transferred his easy weight back to her.

Yeah, this grandma thing would be just fine.

"Thank you," Stella said with feeling. "I didn't know how much I needed that."

"I totally get it, honey. He's perfect and you're doing great. Text me tonight if he's doing that spit up thing again, or whatever. I'm always here for you."

She willingly went into my hug, and I couldn't help but squeeze her extra tight. With both parents deceased and her grandma living in Florida, Stella had been stopping in and calling almost daily with questions. She pulled away.

"You're too good to me."

"Nah." I squeezed her arm. "We've got you, Stella. You're never alone in this Mom thing."

Dahlia fidgeted behind the counter while Stella gathered up her things and I helped her out to the car with the diaper bag. When I stepped back inside, Dahlia burst.

"What is going on with Landon?"

I sighed, having anticipated this exact moment, lowered into my booth and rubbed circles into my temples.

"Landon is trying my patience."

"He's engaged?" she screeched. "Congratulations! Do you like her? How did he ask? When is the wedding?"

"She's not so bad, I actually liked Starla. Yes, I think they've rushed the whole getting-engaged-thing, but they don't have a date set. There's time for them to figure that whole situation out."

Dahlia lifted a dark eyebrow. "Buuuut?" she drawled.

I leaned back. "But he's dropped out of medical school. At least, he said he did. I don't know the details. Maybe he hasn't actually pulled out yet? Not really sure."

Her eyes grew round as globes. "Oh. That seems like a big deal."

"It is a big deal. His decision, but still a big deal. I can learn to live with that, but now he's avoiding me. He won't let me talk to him about it, which has my mama senses tingling. Something is up."

"Can you corner him?"

I shrugged. "Maybe. But should I? I'm not sure it's come to that yet. He's made a series of decisions that I don't agree with, but I'm going to have to get used to. There's no wedding date on the horizon and there could be hope for the future that he's wanted for years. So . . ."

Dahlia nodded. "So you wait."

"So I wait. At least for now. Forcing Landon in the past has never helped."

She shook her head and leaned against the counter behind her. "Wow, parenting looks like it sucks."

"Totally."

The slam of a car door outside drew my attention, and my stomach caught. My ex-husband Ethan stood in front of the Frolicking Moose, eyes shaded by a pair of sunglasses.

He'd cut his shaggy hair short so it looked neat and manicured, giving him a more professional bearing. The mussy HVAC guy that I'd lived with for the last two decades had all but disappeared underneath a button-up shirt and slacks. Had he lost weight? He cut a leaner figure.

I crossed my arms self consciously over my chest.

"Oh." Dahlia straightened. "Is that . . ."

"It is."

Before she could say a word, someone stepped out of the passenger seat. A lovely woman, middle-aged, with streaks of gray in her dark hair. She gave him a smile highlighted by red lipstick. Her gutsy pantsuit reminded me of Celeste. While I wouldn't call her ritzy, she certainly gave off an upper class vibe.

The two of them linked hands and headed toward the door. My stomach twisted in on itself. After the divorce, Ethan had moved to Jackson City. He gave the house to me, took the RV and truck, and rented an apartment. At some point, Blake told me Ethan had purchased a home, but I didn't know much more about his life up there. His HVAC business, I'd heard from someone, had boomed. He paid his child support for Blake, so I didn't care what else he did with his money.

The fact that he'd left Jackson City to come here meant one thing: he needed to speak with me.

But why?

My instincts told me it had everything to do with Landon, and I braced myself for what would be said. Ethan had always put pressure on Landon to get into medical school to avoid *being the HVAC guy*. He wanted Landon to live the life he hadn't managed to achieve. We'd married so young and hadn't given ourselves the headstart we needed to be prosperous. I'd gotten pregnant with Landon within a year, and spit out the other three in the six years following.

Somehow, life had just . . . swallowed those dreams.

The chimes on the door jingled when Ethan pulled it open, allowing the woman to step inside ahead of him. I didn't have the presence of mind to act like I'd been doing something else, I just stared at them like a deer in the headlights. Ethan glanced up, saw me, and managed a warm-enough smile.

"Hey Les. Sorry for dropping in unexpectedly. Do you have a minute to talk?"

* * *

Thanks to limited space in my office, the three of us sat at my usual booth near the back. I put my back to the wall so I could face the rest of the shop and anticipate who came in.

Ethan introduced the woman with a hand on the small of her back.

"Leslie, this is Kate. She and I have been dating for a few months now. We're just heading out of town for a weekend trip and stopped in while driving through."

I smiled. "Good to meet you, Kate."

"Same," she murmured, with real curiosity in her eyes. "The boys have said such wonderful things about you. They really love you."

I'd long ago released any romantic attachment to Ethan. He and I had experienced it, it had flared for a short while, and then dwindled in a slow squeeze that felt like gasping for air. I harbored no jealousy over Ethan dating another woman, but my entire body prickled at the mention of my sons.

"That's always good to hear from another source," I quipped with a quick smile. "Sometimes, parenting feels like shouting into the void."

She murmured something that sounded like, *I can imagine* while Dahlia set several cups of coffee down, then disappeared. Behind them, she gave me a bolstering look that sent a shot of courage through me.

"So." I leaned back and looked straight to Ethan. "To what do I owe this pleasure? I have my doubts you'd drop in to chat without a reason to do so."

"Yes, of course. Nice place, by the way." He glanced around. In all the years that he'd lived in Pineville, somehow he'd managed to avoid coming in, even after the renovations. Then again, I'd haunted Lizbeth here so much in the early days that he probably avoided it just because I loved it.

"Thanks."

"I hear you're doing great things with it."

"I've really enjoyed the job."

Thankfully, Ethan leaned forward, shoulders hunched slightly, as if ready to drop into the trenches. I'd do anything to get out of this small talk and right to the heart of the matter.

"Right," he said. "We need to talk about Landon."

"Landon." I sighed. "Yes."

Ethan sucked on his front teeth, an annoying habit that used to set my hair on end. Seeing it now reassured me that, no matter what he pretended, the grungy Ethan that I'd attempted to spice back to life still lived somewhere beneath all this glittering exterior.

How much of this new person was Kate directly responsible for? Would it fade if she left?

"The quick marriage proposal I can get around," he said, "and I guess I understand his reasons for dropping medical school, even though I don't like them. I think he's going to regret this later. But getting married in February? That seems . . . I don't know. Something is going on."

My blood turned to slush. "I'm sorry," I whispered, "what?"

Ethan blinked. "What, what?"

"What did you say?"

"He's getting married in February."

I recoiled.

Ethan's eyes widened. "He didn't tell you?"

"I met Starla and he told me about dropping medical school, but he *didn't* tell me they'd set a date for . . . two-and-a-half months away."

Annoyance flared in Ethan's gaze. "Well that little—"

"What day is the wedding?"

"Valentine's day."

I fought not to roll my eyes. A thousand questions streamed through my mind. Why *that* day? Why so fast? Did Starla attend school too? What about his classes, his internship, his job? Amidst all of the questions, however, lingered the undying one that had been haunting me all night.

Why didn't he tell me?

Hurt overrode the panic. A wedding could be scraped together—if that's really how they wanted to approach it— but why not tell me about it? Why avoid me? Did my response frighten him? I'd gladly welcomed Starla into my house. I had made his favorite foods, avoided awkward subjects, and let him bring it up. I'd even given him a chance to explain . . .

"Les?"

Ethan's voice pulled me out of a stupor of thought. I blinked. "Sorry, what?"

"I don't know what's going on with him, It's like he's lost his mind."

"Starla is very nice," Kate said quietly. "I don't think she's putting pressure on him. Whatever is going on seems to stem from Landon."

Another knife twisted in my gut. Kate had met Starla before I did. What was happening here? How had my earth tilted on its axis again?

"Thank you for telling me," I said calmly. "Things have seemed fine between me and Landon but . . . apparently we're having a hard time with details. I'm not sure where this break-down in communication has happened. Or why, for that matter."

The dubious question that lingered in Ethan's eyes prob-ably meant that had been part of the reason he'd stopped by—to see what was going on between me and Landon. Did Ethan blame me for this wedding date?

Maybe.

Regardless, something must be bothering Landon for him to avoid me so completely about it.

"He introduced Starla to me and told me about medical school all at the same time," I said, just to fill the silence. "Maybe he didn't tell me about the wedding because he wanted to give me some time to get used to this."

Ethan shrugged.

Clearly, neither of us believed that.

He had a sip of coffee and we all sat in the contemplative silence for a few more breaths.

"Well." I forced more cheer in my voice than I felt. "Thank you for bringing it to my attention. I'll speak with Landon. Can you let me know if you hear anything from him about details? I believe I'm out of the loop and would like some assurance of what's really going on."

"Of course."

Our mostly-amicable divorce meant we hadn't been too uncomfortable with each other since it happened. Granted, there was weirdness there. The splitting of a shared life didn't come without ghosts, but I felt no ill will toward Ethan. As far as I knew, he hadn't cheated on me. I hadn't been unfaithful to him. We'd just let whatever we once had die, then we lived with it for as long as either of us could tolerate.

For fifteen minutes, the three of us shared small talk. I learned about how he met Kate online, and shoved away the question that wondered, *is it time for me to date again?*

When Tanner immediately surfaced in my mind afterward, I knew I was doomed.

When the small talk ceased and it no longer felt simple, Ethan and Kate made a quick exit. I sat at the booth in a storm cloud of uncertainty. New panic, new emotions, new questions swirled up in the wake of their departure.

Since when had *Ethan* been the trusted parent?

When had I fallen from grace?

Did all the boys feel this way?

Landon was the oldest of four. My second oldest, Max, who called every other Sunday, kept in contact with me. His athletic obsession and rising stardom in college football meant if anyone could go pro, it was Max.

The third child, Nicholas, had always been my quiet one. He'd disappeared into work in the mountains hundreds of miles north of here, in a small town called Livvy that I'd never heard of. Last I heard, he'd found work on a logging rig. Before that, he bussed tables at a local diner and split firewood in between.

Twenty years old and living on pure gumption. He texted me more than any of the boys, but rarely called.

Then there was Blake. The only one stuck at home until he graduated and found a trade school that would get him into fixing motorcycles.

The quick scan of my offspring only produced more uncertainty. I hated feeling insecure about my parenting, and the divorce had only compounded that. Thankfully, Dahlia plopped in front of me with her white-toothed smile and curly black hair.

"Rough couple days, boss lady," she quipped.

"Yes, it's been interesting."

She nudged a cupcake my way with a wink. "Here. Eat this. On the house. Every mom needs a little sugar therapy now and then."

I bit into the rich buttercream and let thoughts of Landon dissolve away.

Chapter Eight

TANNER

The urge to call Leslie and ask her on a date was almost overwhelming, but I wrangled it under control through Thanksgiving and into the days that followed.

The end of November slid into the first of December without change. The warm tones of fall were abandoned for the cool ice of winter almost everywhere.

Later the next week, I sat in my truck outside the Frolicking Moose and stared at glittering snowflakes that dangled from the ceiling. White tinsel brightened sparkling lights that blinked. Blue and silver words filled the chalkboard with Christmassy flavors like peppermint and eggnog.

Was Leslie inside?

I forced the question away as Celeste climbed into the truck.

"Hey, Dad."

"Hey sport."

"Good day?"

She reached behind her for her seatbelt and missed my baleful glance inside again. No sign of Leslie. I pulled the truck out of park and forced myself to navigate away. Leslie and I had spent less than a day in each other's company. *Why* couldn't I get her out of my head?

"Dad?"

I jerked back to life. "Sorry, what?"

Celeste peered at me, already suspicious. "I asked if you had a good day and you totally ignored it. Everything all right?"

"Oh, sorry. Yes. Today was fine. You?"

While Celeste chattered non-stop about school, I headed to the canyon and pretended like I wasn't curious about the Frolicking Moose. Like I didn't want to suck all the details out of my daughter so I'd know what happened in Leslie's life.

My forced silence was punishment, pure and simple. If I wasn't going to ask Leslie on a date myself, I didn't get to ask my daughter for an update on Leslie's life.

Simple.

But hard.

Something held me back from asking. Something stupid. Something that stopped me from asking other qualified women out on dates for years.

Stasis.

After navigating a marriage, a pregnancy, a baby, and a divorce, for years all I had craved was stability. A life without the pitching up and down that came with relationships and change and a young kid.

Over time, that's exactly what I'd created.

Even with Celeste living in between both her parents, I'd created a steady career or two, let them ride me out, and now I had no mortgage, two fantastic cars, a girl about to go to college with a savings account that I'd built up for her, and a fairly easy life, all things considered.

What if Leslie was the one who interrupted that?

While the canyon whizzed past us, blunted in the late light, Celeste yawned sleepily on the seat next to me. Her light had been on for far too late last night, probably catching up on homework. Living an hour away from school meant earlier-than-usual mornings, but it was still better than being home-schooled. Mountain life didn't leave a lot of options.

We didn't speak as I navigated back toward home, Leslie still on my mind.

One date did not a marriage make—or so I told myself. With Leslie it was different. I'd been on plenty of dates over the years. Not many of them, because Celeste had been younger and my work as a coach had been more consuming, but enough that I wasn't totally out of the game. Dating never caused me any fear, because none of them had any real chance of going beyond a single date. I'd made sure of that before I asked.

Leslie posed a whole new challenge.

First, she was a real candidate. If I didn't want to spend the rest of my life alone, Leslie was the kind of woman that could be part of a feasible future between us. We hardly knew each other, yet I could already recognize the potential connection. That was problematic for the easy stasis I'd created.

In addition, I loved her kids. Aside from Blake, whom I met only vaguely, I knew her three older sons pretty well. I'd coached two of them, taught one of them in the classroom, and enjoyed them as people. As adults, they'd probably be even more intriguing.

To make the situation worse, my kid loved *her*.

We lived in the same mountain world, knew the same people, and dating Leslie wouldn't dramatically shift the status quo. Which meant that holding her at arm's length wouldn't be easy.

But I didn't like her that far away, either.

These thoughts ran through my head while I navigated through the canyon and back into Pineville. The holidays had delayed my invoicing cycle, so yesterday I'd tucked two paper invoices for Leslie in between my seat and the gear shift, right where I couldn't ignore them. They drew my gaze too often.

Normally, I dropped my clients an email with the invoice, but I was actively searching for an excuse to talk to her again. I'd already cleaned her house a second time, intentionally doing it while she was at work. Now? Now I was ready to face her.

Maybe not to *ask* her on a date yet, but I did walk to talk to her again. See if I had imagined all the chemistry, or if it really existed.

Getting paid for cleaning her house seemed to be the most likely way to get in the door. I'd drop Celeste off at school tomorrow morning, then swing by Leslie's place. All before she went to work. A totally, completely normal excuse to see her.

And then?

Well, I'd deal with that when I got there.

* * *

When I arrived at Leslie's house the next morning, the place lay quiet.

A quick glance at my watch confirmed that it was only 8:15 in the morning. Would she already be at the Frolicking Moose? I had no idea what hours she kept, but didn't peg her as an early-riser. Besides, from what Celeste said, Leslie didn't work behind the counter unless she filled in for a lunch break or something.

Before I talked myself out of a clearly reckless course of action, I shoved open the truck door and started across the lawn. No sooner had I jogged up the three steps and reached for the door knob then the door burst open. I stopped.

Leslie screeched to a halt.

She held an empty coffee mug in one hand. Drops of water clung to it, as if she'd just rinsed it out. The lid was pinched between two fingers and she carried her car keys in her teeth. A purse, two bags full of something that looked like decorations, and other odds and ends filled her arms.

Looked like someone didn't want to take two trips to the car.

"Oh!" she cried, eyes wide. The expression quickly dropped into a hesitant smile. A low drawl followed, "Ahhh hey."

The words were mostly garbled coming out around her keys. She gingerly reached up with the pinky finger of the hand holding the coffee mug and pulled them out. Her hair lay around her shoulders in freshly washed and dried strands.

"Hey," I said. "Looks like I caught you at a bad time. Can I help you carry something?"

Her left arm dropped to catch a bauble that threatened to fall. I reached out, snatching a hollow, plastic ornament. Her cheeks flared with color.

"Thanks," she breathed. "Sorry, I'm just on my way to work. I bought some Christmas decorations to spruce up the tree there. Did you see it? It's a bit thin."

While she hurriedly explained the dizzying array of *stuff* in her arms, I peeled several bags and containers out of her pile.

"Thanks." She smiled. "I just hate making two trips, don't you?"

I laughed and followed her to the car, parked in the driveway a few steps away. "I've been known to load up all the bags of groceries on both arms to avoid that very thing, yes."

"Good. Because you're a psycho if you don't."

The smell of something light and sweet trailed behind her. Vanilla bean, maybe? It conjured up images of cupcakes and frosting and somehow I already liked Leslie a lot more than I remembered.

I mean, I'd brought invoices to her house on a day when I wasn't cleaning. In fact, I'd be cleaning again in two days and could have brought it then.

Who did that?

Someone desperate for answers, and that perfectly described me right now.

Once all the stuff had been unloaded into the back of her car, she faced me. Both hands were tucked into the pockets of a tan jacket that covered a darker shirt. The tones against her eyes and hair had a stunning effect.

For a moment, I fumbled to find words.

"I, uh, brought your invoices." I pulled the folded paper out of my back pocket and held it up between us. "It covers that first week and last week. I went ahead and added this week, but I won't push it through until I finish cleaning. Hope that's okay. Thought it would be easier."

"Oh, great. Thanks."

By sheer force of will, I swallowed back a sigh that meant *I totally overdid it here today.* Because, yes. I could have texted her the amount and all of this would have been totally moot. Except for the confirmation of my interest in her.

That had definitely just happened.

She grinned, and the smile illuminated her whole face. The last time I'd run into her, she'd been carefully fielding several building disasters. Talking to her on the phone had removed the obstacle of her presence, to which I couldn't deny a strong pull. Now, I realized there was something about Leslie Hill that made me just want to stand near her.

How did she work that magic?

With concerted effort, I pulled my thoughts back together.

She waved the paper and asked, "Are the billing details on

here? I think I want to change it so it's not on the credit card. Do you take DollarsApp?"

"Yes. I mean, no. Wait. Let me check."

Feeling like an idiot, I glanced at the invoice. Panic slipped through me again. The papers weren't even an invoice. They were a bill from one of my chemical providers that I hadn't paid yet.

Fantastic.

I folded the page and slipped it back in my pocket. "You know what? I'll just email it to you. How about that?"

"Uh . . . sure."

"Let me find my username on the app. You can just pay me that way now."

My brain felt like a jar of flies as I attempted to find the app where money transfers came in and out. What felt like an eternity later, I pulled it up, found my username, then showed it to her.

"Here you go. Total was $250."

Her eyebrow quirked. "Thought you said $300 for the first one? Then $100 for each after. So shouldn't it be $200 if we're combining this week and last? I think already paid for the deep clean."

If the earth could open a giant hole and just swallow me now, that would be great.

Had I really thought I'd just walk up to Leslie's house and ask her on a date? That I'd *feel out* whether we had chemistry or not? Idiot. Maybe boys didn't grow into men. Maybe all men were just little boys walking around, playing with fire and getting into trouble.

I hadn't done this in years, which was all too clear, because I'd thoroughly botched this attempt.

"Oh, right." I cleared my throat. "Yes, thank you." A chagrined laugh saved this from being too-terrifyingly devastating. "$200."

Did her lips twitch, or was that just me being paranoid?

"Great," she murmured. With a few quick taps of her phone screen, she declared, "Paid!"

Seconds later, my phone buzzed in my back pocket.

"Thank you."

Her nose wrinkled slightly. "I'll keep you updated on future cleans. Let's do this week again, but I'm not sure about after. What with the wedding now . . ."

She trailed away.

Did she say wedding?

Although it was none of my business, having been present the moment that Landon dropped the fiancée bomb, I felt more invested in this outcome than I ever expected to be.

"Wedding?"

Leslie sighed, her shoulders slumping. "Apparently Landon has scheduled a date for the wedding."

"Really?"

She made a face that indicated displeasure, but I saw more concern than annoyance there. The pad of her thumb ran over the screen of her phone, as if she could coax something out of it with a gentle touch.

"I've been texting him, but he keeps saying he's busy and will call later. So far, he hasn't. It's been almost two weeks since that . . . *awkward* . . . lunch and he's dodged all my calls. My ex-husband Ethan was here a few days ago and mentioned the wedding date. Landon has been, obviously, avoiding me on purpose."

"I wonder why?"

"Great question," she muttered.

The details didn't quite stack together. Would I expect something like this from any of the Miller boys? Not really.

"It doesn't make sense."

Leslie illuminated like a Christmas tree. "Right?" She threw up her hands. "Thank you. None of this makes sense. I mean, maybe from Max because he's always found it really fun to play pranks on me, but from Landon?"

"Think he's hiding something?"

"I don't know." She chewed on her bottom lip. "That makes the most sense, but what?" She laughed a little. "Starla already told me she's not pregnant. Besides, why hide that anyway? I've always told my sons I'd love them no matter what."

"Having been on the twenty-something side of the male brain before, I can assure you that that doesn't matter in his decision-making process right now."

She huffed a wry laugh. "Fair." A thoughtful expression came to her face. "How close *were* you with Landon?"

I sensed something coming, but couldn't peg what it was.

"He was one of my favorites. We spent a lot of time working together on his leadership skills as the team captain. But that was years ago."

"Yes, but he clearly looks up to you."

"Why?"

The pleading expression that followed would have kneecapped a lesser man.

"Could you try talking to Landon? I can't explain it, but I get the feeling that he's flailing and doesn't have anyone that he feels he can talk to." She held up a hand with a roll of her eyes. "Never mind that his dear mother is always here for him. He's clearly not talking to Ethan about whatever is driving him to these decisions either. Maybe he would talk to you?"

The lingering question sat in the air between us, and I wanted to counter with *but what if he doesn't?*

From one parent to another, I could appreciate her desperation. As a parent, sometimes it was just enough to know that your kid confided in someone trustworthy, and wasn't totally headed for the deep end. Not to mention my inherent curiosity, but this had disaster spelled all over it.

Still, I couldn't resist the lure of helping her in some way. "Sure."

She let out a long breath. "Oh, thank you. I can't tell you what that means."

"Text me his number and I'll give him a call."

Leslie was already on her phone, head bent to the task, as I said the words. Not five seconds later, she declared, "Done."

"I'll let you know how it goes."

She reached out and a warm hand touched my wrist. A little shiver slipped through me that I attempted to ignore, almost entirely distracted by the gratitude that filled her lovely eyes.

"Thanks."

"My pleasure."

Clearly unburdened, Leslie turned back to her car and slammed the trunk closed.

"Well, now it's time to decorate the Frolicking Moose and put Maverick's Christmas family reunion together. Talk to you soon, Tanner!"

With that, she disappeared into her SUV with a wave. I returned to my truck, my phone burning in my pocket and my skin on fire where she'd touched me.

* * *

My conversation with Leslie haunted me until I couldn't stand it anymore.

Around 4:30 that afternoon, I pulled up her text message, clicked on the number, and pressed the phone to my ear. It rang twice before Landon's voice came on the line.

"Hello?"

"Hey Landon, it's Tanner Beck."

"Coach?"

"The one. Do you have a minute or two to talk?"

He laughed. "Oh, that's awesome. You're the last person I expected to call. I've always got time for you, coach. What's up?"

"We didn't get to talk much the other day with all the excitement going on. Just wanted to tell you congratulations on the engagement and hear more about your life now. It's not often that I get to catch up with my students."

Thankfully, sincerity drove this talk. I really did want to catch up with him. My students had always just disappeared at the end of the school year. A few stragglers made their way back once or twice, but not often. Part of the reason I left coaching was all the questions it left in the air.

"Uh, yeah," he said, his tone long. "Just a second."

The sound of rustling and a lower register of voice followed. I stared out at the road and wondered if this had been a mistake before Landon came back on the line.

"Twenty minutes work?"

"You tell me, my friend," I said. "I just wanted to touch base."

"Sure thing."

For the next seven minutes. Landon did what he'd always done—he spun a great story. I laughed, chortled, remarked, and we had a familiar back-and-forth. Catching up on his foibles since high school ended had been worth the call.

If nothing, it served as a reminder of how much hope I'd invested in these kids. Sometimes, I'd felt like a surrogate father, and that pride tripled through me now.

"You're doing great, Landon, as you always did. But I have to ask about medical school—why'd you drop out? We worked hard on your applications, on your plan. To drop it? I was shocked, if I'm going to be honest."

The first sound of hesitation entered his voice.

"Did my mom send you?"

"Your mom expressed concern to me," I admitted, "but I

don't answer to her. My intention for calling is sincere. Landon, you wanted medical school bad."

Until I said the words, I didn't realize how true they were. Landon's single-handed focus on medical school had been a plan that the whole school knew about. When he graduated as valedictorian, no one had been surprised. Landon had plans, and those plans always seemed to unfold before his feet.

He sighed.

"I know, coach. It's crazy to me too, but this is the right path. The closer I got, the less I wanted it."

I couldn't help but think of his father, Ethan. Very nice guy. Low-key, visited with us often, but didn't show a lot of spirit. He had a quiet life in his work owning an HVAC company and didn't seem to take things too deep. Landon, on the other hand, was the opposite of his father, and I'd always wondered if something in their differences drove Landon to keep that going.

"Had you really wanted it, or were you chasing something for someone else?" I asked.

Landon sighed. "I'm still not sure."

"Your Mom pressure you?"

"Nah, she's cool about it."

"Your Dad?"

"Not directly, but he wanted me to be more successful than him."

"Well, I'm always here if you need it. You know that, right?"

He laughed. "Coach, you never change. I've got your number now, so you can't get rid of me."

"Wouldn't ever think of it. Hey, I liked Starla, by the way."

A moony tone overtook him. "Oh, man. Starla. She's . . . she's the greatest thing that's ever happened to me. I'm so glad you got to meet her, but she's not always like that. She was just terrified to meet my mom."

I rolled my eyes. All of us were Superman until we met our kryptonite, then we became ridiculous puddles that can't hold ourselves together.

"Your Mom isn't so scary."

"I know that and you know that, but Starla didn't. She's cool about her now. She hopes to see Mom again soon."

"Well, you're a lucky dog to get someone like Starla."

He laughed again. "I know it."

Then I threw out the question I'd wanted to ask all along. "So, when is the big day?"

"Coming up really fast. Probably Valentine's, but we're just figuring a few things out. Could be sooner. We'll let you know when we have a firm date. Probably won't be a big deal, or anything like that."

This time, my concern became real. Landon had never been a *play it easy* kind of guy. No, I'd always imagined his wedding being one that blew out speakers and invited everyone and created a reputation for itself.

"Sounds good. I'm here if you need it."

After a few more comments, the conversation ended. I tossed my phone on the seat next to me and stared out the windshield. Leslie would find some relief over my conversation, but we really hadn't gotten to the core of anything. Landon hovered me at 20,000 feet. Enough for details, but nothing I could rely on.

Really, it wasn't my place anyway.

I turned the key in the ignition as the car chugged to life. No further answers with Landon, but somehow I felt better about the situation.

Whatever he had going on in the background didn't sound bad. It sounded . . . uncertain. I couldn't exactly tell Landon to call his mother. Leslie and I didn't have that kind of relationship and I didn't want to make any illusion that we did.

Still, I couldn't help but wonder what I should say to her now.

Because the fact that I wanted to help her fix her broken things—and see her again—was growing more and more problematic.

Chapter Nine

LESLIE

Maverick frowned at the box I dropped onto the table at the Frolicking Moose. His dark brows pulled together in deep grooves. Then his honey-colored eyes darted up to me.

"Are those decorations for the reunion?"

"No, Conan," I muttered, "they're for the coffee shop. We're going to put them up after the party."

He let out a long breath, closed his eyes, then fluttered them back open. With feeling he said, "I'm sorry. I don't mean to be condescending or controlling. Bethany is just a few months away from delivery, my siblings are coming here in a few short weeks, and I think it was a terrible idea to do a family reunion right now."

My lips twitched. Although I wanted to laugh, I held it back. Real stress filled Maverick's tone. For such a big bear of a man, when it came to Bethany, he had an anxiety tolerance of almost zero. His endearing fear for his wife warmed my still-divorce-chilly heart.

"Look, Mav, everything is on track, okay? Your siblings won't arrive for several more weeks. The flights are booked. Serafina and I have confirmed everything with the lodge. The catering company called me today with a confirmation of orders, and the events you're going to in Jackson City are booked out. I even have split firewood getting dropped off." I gestured between us. "I got your back."

He melted under my comprehensive list. If Mav loved anything, it was a plan that came together just right. The strain drained away from his taut features.

"Thank you, Leslie. You're a lifesaver."

"I know. You good now?"

"Yes. Much better."

After he asked a few more questions—and attempted to meddle in my job, which I quickly scolded him for—I shooed him away to take dinner to his pregnant wife.

Their little girl was only a few months away from her due date, and Bethany was more than ready to get it over with. Lizbeth's presence in the Frolicking Moose had waned the last few weeks as she took care of her own baby.

Whatever he thought, the Mercedy family reunion would be an epic one.

The moment Maverick disappeared, Celeste took his place. "Hey Leslie!"

"Hi!"

She dropped her backpack on the floor next to my booth and slid into the open seat. As usual, she was perfectly put together and totally oblivious to my jealousy.

How did they make teenagers like that these days? The only memories of high school I held onto involved very frizzy hair, braces, and an awkwardness that went bone deep. Girls like Celeste, who were all natural ease and warmth from the get-go, boggled my mind.

"So." Her bright eyes met mine. "Did you say yes?"

"To what?"

"My dad."

My brow furrowed. "About what? The invoice he brought over this morning?"

"No." She recoiled, then rolled her eyes. "The date? Duh!"

My throat grew tight and hot at the same moment. I opened my mouth to speak, then stopped. Date? The sound of something crashing followed. Dahlia called out, "I'm good!"

"Date?" I whispered, blinking through blurry thoughts.

Celeste's expression loosened, as if she realized she'd just done something wrong. "Uh oh," she whispered.

"Um . . . what do you mean?"

Her eyes widened like snow globes. Seconds before I thought they'd explode, she burst into a giggle.

"Double uh oh," she sang, a hand over her mouth. "I totally mucked that up. He didn't ask you on a date this morning? Really?"

My mind shuffled through a few questions all at once, but ended on the most pertinent. "Your dad was going to ask me on a date?"

"Supposedly." She shrugged. "Sounds like he lost his courage, or something. He never does that by the way. This is awesome."

The replay of Tanner's conversation at my house wasn't difficult to conjure. He had definitely been more flustered than usual. Fumbling over words, his thoughts, his own invoice, which I'd never even glimpsed.

Had he been nervous?

Was that why he delivered the invoice in the first place? It seemed a weird time to swing by considering he'd be back in two days to clean again. Also, he had my number. Why not just text me? Ultimately, only one question kept replaying in my mind.

Why *didn't* he ask?

I tried furiously to *not* blush and managed to fail on an epic level.

"Sorry, Les," Celeste muttered. She reached across the table and squeezed my wrist. "Dad never chickens out which is, I think, a compliment to you."

Yeah, I wanted to say, *I took his absolute lack of interest as a really positive thing.*

Her gaze traveled from her phone and up to me with a pleading expression. "Please don't tell him I said anything?"

"Promise," I said too quickly. "I won't say anything. To anyone."

"Thank you." She slapped her palm on her forehead. "He'd kill me."

What was worse than being the one that Tanner botched? The one that Tanner didn't ask. Maybe the only thing worse was being the one that your son *didn't* tell about his wedding date.

A quick beep of a familiar horn sounded outside. Celeste gathered her things, sent me one last apologetic smile, and headed out to the truck. I folded myself into my office until long after Tanner Beck had driven away.

* * *

For the next week, Blake puttered around the house as he spoke to a girl across the country via his bluetooth headphones. They alternated from deep talks to intense video games. I buried myself in updating the Frolicking Moose HomeBnB listing, finalizing aspects of the Mercedy reunion, and trying not to think about Tanner.

Turns out, after four years of raising sons and a husband, I rocked at coordinating other people's lives. Something in my work at the coffee shop fulfilled a deep part of me, and I'd grown to love it.

Of course, Tanner messed up all my usually spectacular focus. If he hadn't stopped by last week, I'd be a lot more productive. If I hadn't seen the attractive way his eyes crinkled when he laughed or the rolling way the sound rippled through the air, I wouldn't still be daydreaming about it now.

Whenever I replayed those moments, Celeste's conversation about his not asking me out soon followed. The bottom line was this: no matter what I talked myself into, Tanner Beck wasn't interested in me. If he was, he would have asked me on a date already.

Now, I needed to get over it.

While working at the Frolicking Moose near the end of the week, my mind somersaulted like jeans in a dryer over Landon. My pen tapped the edge of my binder, which was tabbed into different sections and decorated with post-it notes in the shape of a Christmas tree. Not even that cheered me up at the moment.

Katelyn worked alone today while Dahlia and Bastian visited Jackson City to mail Christmas presents to all Dahlia's family around the country. This was her first Christmas away from home and she compensated by sending *loads* of stuff to every cousin and distant relative. Katelyn hummed while she worked, but said little without Dahlia here to start the conversation.

Meanwhile, I couldn't fathom how Landon continued to dodge the topic of his wedding.

Countless text messages, some emails, and a few stilted phone calls led me to no further information. Ethan heard nothing else either, which didn't reassure me as much as I'd hoped. Blake had no reports, and Nicholas hadn't even called. Only Max had called, per usual, on Sunday. He locked information up like a vault, though, so I'd never get news from him.

Would there be a wedding?

Was there trouble in paradise?

So many pieces to this puzzle didn't add up.

With a shake of my head, I yanked my phone out of my pocket. I hadn't heard from Landon in several days.

Leslie: Hey kiddo, just wanted to check in. When do you have time to chat?

I held my breath. Lately, he didn't respond until evening, but I waited for about thirty seconds each time I messaged him just in case. To my shock, three dots popped up indicating a reply.

His response shuttled through moments later.

Landon: Sorry, Mom. Just swamped here with job training and Starla's trying to plan the wedding. What about this weekend? I know you want to talk about Starla. I do too. But it needs to be in person.

Leslie: This weekend is great! Promise you won't dodge me again like you did weeks ago? That hurt my feelings. I'm worried about you.

Putting the words out there removed a weight off my chest, even while they terrified me. Kids-as-adults was weird. The boundaries felt loose, because I couldn't be the buffer that protected him from everything now. Holding them accountable was hard, but it was even worse when they had a cavalier attitude.

Landon: I promise. I'm sorry I hurt your feelings, Mom.

Leslie: Forgiven. Love you.

Relief that *something* had been acknowledged felt slightly less isolating, which led my thoughts right to the conversation with Tanner when I asked him to reach out to Landon.

Should I have asked him to help me? Maybe that had been a mistake.

Tanner had never mentioned if he'd been able to call. I'd asked a week ago, but didn't want to follow up on it myself.

Maybe asking Tanner for help had been a step too far. It felt a little too desperate.

Either way, I still had no idea what else to do, or who to turn to. Parenting had always been a comedy of errors. While everyone had sympathetically tut-tutted over my position or laughed over what my kids said, I just wanted someone to *help*.

Ethan had been a little too focused on work for that.

"Hey, Blake," I called over the sound of violent shooting and shouts of pain from his console. "Have you talked to Landon lately?"

"No," he called.

"What about Nicholas?"

"Nope."

"Max?"

"Yeah. Had a practice and called me on his way there. Said it went well and things are looking up. Might be some scouts for him."

I frowned. Of course, I had to get the most pertinent updates through my youngest son. Max was going to suffer for not mentioning that the last time we spoke.

"Said he'd tell you about it on Sunday," Blake quickly added. "He only had a minute and I had a question about something on my video game that Missy couldn't answer."

Reality didn't soften the blow much. It felt like my relationship with all my boys slid down a wet slope. Then again, all of them still grappled with undeveloped brains, so what did I know?

Just as I'd resolved to keep showing up and let them know I cared, my phone rang. I glanced down, then muttered a swear word. Tanner's name appeared on the screen. A simple call from him created a storm of butterflies in my gut.

What would a date do?

I banished the thought. Didn't matter because it wouldn't happen. With a deep, slow inhale through my nose, I forced myself to answer.

"Hello?"

"Hey," Tanner said easily, as if we talked every day so casually, "just wanted to let you know that I got a hold of Landon. A couple of days ago, actually, but I . . . I got wrapped up in stuff. I also thought about calling him again but haven't done it yet."

I slipped out the back door and closed the door behind me. The shock of cold air woke me out of my thoughts.

"Awesome, thank you for reaching out to him. I don't expect you to recount everything, or whatever. I just wanted to know . . . did he mention anything I should be worried about?"

"Nothing noteworthy."

A boring explanation of their conversation followed, which gave me some relief. No massive gaps in Landon's life that he sought to hide from me, at least. Perhaps that was one of my biggest fears as a parent—that my kids would struggle but not come to me for help.

"Well, that's something," I said. "I just got a few text messages from him. He promised me we'd talk this weekend."

"Good."

Tanner's confident tone helped all the ruffled edges in my body smooth back out. Instead of feeling prickly and rankled, I had a moment to breathe.

"How are you?" Tanner asked. Thankfully, his tone hadn't grown stilted. The phone had always been forgiving that way. You couldn't read body language, even if you could read the tone.

"Stressed," I admitted.

"Oh? About what?"

"Landon, mostly. My boys, always. Maverick's family reunion a little, but that's coming together well."

"Tell me about the reunion. Sounds intense."

His melodic voice came out gentle, but this time with an unusual roll to it. It sent a shiver down the back of my arms, and I felt a moment of gratification that at least aging hadn't taken away *that* response.

Everything changed in your forties—some of it for the good. But I missed the naiveté of youth sometimes. When you had a whole life of *first's* ahead of you. First butterflies. First kiss. First boyfriend. First hickey. At forty-something, I'd done and felt most of it. I missed feeling uninhibited and naive about what came on the other side of emotions.

"You really want to know?" I asked.

"Yeah."

"But . . . why?"

He laughed. "Because I can *almost* competently coordinate my life and my teenage daughter's life. Can't fathom a powerhouse family like the Mercedy's swooping in and expecting me to make it perfect. Not to mention four boys, a career, and a house. It's fascinating to watch."

When he stated it like that, it sounded far more flattering than it was.

"Well, it's stressful, but it's mostly about organization. Maverick is a teddy bear that's secretly a hot mess, Bethany is pregnant so she doesn't care about anything but sleeping and getting the baby out, and Serafina is just trying to keep Benjamin from imploding while around his family for so long. In the end, the bar isn't set that high."

Tanner laughed and the sound brought a reluctant smile to my face. Yeah, I could deal with more of that in my life, even if I'd spent all this time trying to pretend I didn't care.

I leaned against the house and peered out on my dead garden.

"I take it you don't come from a big family?" I asked.

"Nah. One brother, younger than me. Celeste is my only daughter, and my parents died a couple years apart around ten years ago."

"Lone man."

"Not really." He had a shrug in his voice. "I'll always have Celeste, in some form."

"Do you ever get tired of being the only parent? This crap isn't easy. I mean, Ethan didn't do a lot but once he was gone I realized his presence was more helpful than I thought. He at least took out the garbage, or got after the boys when they didn't."

The question slipped out of me before I could stop it, but I couldn't say that I regretted it.

Ethan and I hadn't been bastions of communication at any point in our marriage, but there had been connection in the mindless prattle of *someone* to talk at that I missed. I kept some of that from my boys. Blake didn't need the burdens of his mother, and Ethan hadn't, apparently, wanted my prattle anymore.

"I think you get used to it," Tanner replied. "It just becomes the new normal."

My brow furrowed. "I've only been divorced a year—almost two if you count when we started to talk about separating—and I've been fine with it so far. Even if I act dramatic about it. I wonder sometimes what this will feel like in five or ten years, though. If the quiet just becomes too much."

"Depends on how quiet you let it get," he said.

"Fair."

"What about you?" he asked. "Siblings?"

"Three. I'm the oldest. My younger siblings all have similar versions of a family and a picket fence, just scattered across the country. My parents are both alive, happy in a retirement home near a golf course. I'm absolutely as ordinary as it comes."

"That," he said quickly, "doesn't seem right at all. Ordinary is not a word I would have used to describe you."

"You're kidding."

"Not even a little."

The last thing I wanted to do was fish for compliments, but he'd baited me there. How could I *not* press for details?

"I'm a previous stay-at-home-mom that divorced after twenty-five years of marriage. I manage a coffee shop to keep food on the table and I have four intelligent boys with varying levels of stupid they interact with on a daily basis. There's not much less exciting than that."

"Huh. That's interesting," he murmured, "because I see someone totally different."

My mouth went dry, hungry to beg him for details. Desperate to know what could set me apart in this world that didn't relate to my last twenty-five years of life.

Some shred of evidence that proved I hadn't given my entire self over to marriage and babies and now had nothing left to hold up and say, *this is me*.

"Oh, sorry, Les. I gotta take a call. It's another client coming in. Let's resume this later, all right? We aren't done."

His casual nickname sent the butterflies back into a whirl.

Were we there now?

"Oh. Right. Sure. Later."

"I'll call tomorrow."

The call ended. Stunned, I pushed the phone into my pocket and stared out into the night, utterly at a loss for what the jumbled emotions in my chest really meant. Amidst all the chaos lingered the most unexpected emotion of all.

Giddiness.

* * *

My pen tapped another furious staccato on my notebook the next day.

My left leg jumped up and down, and I felt like I'd had three cups too much coffee, although I hadn't even finished my first.

Unable to stop myself, I replayed how the conversation with Tanner ended over and over again.

I see someone totally different.

I'll call tomorrow.

"Hey, boss lady!" Dahlia called, breaking into my reverie. "You're required out here."

While my brain remained on a spreadsheet of orders for our food supply company, I stepped out of the office and into the shop. Starla stood there, a tentative smile on a pale face.

All other thoughts fled.

"Starla?"

She fidgeted with the strap of her purse as she smiled. "Good morning. I wanted to stop by to see if you're busy?"

"Ah, no. Not at all."

"Do you have a minute to talk?"

A bump of hope welled up in my stomach and I had to hold back my shout of *yes please right now*! There wasn't a soul I wanted to talk to more than her, but I held onto my restraint.

Instead, I gave her my warmest smile to set her at ease. She seemed so colorless and fragile, her skin almost onion-paper white against the backdrop of snow behind her. A thick coat and scarf wrapped her body, but she still looked cold to me.

"Anything for you. Have a seat." I gestured toward my usual booth in the corner. "Want something to drink?"

"Herbal tea would be great, thanks."

Dahlia held up a hand, "Got it. And your usual is coming."

Starla and I sat across from each other while Dahlia bustled in the background, humming a Christmas song. Starla didn't remove her coat as she settled into the seat with a sheepish expression.

"Landon doesn't know I came here today. I'm not hiding it from him," she quickly added, "Just . . . I think he'd want to be here and I wanted to talk to you alone."

My brow rose in silent encouragement.

Starla let out a long breath. "I know how uncomfortable it must have been for you to hear that we were engaged after only dating for four weeks. I wish I could paint a better picture for you. Maybe tell you that we'd known each other for a year before we actually began to date, but that wouldn't be true either."

Her bottom lip blanched under her teeth as she paused, then regarded me through her eyelashes.

"We are a classic love-at-first-sight situation, if you believe that's possible."

I didn't, but I wasn't about to betray that to her. "How did you meet?" I asked instead.

Dahlia set a steaming cup of tea in front of Starla and a coffee with lots of cream and a dash of sugar in front of me. The steaming drinks filled the air between us, countering the cold waves of air from the nearby window. Starla hooked a hand around the cup and pulled it closer, but made no move to drink.

A soft expression stole across her face.

"At a party, actually. Not super romantic," she said with a laugh, "but I guess the details don't really matter. He caught my eye from across the room and . . . the feeling that my life had just irrevocably changed came over me. I can't describe it."

She chuckled, still a little breathless from the memory. I doubted she knew it, but she'd put a hand on her stomach.

Could she imagine the butterflies again?

"Sounds magical," I said.

Starla nodded, but the whimsical expression faded.

"Yes. It really was. He came over, introduced himself, and we talked until the party ended around 1:00 in the morning. He walked me home. We stayed up talking until 6:00. I was late to work because I made him breakfast, and he was late to class because he stayed to eat, and we haven't been separated ever since."

"Of all my boys," I said with what I hoped was a diplomatic tone, "he's the one I never expected to do something like this. He's not usually impetuous and is, despite all appearances, a careful decision maker. Max? Definitely something he would do. He's a knot head sometimes. But Landon . . ."

I trailed away, not certain what I really meant to say. Starla had sobered, her long, pale lashes blinking.

"I know," she whispered. "It's not like Landon at all, which is why I wanted to talk to you about it today. Miss Hill, I *love* Landon. I love him more than I've ever loved anything in my life, even if we've only known each other for four weeks. I love him in a way that I never believed possible. I'm not a romantic girl. I live in a world of expectations, responsibilities, and reality. What we have is . . . special."

Words fled at the gravity in her tone. I opened my mouth to speak, but didn't know what to say. Part of me admired her gumption. She clearly wasn't a weakling that hid behind my son, at least. She'd need a bit of power in that spine to deal with him all the time.

But did that mean I was willing to surrender my oldest to her?

Not yet.

"Why are you moving so fast?" I asked.

Her lips pressed together as she studied me, then quietly said, "Because it's the right thing to do. For both of us. Yes, there is information we're not telling you yet. But we will. I promise.

A dozen other questions flooded my mind. With them came the fear that it wasn't my place to ask those questions anymore. Landon was twenty-three years old. The woman that he loved had come to seek me out and give me reassurance. He'd already found the most important woman in his life. That ceased to be me.

What could I possibly do or say to change it?

And should I?

Memories hovered on the edge of my mind-plunge. Ethan and I had a quick engagement, caught up in the whirl of romance and twitterpation. My mother had been uncharacteristically concerned. I'd seen it in her thin lips, her drawn eyes, her forced excitement as I extolled all of Ethan's virtues. When the divorced had finalized, to her credit, she hadn't breathed a word of *I told you so* to me.

Because she *hadn't* told me so.

Whatever reservations my parents held, they hadn't stated them, and I wondered if they felt caught in the same paradox as me.

Did I let Landon make this mistake on his own? Or did I warn them of my own path? Landon already knew what happened with his parents. Likely, he didn't need reminders of the pain of divorce.

Besides, Starla and Landon weren't Ethan and me.

Parenting, I'd always found, had been a delicate dance between what I wanted to say and what I *should* say. Staring at Starla made it clear that what I wanted and what I needed here wasn't the same thing.

"Thank you, Starla." I reached across the table to take her hand in mine. "I won't pretend that I'm not concerned or hurt that Landon has been avoiding me, but I appreciate you coming here in person. I have concerns, yes. I'm not ready to let Landon go onto a path so similar to mine. But if he's going to do this, I believe he has his best chance with someone like you."

For a moment, I thought I saw a glimmer of tears in her eyes, but she blinked so quickly I couldn't be sure. Her fingers squeezed mine.

"Thank you. Can I make one selfish ask of you?"

"Of course."

Our hands untangled as she reached into her purse and pulled out several papers folded in half longways. Her hands trembled a little as she opened them, then flipped them so I could see.

Lists cluttered the front and back of two pages. While I studied the words, she had a sip of tea. It took only a moment for me to comprehend what she'd just given me.

"A wedding list?" I asked.

"Landon and I are very busy with the end of semester finals and his new job and . . . a few other things." She waved a vague hand and had another sip of tea. "We were wondering if you could help us pull the wedding together?"

Whether it was the warm drink, the coffee shop, or having spilled her thoughts, her cheeks had pinked up a little bit. When she had more color, her face flushed out in a lovely way. I had no difficulty seeing in her what Landon must see.

I studied her eager eyes for any sign of pity. Was she giving me something to do to help me get used to this? I found none. Instead, a sense of hope mixed with despair lived there.

Whatever they faced in their life that they weren't disclosing, it certainly seemed real enough.

"Yes, of course."

She tapped a finger at the top of the list, and I felt a thrill at her organization. A girl after my own heart. Maybe boys *did* marry different versions of their mother.

"Here are a few simple things I need help with," she murmured. "It's mostly coordinating, like what you said you were doing for a family reunion here. Calling a few places, that sort of thing. We aren't going to have anything big. We just need to find a venue, an officiant, and invite Landon's friends and family."

"What about yours?"

"Ah . . . there won't be any. Just me."

My gaze darted to hers, but she kept hers studiously on the papers. "See this list? Landon wondered if we could have the ceremony here." Starla gestured around us. "At the Frolicking Moose. I thought I'd ask if it was available."

I skimmed the page, sliding past completed details like *wedding dress* and *budget*. Their total budget of $500 sent a wince and a giggle through me at the same time. Easy enough to fix. If she let me help with the planning, my credit card could also help with the expenses.

"Winter theme," I murmured as I read the top of the second page. Underneath that were doubly-underlined words. *Lots of snowflakes and glitter*. I grinned.

"Snowflakes and glitter. Girl after my heart."

Starla smiled unapologetically. I kept perusing past a list of bridal necessities—comfortable shoes, groom's ring, and hair-style picked—and into a detailed explanation of the generalities. Simple catering. Easy wedding cake design. My eyes skidded to a full stop on the date.

New Year's.

I blinked.

What?

She'd tensed when I looked up at her, clearly anticipating what I'd just seen. "New Year's?" I asked.

She rolled her lips, looking uneasy again. "Yes. We, ah,

moved up the date from Valentine's Day. It will work best with training for Landon's new position and a few other things."

The *few other things* is what had my curiosity. Whatever it was, those *other things* clearly drove the agenda here. She'd appeased some of my concerns, but new ones grew. While I had a greater trust in their inherent care for each other, I still couldn't believe that they were making the right decision.

What drove them to such haste?

"Do you think it will be possible?" she asked. "Could we pull something like this off, or is it too late?

A note of concern filled her tone, and I found myself wanting to allay it.

"Yes, of course."

"Would the Frolicking Moose be available?"

She glanced over her shoulder, past the counter where Dahlia filled a drive-through order, and into the doorway that led to the back room.

White twinkle lights, fake snow, and far too much Christmas glitter already decorated the back room now. Except for a Christmas tree in the corner, I'd insisted on avoiding Christmas decorations and keeping it solely winter themed to avoid decorating twice. Maverick had been resistant, but eventually saw my way.

It wasn't difficult picturing a wedding there. Small, of course, but it looked like that's what they wanted. With Landon having the only guests, I'd wager that all of Pineville would show up.

"It's free then," I said. "All of New Year's day and evening. I'll make sure to book it today."

Starla sighed, like a burden of relief had been removed. "That's wonderful to hear."

I waved the papers. "You trust me to help you with this?"

She nodded firmly. "It would be most helpful if you take it

over. Surprise us. You have in your hand the only decisions that I'd make and want in there, the rest can be yours. Maybe . . . consider the execution of this as a Christmas gift? I can write you a check for the money right now, if you're willing."

"Oh, no need." I waved a hand. "The expenses are on me."

She opened her mouth to argue, but I set her my sternest Mom-glare.

"No, neither of you are going to pay for this. You're both college students that have a lot going on, and you want it small anyway. Ethan and I will cover the costs."

Her eyes filled with tears. "Thank you."

I smiled. A limited carte blanche on a party of my own planning sounded divine. Planning my first son's wedding?

The ultimate.

"Of course. I'm honored you asked and excited. I'll get started on this right away." I stacked the few pages together and folded them again. "Thank you for allowing me to help."

Starla swallowed hard. "Thank you for helping and . . . for your patience. I hope this is the beginning of a wonderful rela-tionship."

Despite my reservations, I gave her my biggest smile.

"I have a feeling it will be."

Chapter Ten

TANNER

When my phone rang in my pocket after finishing up yet another failed interview to replace Yessica, I glanced down to see Leslie's name.

Shocked that she'd call me—I'd been the one calling her—I stared at it for two full rings before I hit accept.

"Hey, Leslie."

"Hey! Got a minute?"

"Sure." I set my pen down, transferred the phone to my other ear, and leaned my elbows onto my knees. "What's up?"

"This . . . thing happened with Starla yesterday and I wanted to . . . well, I guess that I wanted to see what you thought of it. I've been thinking about it all night."

"Sure."

Why this phone call felt like it meant something, I had no idea. But her hesitation clued me in that she'd shot from the hip. She called me without really thinking about why, and although I couldn't peg it, it seemed like a good sign.

"Starla stopped by the coffee shop," she said.

"Really?"

"Yeah. On her own. She wanted to talk to me about everything."

For the next five minutes, she recounted a startling visit that, while revealing about Starla, still didn't tell us much about the situation. In the end, Leslie summarized my own thoughts.

"I might like her more," Leslie admitted, "but I feel like I know even less about what's really going on. That's frustrating, now that I've stepped away from the situation and spoken it out loud. At the time it just seemed . . . I don't know."

"It's certainly unexpected."

She sighed, and I heard a burden of care in it. I didn't know what to say now. She had a big mystery on her hand that had no clear answers yet. So I said the only thing that seemed pertinent.

"I think this is going to work itself out, Les. I really do. Landon is a good kid with a smart head on his shoulders, impetuous decision notwithstanding. Starla seems to have it together and has no apparent ulterior motives. Right now you have a choice: you can trust Landon or not."

"I know."

"And?"

"Of course I trust him. I just . . . I'm sad that the dynamic between him and me is different. There's a lot to get used to here. I've never been usurped before," she added with a dry chuckle.

I laughed. "Yes, well, that's certainly one way of looking at it."

I thought I heard a smile in her voice when she spoke again. "I just mean that I've never given one of my boys away, and I'm not ready to do that. I've already given away my old plan, my husband, my old life, and now my oldest kid? Blake is months away from me giving him his own life too. It just . . . it sucks."

"It does suck."

"Parenting, right?"

The exasperation in her voice set me to laughing again, but this time I schooled it by clearing my throat.

"Right."

"Listen, thanks. I'm sorry if this isn't something you really wanted to hear about but . . . I guess I needed a friend. You seemed to see the same things in Landon that I've always seen, and I'm grateful to know that I'm not crazy. My son might be," she added as a witty aside, "but I'm definitely not."

"No," I said through a chuckle. "It's definitely not you."

"Have a good day, Tanner."

"You too."

Reluctantly, I let the call end. For several minutes I stared at the phone, lost in thought. I'd dropped so deep into my internal meanderings about Leslie and teenagers and *giving away* parts of our lives that I almost didn't recognize that the phone rang in my hand, even though I stared right at it.

When the name registered on the screen, my brow furrowed.

Landon Miller

Now what were the odds of that?

Concerned now, I accepted the call and said, "Hey Landon."

"Coach. You got a minute? I need some help."

* * *

Landon waited for me just outside the Jackson City hospital pick up lane.

I pulled up in my work truck less than twenty minutes later. When I rolled to a stop, he yanked open the door and peered inside. Fatigue lined his eyes, making his expression drawn.

"Thanks, coach."

"Anytime."

"Starla's just in the lobby. I'll bring her out, just wanted to make sure there was room for both of us to sit together up here."

I motioned to the empty bench chair between us. "All yours."

Stuffing my concerns and questions aside required concerted effort. He disappeared inside while I waited. When he returned only a few minutes later, he carried Starla in his arms.

Her face was buried in his neck. I hopped out of the car and opened the passenger door for them. Starla kept her eyes tightly shut, her lips thin and face a pasty shade of not-feeling-so-good.

I returned to the other side of the car while Landon settled her in. The moment Landon clicked his seatbelt into place, he pulled Starla into his arms. She leaned into his side, head on his shoulder. His arm circled her whole body like a tight anchor.

"Our apartment isn't far away," he said quietly.

Our apartment rang like bells in my head. After he told me his address, I pulled away without another word. Landon murmured quietly to Starla every now and then. The gentle man that Landon had become felt like an odd juxtaposition to the ferocious, competitive athlete I used to coach.

She lay limp at his side, and I pulled a few crumpled grocery bags out of the back when we stopped at a light. Landon nodded as I passed them to him, then kept them handy—just in case she spilled her stomach all over the place.

Whatever had happened, Starla didn't look well.

Twenty minutes later, I stood in the doorway of a run-down apartment complex on the other side of the city. I wouldn't say the neighborhood had questionable tenants, but I also wouldn't let Celeste live here.

Landon's keys rattled in the doorknob as he carried Starla into the apartment. They disappeared down a hallway to the right while I yanked the keys free, locked my truck with the fob, and advanced inside.

Clearly, they'd just moved in. Maybe only a few days or a week ago. Three cardboard boxes lined up against one wall, near a ratty couch that looked like someone had just offloaded it on them for free, and a vague array of paper plates and plastic cups in a small kitchen. A laundry basket full of mixed dirty clothes wasn't my first clue that these two weren't *just* dating.

The whole thing had a hasty feel to it, like they just moved in, hadn't expected it, and didn't know what to do now.

I stood in the middle of the room until Landon showed back up. The dark hallway that he'd stepped into wasn't long —I could see a bedroom door at the end of it, closed tight. The immediate concern had faded from his expression. Now, something haggard lay in its wake.

"You need to talk?" I asked.

He lifted an eyebrow. "You want to listen?"

I nodded.

He motioned to the couch with a wave of his hand. Out of the kitchen he conjured a folding chair, opened it, and sat across from me. Once there, he ran a hand through his hair and let out the world's longest breath.

"Started a month ago."

For the next half hour, Landon spun out a story I would never have expected.

"Non-Hodgkin's lymphoma," he murmured with a shake of his head, as if he couldn't believe it himself. A slight tremor of his hand accompanied the words. "She was tentatively diagnosed three weeks ago, but the doctor just pushed the official diagnosis three days ago, when the final results came in with a bigger picture. Non-Hodgkin's lymphoma has a huge range of things that go with it. It's hard to nail down what's going on and . . . anyway, there's more involved than I ever thought."

He trailed away for a moment, and I was grateful for a chance to grapple with what he'd just said. Cancer? In a girl as young as Starla? Fate had always been mean, maybe downright catty, but this just seemed diabolical. Granted, I hadn't seen her cumulatively for more than a few hours, and we'd only directly spoken once or twice, but I sensed enough life and zest in her that this felt terribly wrong.

"Landon," I said quietly. "I don't know what to say."

He shrugged. "What can you possibly say?"

He rattled details about doctors, treatment options, potentials, different diagnostic imaging, and words I only knew existed because I'd once dealt with player injuries. Hearing them rattled off so quickly from Landon meant he'd been living this reality with her for all the weeks of their existence together.

"Did you really meet only six weeks ago?" I asked.

He hesitated, then nodded. "Yeah."

"And when did you marry her?"

He paled. My hunch had been something of a long shot, but not really. The picture stacked up quickly now that I had concrete details. Landon's jaw tightened as he looked away.

"Four weeks ago."

My eyebrows shot up. "For insurance?"

"No," he snapped, "because I loved her then and I love her more every day. Yes, we were married at two weeks but . . . we knew already that it would happen." He held up two hands, his voice softening. "It's insane, I know. But until it happened to me . . . I would have never thought such a thing possible."

The pragmatism of his mother set against this story created a wild twist that I both dreaded and anticipated. What would Leslie have to say to such a romantic notion? At such a decision?

Pride, I hoped.

"You're a good man, Landon."

He scoffed. "This has nothing to do with being a hero and everything to do with keeping her on this planet with me. That's it. I'm a selfish bastard at the core, really, because I don't want to lose her."

The ferocity of his expression convinced me, if the force of his voice hadn't.

"How are you going to make this happen?" I asked. "Looks like she has a stack of medical bills awaiting her, a long, uncertain road ahead, and it sounds like you have a job or something?"

"Or something," he said and nodded. "Yes, I found a job. I've become a drug rep for a pharmaceutical company that wants to emphasize more offices in this area."

"Drug rep?"

"Yeah." He shrugged. "They take people that don't get into medical school all the time. It's a good fit. It kind of keeps me in the medical sphere without having to go to 8,000 years of college."

"It's a far cry from a cardiothoracic surgeon."

Landon met my challenging gaze. "I know," he said without wavering, "but none of that mattered once I found her. And I really wasn't sure I wanted it anyway. Before I met Starla, I'd been seriously questioning medical school. Four years of college is enough for right now. Something else *will* come. For now, however, my focus is Starla."

I made a mental note to coach him on what *not* to say to Leslie when he explained this situation.

"You have insurance through this new job?" I asked.

He nodded.

"Good. Do you have enough income?"

He nodded reluctantly, his gaze darting a skeptical glance around the apartment. "For now," he said.

"Good. You've got a good start, college degree or not. Sounds like she won't be able to work?"

He hesitated. "She wants to, but she was working at a daycare when she got the diagnosis. With treatment—probably chemo and radiation—she can't work there. She had to quit a week ago because her symptoms have gotten worse."

"So, no."

"No."

"Will she be safe here while you're gone? What if she needs to get to the hospital? She clearly can't get herself there on her own."

His brow furrowed with the first sign of trouble. I glanced around.

"Let me help you answer that," I said. "No, she definitely won't be able to keep herself safe or take care of herself. I know people everywhere, Landon. Let me help you find a better place to stay where there is more support for you *and* Starla."

Landon's nostrils flared for a moment, and I saw the struggle. A man like him thrived on pride. On the ability to take care of the woman he loved and the life he chose. He was young and eager to prove himself. My offer wouldn't be easy to take, but the guy had plastic forks and a ratty rug to his name. Not to mention inherited medical bills, and who-knew-how-many-more on the way.

Finally, he nodded once.

"Sounds good." He swallowed. "Thanks, coach."

I stood up and clapped him on the shoulder. He squared to me and tilted his chin back. Though still smaller and leaner through the shoulders, he wasn't far away from finally being stronger than me.

"You've got this, Landon. It's an impossible situation, but you've always thrived in those. One last question."

"Why haven't I told my Mom?"

I nodded.

"Starla asked me not to, not with Christmas coming up. She didn't want my family's first impression of her to be one of *the sick girl*. Doesn't want anyone to think she married me for the insurance or anything like that. She has a really ugly road ahead and she just wants our first Christmas together to be normal. As normal as it can be," he added quietly, with a vague wave to the back room.

"Okay."

"Will you please keep the secret? We're going to tell Mom, I swear. But we want the wedding and Christmas to be happy. Not . . . loaded with whatever."

I hesitated. Keep this secret from Leslie? The Landon mystery had been one of our main connecting points. One of the things that kept me in her brain. The fact that I could stay top-of-mind for Leslie by asking her on a damn date, already, was a thought I sent away. The siren song of *stasis* always sang in the background when I thought of dating.

Though it sounded a lot smaller these days.

"I'll keep your secret," I said.

His shoulders eased back. "Thank you. I . . . thank you. My mom isn't exactly the most romantic person. She won't understand if we tell her it was love at first sight."

Leslie's previous conversation whipped back through my mind.

"I don't know," I drawled, head tilted, "you might give her a chance. She could surprise you. I know she surprises me all the time."

A funny look came on his face, but I grabbed my keys and headed toward the door before he could think too hard on it. Or me, either. The last thing I needed to do tonight was stake a claim on Leslie Hill with her oldest son.

We weren't there yet.

But maybe we wouldn't be far off soon.

"Thanks again," he said as he followed me to the door. "I just . . . I didn't know who to call without worrying anybody or giving everything away. Plus, she would have had to drive so far, it didn't make sense. Starla suggested you. It was the right move."

"It was." I agreed with a nod. "And I'm always here. I'll talk to you tomorrow about a better place, all right?"

"Thanks, coach."

* * *

My fingers drummed the edge of my steering wheel as I navigated through Jackson City and back to the office. Thoughts fluttered through my head like a murder of rising crows.

Foremost on my mind was my promise to keep their secret. I didn't like the thought of not telling Leslie what I'd learned—that didn't sit right. Which meant that I might need to avoid her, which I also didn't want to do.

Eventually, she'd find out that I knew. She'd probably be upset or never speak to me again or . . . any number of things.

But it still wasn't my story to tell.

The office lay quiet when I stepped inside. I gazed around, muttered a swear word under my breath, and headed back out. My worry over keeping a secret from Leslie had me too distracted. I'd never be able to focus on new applicants.

Half an hour later, I made it back home. Celeste's extra day off of school meant she'd be there too. I flipped the kitchen lights on as I navigated into the house, grabbed some leftovers, and watched the container spin through the microwave. The sound of Celeste laughing—she probably video chatted with one of her friends—drifted down the stairs.

"I'm home!" I called.

"Hi Dad!"

When she didn't appear, I took my lunch into the other room.

Just to have sound, I flipped a game on and lowered to the couch. The rewarmed potatoes and chicken hardly had flavor as I attempted to track the game and think about Landon.

In the end, I finished the food, leaned back, and closed my eyes.

Who was I kidding? Myself? This whole thing was a friggin' mess, and somehow I stood at the very center of it. The moment she found out I knew the truth about Landon and Starla and she didn't, Leslie would flip.

My goal to ask her on a date seemed far, far away now. Not only was she going to plan their entire ceremony and wedding —which made sense in new ways considering Landon's revelation—but she had the Mercedy reunion on her plate.

I wanted to ask her out more than ever. Snag some one-on-one time with just the two of us and *really* see what this woman was about, but her life had a chaos about it that wouldn't allow free time anytime soon.

Maybe that was for the best.

Because I had the feeling that Leslie was a heavy rock rolling down the mountain of my life. Once I let her go, she wouldn't stop. Then I'd slide with her, lost to it. Was I ready to be lost to any woman again?

Not by a long shot.

My hands itched to call her, but I held them back. No, this wouldn't be the right time to hear her voice. Besides, we'd already spoken today. She called me. What would I even say to her?

So much. I would say *so much* to her.

Just to hold myself accountable, I grabbed my dirty dishes, walked into the kitchen, set my phone on the charger, and walked upstairs to take a nap.

Instead, I'd call her tomorrow and the next day. And the next. Just because I wanted to. Maybe I wouldn't ask her on a date yet, but I would talk to her. Talking to her on the phone might allay the driving need to be part of her world. Then I wouldn't entirely tip mine upside down, wreck the stasis I'd maintained for years, and throw it all into chaos.

Or so I told myself.

Tomorrow, I promised as I dropped onto my bed. *I'll call her tomorrow.*

Chapter Eleven

LESLIE

The hum of the dishwasher gave me a sense of satisfaction as I walked out of the kitchen the next day.

My phone buzzed with endless text messages from Maverick, and a couple from Lizbeth, but I ignored them for now. One week away from the Mercedy family reunion, and I'd have plenty of time to deal with crises. Christmas loomed eight days from now, and I'd just finished all my shopping.

With my life packaged into a neat bow for the time being, I wanted my garden. My dead, cold, dark garden that held no real appeal except for a mostly-false sense of escape.

I had a niggling suspicion I was about to get a phone call anyway. Tanner had been calling me most evenings. We had short, easy chats. They dove deep, and fast, and ended before it became awkward.

Yet, no date.

Nothing more.

He either flirted with a fear of dating or just needed someone to talk to. Either way, I'd take it. The smooth cadence of his voice in my ear felt like a warm bath. The sense of taking something slow came from our conversations, and helped me remember what it felt like to make a new friend.

December unfurled around me when I settled onto my swing. Frost-tinted air constricted my lungs with the cold. My breath fogged ahead of me, and the stars grew dim in a dark backdrop.

With Thanksgiving behind us and December speeding by, I let myself finally relax. For just a few minutes, I sat on my bench, closed my eyes, and released long breaths. I slouched further down the bench, canted my head back, and stared up at the dark sky.

More stars winked into sight overhead, Distant, cold, and quiet. I stared at them with a feeling of relief that they were still there. The night air pinched my cheeks and prickled the inside of my nose with each chilly breath. This was far more comfortable in the summer, when warmth unfurled instead.

My fingers tightened around my phone, which I held in my pocket. *Tanner,* I thought. *Tanner, Tanner. Will you call today?*

Questions had been populating about him for days now. What was he doing? Why did he call so much? For the past week, he'd called about this time every evening. No intention had been stated. We talked about our days and he asked questions almost too intense for a blossoming friendship.

Questions like *what's your opinion on financial savings* and *where do you stand on the political spectrum?*

None of the basic *what's your favorite color?* or *where would you go if you could go anywhere in the world?* kind of stuff.

No, Tanner was a deep dive into complexities, and I loved it.

Would it be weird if I called him this time? His propensity to drive right into the heavy stuff, then back out before it became burdensome, left me equally breathless. Like when he asked, *what was one night when things went really wrong with you and Ethan?*

I'd spent half an hour explaining the darkest night of my marriage three years ago when I thought Ethan had been cheating on me. Tanner listened the whole time. Not a breath of advice or one-upmanship.

He listened.

How long had it been since anyone had done that?

Did *never* count?

Ethan and I had been too young to really understand how important the depths of our relationship should be. If we'd dug a little deeper, maybe we would have been more open, more vulnerable, when it mattered most. By the time it *did* matter, we were too far gone. Tanner swept that problem right out of our friendship.

I *really* liked that.

When the cold drove me back inside, I headed to the fireplace and stoked a low bed of coals back to life. The snapping fire crackled again, the flames putting me into a trance, when my phone gave a little trill.

I grabbed it from my pocket as I shook out of my mesmerized stare. My heart hiccuped at the sight of Tanner's name. I couldn't answer it fast enough.

"Hello?"

"Hey."

He said it so easily, with eagerness to chat, I hoped. As if he weren't scared to call me, the way I was scared to call him. It had taken me almost an hour to muster the courage to tell him about Starla's visit. Once I had told him, I'd instantly felt better.

Dahlia was a fantastic sounding board at work, but she didn't have the same life experience as Tanner. She didn't know what it was to love and lose at a decades-long level. To scrape and change and sacrifice years of youth and sleep for children that you didn't ever stop worrying about.

Tanner, though.

Tanner got it.

"I wasn't sure if I'd hear from you tonight." The poker clanged as I set it down, accidentally hitting the fireplace.

"Is this a bad time?" he asked.

"No," I said quickly. "No, not at all. I didn't mean that to sound the way it did. I . . . I'm excited to hear from you. I just . . . I guess I don't know why I doubted."

Because inside I'm a twelve year old girl that just wants you to like me, I silently added as I clenched my eyes shut and let out a silent breath. Really, I needed to get this crush back under control.

"Good," he murmured. "I wanted you to know I saw Landon again yesterday. Brief check-in with him. He needed help finding a new apartment so I set him up with a friend of mine. She's a sweet old lady that lives in the apartment next door in case they need anything, you know. He'll move next week."

"Oh." My voice lifted. I cleared it to hide the shock there. Landon was moving? But why? And why did the old lady have anything to do with it? "Thanks for helping him."

"No problem. He seems good. I've been thinking about your visit with Starla and Landon and . . . you know? I think it'll work out. Whenever you get the whole picture, it's going to be fine."

Something in his tone set my hair on edge. *Whenever you get the whole picture.* What did he know? Was he not telling me everything? Before I could ask—and maybe I wouldn't have even done that—he kept going.

"But that's not why I called."

"Oh. Okay."

"I wanted to ask you how you stand the quiet."

My eyebrows rose. Intrigued by the question, I lowered onto the couch. "What do you mean?"

"The quiet house. You have one kid left, just like me. I'm assuming that Blake is gone as much as Celeste manages to be. She's with some friends right now," he added as an aside. "Yesterday night she did homework over video chat and I had the evening to myself. Same as tonight. It's too quiet when she's gone. You must grapple with the same thing?"

I drew in a deep breath. Several answers streamed through my mind all at once.

"I spent years craving the quiet," I said softly. "Four boys, a busy husband, and chaos all around me. There were times it felt like I had no escape from the noise and emotions of others. And now . . ." I trailed away, unable to articulate the jumble of emotions warring in my chest. "I don't know."

"Does it drive you crazy?"

"Sometimes. I think it's more the absence of what used to be."

"Huh."

"You never had that level of crazy though, did you, with one child?"

"Not that four boys would create," he said, laughing.

The easy roll of his amusement sent a thrill through me. I couldn't help but wonder if it would sound more resonant in person. His voice had such a calm way of unwinding, like someone who constantly spun a story. He often seemed unconcerned.

Was there anything that truly ruffled this guy?

"What are *you* going to do when Celeste is gone?" I asked, sensing that a deeper question lingered under his.

"I don't know."

He sounded like a lost boy for a moment. I tucked my feet deeper beneath me and burrowed into the couch, relieved to have his voice in my ear again. The snap of the fire lulled my muscles into a more relaxed state.

"I haven't even figured out what I'm going to do for Christmas this year," he added with a wry twist. "Celeste is with her mom and her stepdad. Normally, I don't really care. They're just outside Jackson City so she's not that far away. But this year? I don't know . . . It feels like it's different. Like it's her last year at home for Christmas."

"Feels that way," I said, "but she'll come back."

"It'll be different when she comes back."

"True."

"I don't like *different*. I've managed to keep a pretty steady state of life for us. Now everything feels like it's that unsteady moment right before massive upheaval, you know?"

My lips twitched, but I managed to keep amusement out of my voice by sheer willpower.

"Different is hard," I said, "but it can also be a great thing. I don't know the details of your divorce, but I'm going to assume it was a good thing?"

"Yes," he said instantly. "It was the right thing. Good point."

I held my breath, secretly hoping for more information, but he canted the subject just enough that I couldn't tilt it back without it being obvious that I wanted more details on his secret life.

"Do you have plans for when Blake leaves?" he asked.

"Oh, loads of them. Sometimes it feels like I've been waiting the last twenty years for this moment."

"Really?"

The genuine shock in his voice almost made me laugh, but I let it go again. I didn't know for sure, but I thought he'd been divorced from his ex-wife for most of Celeste's life, based on what she said. At least since elementary school, because she'd spoken about the difficulty of living in two places all her life.

"Yes. I was a stay-at-home mom. I didn't build as much of a life outside myself as I could have. I just . . . I wanted to be home with my boys and it was great. I wouldn't change it. But toward the end it felt stifling. So I started a picture of what I wanted after this phase of my life as they left the house."

"And what is it?"

I laughed. "Oh, look who thinks he gets to know everything!"

"Too much to ask?" he asked wryly, and I laughed again.

"No, not really. Some of my plans are very vague, like *have a career that feels fulfilling*, or *travel somewhere I'd never thought of before*, and *meet new people*. Others are really specific, like *pay off the mortgage, get my passport,* and *learn how to cook for one person instead of six. House swap with someone in France*. That kind of thing."

He whistled. "It's a good list."

The contemplative tone that had taken over his voice made me wonder. Had he *not* thought about life after kids? What did men think about the shift into something else?

He'd had the majority of Celeste for years, so he'd probably understand it more than Ethan. Ethan had spent most of his time at his office. To separate himself from the boys had always been easier—that had been built into his life.

Not for me.

"Thanks," I said and tucked my toes into the cushion. "As far as lists go, it's my best one. Totally focused on what I want, no one else. The list is about me living out my best life with no husband and no small kids around my legs."

The assertion came out stronger than I expected. Had I come on *too* strong? Did I feel an unusual need to assert my independence right now?

But why?

"You've earned it," Tanner said, and with feeling. "I hope you make it happen."

"Thanks," I murmured, at a loss. "I appreciate that."

"Word around town is that the Mercedy family reunion is coming up soon. Rumor also has it—and by rumor, I mean Celeste—that you've been preparing this for them for the last two months?"

I laughed. "Yes, that would be right. I think I will be the most excited person in Pineville when this reunion is over, and that's saying something, because Benjamin dreads it when his family is in town."

"Do you need any help?"

My mouth opened, then closed. Was he offering? Sure sounded like it. Having more of him around would be an acceptable and a terrible idea at the same time. How would I focus with him near?

In fact, I might like that a little *too* much.

"What kind of help?" I asked instead.

"Whatever you need. Celeste is going to her Mom's on Christmas Eve morning to be with them, and we don't have any clients booked that day. You know that whole it's-a-holiday-thing."

"So I've heard," I murmured vaguely, just to buy time. There were dozens of things that needed to happen just right in order for the Mercedy reunion to come together without a glitch, the way Maverick wanted. He didn't care much about impressing his siblings, but he had wealthy cousins attending that held power in impressive business circles. Not to mention his mother's failing health.

Plus, Maverick didn't do anything small.

"If you're going to be bored and you're offering help," I said, "I will gladly take it. There are a lot of places where I could use an extra pair of hands."

"Really?"

Anticipation filled his voice, which completely gratified me. In the span of a finger snap, Christmas Eve had shifted from something I'd stressed over to a day I couldn't wait to happen.

"Really," I said. "I appreciate the help."

"Tell me when and where."

"Meet me at the Frolicking Moose on Christmas Eve in the morning. Dahlia's working the early shift. You and I can start coordinating arrivals then."

"We're what, ten days away?"

"Yes, sir."

"Easy. I'll be there. But we'll talk before then, anyway."

A smile crossed my whole face. He shuffled around, doing what sounded like dishes in the background. Had he called me over dinner again? My eyes flitted to the clock. The time certainly suggested it.

"Listen," he said, and I pictured him standing at a sink, sleeves shoved to his elbows and the phone propped between his ear and his shoulder. The sexy image had me tugging at my flannel shirt collar while he spoke. "Thanks for letting me talk to you about the whole Celeste- leaving thing. I know it might be weird to fear the quiet, but . . . I don't know. I'm just trying to figure it out."

"I don't mind at all." I glanced around. "I like it, in fact. It was one of those quiet nights over here, too. I'll think more about how I process the quiet days and let you know."

"Thanks. It's good to have someone that'll talk it out. Sleep well, Leslie."

"You too, Tanner."

"Talk to you later."

The phone went quiet against my ear. I let it drop back to my lap while I stared at the fire, lost in words.

* * *

Christmas Eve popped up so suddenly, I felt whiplash the morning I woke up.

Buzzing excitement lingered in the pit of my stomach as I hopped out of bed. Not only would I get the Mercedy family reunion off my back, but I'd spend all day with Tanner. Tanner who existed mainly as a voice in my ear and a vague figure that picked up his daughter from the coffee shop.

Despite our nightly phone calls, the man had serious holding-at-arms-length tendencies. Fortunately, I could deal. The attention was flattering all the same. Because of his penchant for staying back instead of moving forward, I had a feeling today would mean something. At the very least, by the end of the day, I hoped to understand where we stood.

Friends or more?

For my part, I leaned far, far, far to the side of *more*, but that didn't speak for him. Maybe Tanner did just need a platonic friend.

I shoved that thought aside as I plunged into the steamy shower. No need to get ahead of myself. I still had an outfit to pick out and that would probably take awhile.

Before Tanner had entered my plans, I hadn't thought about what I'd wear to the reunion. Now that he'd accompany me, everything mattered. My hair. My clothes. My scent.

Did I smell like my deodorant, or something better? Did my shoes match *and* provide protection from the snow? No. Of course not, because when had anyone ever thought of *that* before?

Never.

Now *never* haunted me.

The quiet of the house without Blake bustling around or blowing something up on his video game with Missy kept my thoughts on Tanner.

Did I hate the quiet? Did I enjoy it? What did I think about it? Until he'd asked, I hadn't thought much about it.

Now, I couldn't stop. The quiet was a blessed change from what I'd had the last twenty-something years.

After ten outfits, I settled on a simple pair of black pants that had a flattering effect on my derriere, a pair of sensible snow boots with a fluffy top of fur that added a dash of white and sensibility, and a long-sleeve shirt beneath a vest. My favorite coat would top it with a fur-lined hood that complimented my eyes. A swipe of eyeliner and mascara finished out my process.

I hurried out of my bedroom to the sound of the weather forecast on the TV.

"Snow, snow, and more snow," boomed the weather-woman. "Get ready for Christmas, because snow is falling all day long—to the tune of up to sixteen inches."

"Ho, ho, ho," I murmured as I peered at a slowly dawning world.

Max's flight was supposed to arrive later this morning and Ethan would pick him up at the airport. Nicholas flew in after Christmas because he didn't want to see his father—and who knew why. He'd certainly never told me, so I'd pick him up and the other boys up in a few days.

With a wish that they were having fun at their dad's, I grabbed my keys and headed out, giddy for the day ahead.

Checklists, dates, timestamps, and things that *had* to happen sailed through my mind. Easy. I had this. Today would be a great day.

When I stepped into the shop, flurries accompanied me. An inch of snow had accumulated on the bright windowsills, and more fell in a dizzying array. Cars lined the drive-through with glowing red brake lights, illuminating the gathering moisture.

I shook off my hood.

"Merry Christmas!" I called.

Dahlia groaned behind the counter. "This place is too

freaking cold!" she squeaked, then turned back to the drive-through. A puffy winter coat kept her warm under her apron. Her hair was pulled away, tucked back into a fur-lined hood that made me laugh. She glared. I sent her a sympathetic look.

For the past month, she'd walked around the shop clutching something hot, asking when it would stop.

"Sorry, Dahlia," I said. "I didn't order this."

But secretly, I loved it.

She muttered something unintelligible and let the window slide shut. This would be the last Christmas for Bastian's older sister, a woman with Down's Syndrome named Inessa. She lived in a care facility in Jackson City. According to the latest report, the doctor expected Inessa to pass after the first of the year. They stayed to spend the holiday with her.

Bastian sat tucked in his usual corner and waved without looking up when I entered. A Christmas miracle, for sure. The man hardly said a word to anyone now that Dahlia entered his life. Like he used up all his words on her and wouldn't extend any others to the rest of us poor suckers. Dahlia only worked until ten, when Katelyn took over.

I pulled in a bolstering breath. The next part of the conversation had to be broached very carefully.

"Have you seen Tanner here yet?" I asked as nonchalantly as possible. Another car whizzed through the drive-through, leaving an empty space. Dahlia's gaze tapered into slits over the top of her coffee mug.

"What do you mean?"

"Tanner." I met her gaze. "Has he stopped by?"

Her cup lowered. She straightened. "No, why? Is he supposed to stop by? Do you have a date with Tanner?" She squealed. "Is he coming *here*?"

"Yes, no, and yes."

"Boss lady!" she cried. "You're killing me. Tell me everything."

With the most reserved voice I could muster I said, "Tanner offered to help out with the reunion today because Celeste is at her mother's house. I accepted his offer."

Dahlia grinned slowly, and it reminded me entirely too much of the grinch.

"I bet you did," she drawled.

I pointed at her. "Don't do that. This only means that he's bored and wants to help. That's it."

She rolled her eyes. "Tell yourself that if it makes you feel better, but we know the truth. He's going to ask you on a date tonight, guaranteed."

"He would have asked by now if he was going to, don't you think?"

She shrugged. "Maybe he's working up his courage."

"We talk every day! And none of it is trivial. He asks me big stuff, like what spending tendencies I have with discretionary cash."

Dahlia lifted an eyebrow. "Is that dating in midlife?"

My nose wrinkled. "No idea, but if it is, it's refreshing."

"He's going to ask you about your mortgage amortization schedule next."

I rolled my eyes, but still felt compelled to defend Tanner. "Can you imagine if Bastian had asked you that at the beginning? Gamechanger, right?"

She burst into laughter. Bastian sent her a slitted glare, which only made her laugh harder.

"Sorry." She waved a hand in front of her face. "Getting him to say two words was a miracle then. Sometimes now, too," she added with a lift of her mug in his direction. "Not sure he'd care enough to get *mortgage amortization schedule* out."

He ignored her, gaze focused on his computer screen. His fingers flew across the keyboard with practiced speed.

"Doesn't matter anyway. Dating isn't on my list," I said as

I yanked my coat off and pulled my phone out of my pocket. "Besides, we're . . . friends more than anything else. If he was interested in me romantically, he would have asked me on a date by now. Or, you know, walked into the shop to say *hello* instead of picking his daughter up outside and waving."

Dahlia opened her mouth to rebut, then stopped and closed it again.

"A ha!" I cried. "See? You agree."

"Not agree!" she cried, wagging a finger at me. "I just have no . . . formed opinion or response yet."

"Still, proves my point."

"Me thinks," Dahlia murmured with a brightness in her eyes, "that she protests too much."

She sent a knowing look my way that I blatantly ignored. Maybe I did feel a little *too* motivated to prove myself indifferent. Hadn't I been giddy with hope at home? Yes, but carefully so. This situation felt like I had to brace myself for the inevitability or convince myself that I didn't want more.

A lie.

But I'd lived lies before.

"Anyway." I spun my phone around to face me. "I have a reunion to focus on, and he's here to help. That's it. No comments, no matchmaking, no attempts to get us together. Capeesh?"

Dahlia sighed.

"Fine," she muttered into her coffee. "I'll . . . drive Bastian crazy instead of you."

Bastian lifted an eyebrow at her.

"Besides," I added, my finger twirled in the air to indicate the greater Pineville area. "There are going to be Mercedys all up in here all day long as they start arriving from the airport and shuffle to the lodge and other events. It's going to be insanely busy and Tanner's done me a huge favor volunteering to help out."

"What will you do tonight though? It's Christmas!"

I shrugged. "Not even sure what I'm doing for lunch," I said as I accessed all the messages that Maverick had sent this morning. "Don't ask me about tonight yet."

A bevy of text messages followed. Mercedys checking in with me as their flight arrived or asking questions about their arranged drivers. My fingers went to work as I slid into full coordinator mode.

By the time I'd answered all of the initial questions, the tinkle of the door opening came behind me.

I glanced back as Tanner strolled inside. He ran a hand through his hair, dusted with snowflakes, to shake them free. They turned to droplets on the black parka that he wore as he entered the room, clad in a pair of jeans, snow boots, and a quick smile. Stubble had filled out his face, giving him a softer appearance. I wanted to run my fingers down the hollow of his cheek.

Sweet baby pineapple.

I was in trouble.

"Good morning," he said, his voice ringing with its usual caress. I forced my brain to work and spit out a smile.

"Hey! Glad you made it down the canyon. Roads okay?"

"Not bad, considering. Plows are out."

He stomped his boots and advanced farther into the shop.

"What's your poison, boss man?" Dahlia called. "Espresso, cream, no sugar?"

He grinned. "Spot on."

She fist pumped and grabbed a cup. Thankful for the quick chance she bought me to gather my wits, I let out a deep breath.

"Thanks again for coming," I said as I tucked my phone back into my coat pocket and reached for my car keys. A mental to-do list had started to overtake my mind. Time to get started and get my mind off his delicious silver-and-black locks of hair.

"My pleasure," he murmured. "The Mercedy's are always making history one way or another when they get together. Figured I didn't want to miss the party."

See? I wanted to say to Dahlia as I sent her a smug look she couldn't see. *Totally platonic, and platonic is totally safe.*

She ignored me and handed Tanner his coffee.

I spun to fully face him. Quick as lightning, his eyes dropped to my feet and rose all the way to my face in an encompassing glance. My breath caught. I had to stop myself from doing the same to him. I'd already drunk in those delicious shoulders packed with muscles and arms I wanted to wrap around me.

I blinked out of those thoughts.

Right.

Time to move the Mercedy party forward and me out of the danger zone of stare-at-Tanner-all-day-and-never-stop.

"The first thing we need to do is head to the lodge and make sure that everyone's bags get over there from their various hotels, houses, or places they've been staying. The Big Cousins are arriving right now in Jackson City."

"Big Cousins?"

I grinned. "Really important, really rich, cousins from the other side of the country. Mav calls them the Big Cousins. He says that his family doesn't see them much. Mav's siblings are all already here so they're all going to congregate at the Diner as the final people arrive for breakfast. You driving, or am I?"

He held up a ring of keys on one finger.

"I got this."

I grabbed my folder filled with organized pages, a pen, some highlighters, and followed him out, studiously avoiding Dahlia's wicked smile the entire time.

Chapter Twelve

TANNER

I'd thought I'd seen Leslie in her element the day she coordinated the lunch with Landon and Starla, but that was nothing compared to what I witnessed on Christmas Eve.

While we moseyed our way through Pineville and over to the Great Lodge, small talk came easily. Non-pressured and didn't feel awkward. Part of me had wondered if we could be as natural again in person as we had been over the phone for weeks now.

Confirmed.

The Great Lodge was a massive place that rented out it's twenty plus rooms for big business retreats or sprawling family reunions like this one.

Although Maverick and Benjamin Mercedy were relative newcomers to Pineville—they'd only been here a few years each—they'd quickly become local favorites. To have their whole family here felt . . . natural.

"Should be over fifty people," Leslie said. A bright yellow folder lay sprawled open on her lap, belching papers that were organized, color coded, and messily stacked. Leslie had it together, but she didn't do it neatly.

"That's a lot of family."

Her face contorted into an expression I couldn't hope to read.

"No kidding," she murmured. "It's a lot of people. Regardless, the final twenty come in at various times today. Their cars will arrive around nine, which is why I wanted to get to the lodge early. It was *very* inconvenient that the lodge wasn't available yesterday. Mav and Ben made it work between their houses and Lizbeth's, up in Jackson City."

She prattled off other details that didn't need any reply. The background chatter was a comforting difference to what I usually faced on my own, and I sank into it. She didn't require much, but I'd insert an observation or answer here or there, she'd tut over it, and make a decision.

In a word, it felt just right.

Less than ten minutes later, I pulled to a stop in a far parking space of the empty lot. The Great Lodge towered three stories overhead, encompassing well over 15,000 square feet. Rooms packed both upper floors, including a chrome kitchen and dining area on each floor. Such a massive place would easily house all fifty Mercedys.

Leslie drew my attention when she faced the building, drew in a deep breath, and said in a small voice, "I got this, right?"

"You totally got this."

"There won't be really important details that I missed?"

I shook my head. "Nope. You're on top of all of that."

Her wide eyes watched me almost owlishly for a moment, like a small child begging for scraps of praise from a parent.

A stark reminder that for all my gentle adulation of Leslie Hill, I hardly knew her at all. We'd talked on the phone while I took the chicken's approach to asking her on a date, but this was only the second time we'd been in close proximity.

Yet, for all the times we'd passed in the street and head

nodded and maybe even interacted when I coached her boys, you could know someone for an eternity and still not understand everything about them.

She blinked that expression away and my thoughts broke. With a bit less power in her voice, murmured, "You'd think that, after almost fifty years of life, I'd have a bit more confidence."

"You have the confidence. You're just doing something new. It's harder to access when that happens."

Sometimes, I should take my own advice.

Her lips twitched. She nodded once, as if making a decision, and said, "You're right. Thanks. Shall we?"

"We shall."

* * *

The spacious, glorified-mountain feel of the interior of the lodge felt strangely empty as we strolled through.

Giant wooden beams. Evergreen banners over sliding glass doors that led out to a porch. Stained wooden cupboards above a black, polished sink. The ritzy mountain esthetic reminded me of the Frolicking Moose.

Leslie clutched her folder to her chest, pen tucked behind her ear, as we strolled through each and every room. She murmured at the bedroom door, then wrote a name on the whiteboards that hung from a peg on the wall. A paper lay between her shirt and the folder that she kept glancing at.

With a low mumble every few moments, we toured the entire lodge as she ticked things off her list.

I kept my hands tucked in my pockets and watched her.

A strand of hair kept escaping from a loose ponytail she'd tied away from her face. Impatiently, she kept batting it back or tucking it behind her ear in a youthful gesture. Her teeth worried her bottom lip, which hadn't lost any fullness over the years. I had to look away before the temptation to tuck that hair out of her lovely eyes overcame me.

"They didn't stock the right kind of milk," she declared, her voice an echo as she rummaged through the fridge. "Maverick's sister-in-law, Mallory, prefers a specific kind of almond milk."

I spun away from my perusal of the river outside and walked closer.

"Need me to run to the store?"

She hesitated. "No, let's do that together. I totally forgot to grab breakfast at the shop and I'm starving."

"Sounds great."

Secretly, I was relieved she didn't want to send me off without her. Time alone with Leslie would be at a premium and I didn't want to miss the chance.

She pulled out a separate paper, made a note, and then straightened up. A clatter came from just outside.

Without missing a beat she said, "Oh, that must be Jax. Benjamin recruited him from the gym to bring all the luggage over from Maverick's and his place while the Mercedys are at breakfast."

"Where is the Mercedy family eating?" I asked as I leaned against the fridge. Leslie had spread out some of her papers— it looked to be a timeline that she'd put together—and she consulted it with a click of her teeth now.

"I booked out the whole Diner for them this morning. They're eating there from 8-10, and then they'll be here. The Big Cousins are getting rides right to the Diner."

A metal clock set in a moose head with antlers coming out the side revealed the time as 8:05.

"We have time."

"We do," she murmured.

Once her initial checks were completed, we stepped back outside with a new list of things to grab at the local market.

Leslie seemed to mentally set aside that task, because she looked over to me with a little smile as we approached the truck. Snowflakes twirled around her as she pulled her hood over her head, white and gray fur framing her face in a lovely way.

"You sure you're up for this all day?" she asked. "It's glorified parenting, that's all. After we get the final missing touches that Maverick asked me to make sure we have, we need to round up the rental ski gear from Pineville Outfitters. There's a group of them going cross country skiing, another group that'll have a rental van drive them to Jackson City for downhill skiing and snowboarding, while yet another group stays here for board games. After that's settled, we confirm catering."

I grinned. "Never wanted to be anywhere more than this."

And I meant it.

Chapter Thirteen

LESLIE

If you counted all the little things that *didn't* go wrong, the launch of the Mercedy family reunion was an utter success.

Aside from a catering snafu, some lost gluten-free bread that later reappeared in a toddler's bag, and a few breakdowns amongst the children who didn't want to share beds, very little fell apart.

Tanner followed along like a quiet shadow, but it didn't bother me. He found his own things to take care of that I didn't notice, like a screen door that hung loose and a couple of lightbulbs that needed to be replaced. When it was blatantly clear that the cleaning crew had forgotten to sweep and mop the laundry room, he had it whipped together in a trice.

My hero, indeed.

His calm presence grounded me during a day when I felt fear all the way to my bones. Impressing Maverick and Bethany hovered at the top of my to-do list. Although they were practically family, I still wanted to do my job well. It had been far too long since I had something to own and take pride in outside of my house.

Toward the end of the day, when dinner arrived and Maverick's sisters set it out on a long buffet table, Maverick caught my eye. He motioned toward the butler's pantry with a tilt of his head and I nodded.

Without thinking, I reached over and put a hand on Tanner's arm.

"I'll be just a minute," I said quietly. "Mav needs something, but then I think we can go."

Tanner nodded and gave me a smile. I returned it, feeling like he'd just dipped me in a warm bath all the way to my toes.

Maverick stared at a box of cereal with a critical eye when I slipped into the butler's pantry. He put a heavy hand on my shoulder and said with a grin, "You killed it, Leslie. This is absolutely perfect."

Relief slipped through me, but I attempted to hide just how deep it went.

"We both know that hiring me was the smartest move you've ever made."

He held up both hands. "Can't fight the truth. Listen, we've got this from here on out. Mallory is obsessed with your folder and has been delegated full responsibility of the happenings for the next three days. You've detailed everything out perfectly and I'll text you if I have any questions. Now, it's time for you to let go of my family and have a good evening with Tanner."

My mouth dropped open to protest, but I couldn't.

Have a good evening with Tanner? How did he know?

"You don't want me to help?" I asked, just to stave off the Tanner line of questioning. Maverick rolled his eyes.

"We've got this."

"But I've planned this for months. The Big Cousins are here. You said . . ."

"Leslie," he drawled.

I floundered for a moment. Maverick and I had worked together on this since late summer. In all that time, I'd meant to still be somewhat present throughout. I planned to check in, stop by, and make sure everything worked smoothly. My boys were with their dad for several days. The Mercedy reunion is what was supposed to fill my time while they were gone.

Maybe I *did* grapple with the quiet.

But, if Tanner didn't have Celeste and didn't seem particularly inclined to leave, then why *not* leave the Mercedys and do something far more fun? Today had been an absolute dream with Tanner at my side. A quick flash of him and me at my fireplace for the night went through my mind, but I shuffled it away.

No.

That wasn't . . .

I mean—

Wait. When had I started to daydream?

My question remained unanswered. A quick smirk on Maverick's face meant he'd just tested me and I'd inadvertently told him everything without even saying a word.

"So, you and Tanner, huh?"

"It's not . . . I . . ."

"Sure." Mav held up both hands, as if to surrender. "You can say that *it's not like that* or *you're just friends* or whatever, but you and Tanner have some serious chemistry going on. Maybe you should lean into that a little bit, Les."

I scowled. "Thank you for the dating advice, he-who-left-Bethany."

Maverick laughed. "Fair jab. Low, but fair jab. All I'm saying is that Tanner is a great guy and the two of you seemed like you had fun today." He pointed to the door. "Now get out of my house and let me take care of my family. Because, you know, I'm supposed to be able to do that. It's sort of all my idea."

* * *

Less than twenty minutes—and so many hugs later—Tanner and I headed into the cold Christmas Eve night.

Darkness had already wrapped the earth. In the distance, I thought I heard carolers singing. The snow that had fallen all day continued gently. Every now and then, a car hissed by on the road nearby with a splash of slush. My breath fogged in front of me as I yanked my zipper up and shivered in the confines of my coat. Bitter cold. No garden meditation tonight.

"Seems strange that it's Christmas, doesn't it?" Tanner asked.

"Today was so busy that I hadn't thought much about it," I admitted. "Even if it is the perfect Christmas setting."

The lodge had been gorgeously decorated with garlands, Christmas trees, and lights that illuminated the parking lot as we strolled through. Snow accumulated in a sheet on the parking lot and eaves of the lodge.

Tanner followed me to the truck, then opened the door. I smiled as I climbed in. "Thanks."

He didn't say anything, but a musing expression filled his face as he strolled around the other side. The truck cranked to life after he climbed in and a blast of cold air hit my face. I turned the vent away.

"So," Tanner drawled. "Your place?"

A quiet invitation existed in that question. He'd given me the power. I could feign fatigue and I sensed he'd understand that it was true. But now he was giving me a chance to turn him away.

Yet, I didn't want to.

The quiet of my house would be vast tonight indeed.

"My place," I said firmly. "If you swing by the coffee shop, I'll pick up my car on the way back."

He shoved the truck into drive.

*** * ***

"Where are your boys?" Tanner said as he stacked wood into my fireplace.

"With Ethan. Landon and Starla have been busy with finals and some other things at work, he said. They're going to come down for New Years. Nicholas flies out in a few days. Max flew in yesterday."

"Do you miss them?"

I shrugged. "Yes. No. I don't know. I miss the full, bustling Christmas's we used to have. Miss picking out Santa's presents and stuffing the stockings."

His gaze twinkled when he asked, "The party planning aspect of the holidays?"

"Yes," I said, laughing. "That's exactly right."

I bustled around the kitchen, pulling food out of the fridge. Christmas music warbled in the background with a vague song. A wrinkled, cooked-apple danish that JJ had made for me—my grandpappy's recipe—waited in the fridge while I gathered ingredients for a hasty Christmas Eve dinner.

Cold, boiled potatoes and hard-boiled eggs for a quick potato salad. A rotisserie chicken from the fridge, still whole and browned and delicious, even if chilled.

While it wasn't exactly a Christmas feast, it would be just right. The real food party would happen once the boys came home and I indulged them with all their favorite dishes in the greatest gluttony of the year.

"So," I drawled. "Why did you quit coaching? I've been meaning to ask for a while now."

He grunted. "Good question."

"What, you don't know?"

"I do. It's just that quitting coaching was a hard decision. I really didn't want to leave the kids but there wasn't enough money in it for Celeste to afford a college education. Besides, I wanted her to learn how to work. When T&C took off, I just went with it."

"My boys loved you as a coach and a teacher," I said, parroting what all three of them had mentioned. Nicholas had said, *yeah, he was cool* when I talked to him about Tanner on Sunday.

From Nicholas, that was high praise.

"They were great students. Landon had determination a mile wide, and I'd never seen such innate competitiveness as I did in Max."

"Gets it from his father."

"I dunno," Tanner drawled. "I think I see some of that in his mother."

I laughed. "Fair's fair."

The compliments he'd given about my boys, and about me, rang deep. Truly, they were amazing sons. Rambunctious and tiring and sometimes utterly exhausting, but still amazing humans. I couldn't be more proud.

"And you like cleaning other people's houses?" I asked with just enough humor in my voice that he wouldn't take me too seriously. "I mean, you essentially went from babysitting other people's kids to cleaning up after them."

He laughed, and his teeth appeared white against the stubbled growth of beard. Behind him, the fire flared. How odd that we'd be getting this very general basics out of the way after weeks of talking nightly about the deep stuff.

"I like the money that comes from it." Tanner straightened, clapping wood shavings off his hands. "I like the flexibility. At least, when I have employees that actually show up."

I gestured around my house with a wave.

"Well, you've certainly outdone yourself here."

The snap of the growing fire replied. I glanced up but he stared at the flames contemplatively.

"What about your ex-wife?" I asked. "What's the story there?"

Over the phone, the question would have felt risky. In person, with his expressions to gauge, it seemed simple. While I scraped mayo and paprika out of a bowl, he turned his back to the fire and faced me.

"Her name is Whitney," he said. "We were young and stupid."

"How young?"

"Twenty-two when I married her. Twenty when we met. I would have married her sooner but she was busy with a growing modeling career."

Landon was only twenty-three, and Starla appeared even younger. I had been twenty when I married Ethan.

Maybe we were all fools for love.

"That is young," I said.

He shrugged. "Felt like I had plenty of life experience at the time, thank you very much."

I laughed. If that didn't describe Landon, nothing else did.

"We'd gotten married because it pissed off her family, and then realized that we weren't really old enough to understand what that kind of a commitment called for. Right when she decided that her pride would recover from the blow of her parents saying *I told you so*, she found out she was pregnant."

I continued to peel the hard-boiled eggs, grateful to have something to do with my hands. There wasn't any pain in his voice, mostly a sense of history. Maybe a dash of nostalgia and resignation.

Was there ever any true letting go of a marriage?

Failed or not, abusive or not, difficult or not, ties

formed in the back-and-forth exchange of signing your lives over to each other. Commitment created a bridge you couldn't truly break. To close a door through divorce meant to *make* a different path, but different paths didn't erase scars.

"Did you stay together for Celeste's sake?"

"We tried for several years and it was a good thing. We were able to tag-team and worked well that way, but we weren't in love. We were . . . roommates, at most. Our resentment of each other started to get between us. Whitney was two years younger than me and wanted to travel and live her life and work on her career. What she could salvage of it after having a child, anyway."

"So did she?"

He nodded. "A little, yes. I gained custody of Celeste and Whitney went off to find herself. She'd come back and visit, but for a couple of years, she had wild oats to sow. I let her, because I wanted Celeste. Now, they have a good relationship. Whitney settled down with her current husband years ago and they moved close to be near Celeste. Had a few other kids. Whitney seems happy, and I'm glad because it wouldn't have happened with me."

"Thanks for telling me," I said as I glanced up.

He smiled, a lopsided, quiet thing that was more boy than man.

"Sure."

"Celeste is amazing." I scraped crumbling yolk off the cutting board and into a bowl. "I genuinely look forward to seeing her when she comes to the shop."

"She feels the same way about you."

While the chicken rewarmed under the broiler in the oven, I grabbed two plates.

"This dinner is not exactly a Christmas ham with piping hot mashed potatoes, all the drippings, and spiked eggnog, but it will be delicious. There are pastries from JJ in the fridge. Trust me, you want his pastries."

He accepted the extended plate with a grin. "Sounds like a perfect Christmas Eve dinner."

Tanner kept me entertained with stories about Christmas dinners gone wrong in the past, when Celeste and he were on their own and he was still learning the subtle art of holiday cooking.

After loading up our plates, I motioned toward the table, not far from the crackling fire that had gently warmed the house.

While we ate, I became a little too wrapped up in watching his expressions. The way his white-streaked hair scooped away from his face and stayed there. The laugh lines around his eyes, deep and attractive. Firelight danced a gentle glow across his features.

Thankfully, the food forced my eyes away from him often enough that I didn't actually drool, but my heart was ready to.

Most of the time, I just kept wondering, *how is this real?*

One topic led to another, and we stumbled onto Ethan and me. I leaned back in my chair, a glass of wine at my fingertips. One leg propped in front of me, braced against the table. Remnants of chicken breast and potato salad lingered on my plate. Too many more bites and I wouldn't have room for JJ's dessert, which would be an utter travesty.

"Ethan and I . . ." I trailed away, searching for the right words. Despite telling my divorce story time and time and time again, I still didn't know if I explained it the right way.

Did a word exist in our language that would encompass how it felt to release the one thing and person I should have held onto all of my life?

"I think we just forgot each other."

Tanner's expression softened. My forehead wrinkled and I shook my head in frustration.

"Honestly, I don't even know if that's the right way to say it. We started romantically and sweetly and it all seemed like a dream. Then a mortgage, one kid, two kids, four kids came. His job became his escape from the chaos and I grew resentful that he had one. I kept the house running and the kids happy and the mortgage paid. We forgot, at some point, that we were supposed to be a team. I stopped telling him things. He stopped asking. Then, one day, I think we just realized that it was sort of . . . gone. That realization happened when we stopped fighting," I added quietly. "When we stopped fighting, I knew it was over."

Though the demise of my relationship was years old, I still felt fresh wounds at the failure of it. I lifted my gaze to Tanner and wondered what I'd see there. Nothing but curiosity, maybe a deep sense of knowing. I didn't have to perfectly explain it to him. Didn't need the exact words to convey how I felt.

He already got it.

Despite all Lizbeth's best efforts, and advice from the book club—mostly Stella, a sixty-something woman that managed the local grocery store and had been through three divorces—none of them seemed to understand. In a glance, I knew Tanner did. It sent my whole body into a loose-as-jello feeling.

"Really rots, doesn't it?" he asked quietly.

"I feel like I failed. Sometimes, I wonder if it would have been easier if he'd just cheated on me or something. The way it happened for us, it feels like I made the decision and that's a lot of weight to carry. Our divorce was amicable, but I worry that one day my boys will hate me for not trying harder to fix it."

Tanner shook his head. He leaned back in his chair in a casual pose, and I felt the edge of his sock accidentally brush my bare foot. Any contact sent a little shiver through me, but it seemed ridiculous that one so innocuous engendered such a strong one.

"No," Tanner said, "it would have been harder on them if he'd cheated on you. Harder on you as well. Much harder."

I thought of what I'd said, and felt silly. Of course that situation would be so much worse than this one.

"You're right."

"There would have been more betrayal, more insecurity. This is just something you need to let go of within yourself. It comes with time. Or maybe never." He shrugged. "Sometimes I still feel the effect of our divorce, even though Brooke didn't cheat on me. It's been almost fifteen years."

"Really?"

He nodded.

"Good to know. Thanks."

He did that half-smile again and it sent butterflies all the way to my toes. I let out a sigh and wondered where to steer this next. Did I ask him to watch my annual Christmas movie with me?

The thought of snuggling up to hot chocolate, Irving Berlin, and a fire while snow fell outside was utterly and irrevocably the most romantic notion I'd ever had in my entire life. All the book clubs I'd ever had with Grace, Stella, and Lizbeth built up behind this very moment.

Nothing in my life had ever seemed all that romantic now that I looked at it through the lens of time and experience. Yes, Ethan and I had started out in romantic ways but they'd deflated almost as quickly as they'd come.

Tonight, however, felt far more potent.

As if on cue, the music playing in the background shifted to a gentle Christmas song. My mouth opened to ask if he wanted to stay, but before I could get a word out, he spoke first.

"Can I ask you something that's going to sound ridiculous, but is something I'd really love to do?"

"Of course."

A hint of nerves appeared in his eyes a moment before he held out his hand.

"Will you dance with me?"

Chapter Fourteen

TANNER

I thought Leslie would say no.

Her gaze arrested on mine, startled but not displeased. Her lips parted for a moment, as if a stalled response lingered there.

I held my breath and hoped she'd say *yes*. Seconds before I withdrew the request and attempted to restore my pride by laughing about it, she slipped her hand in mine.

"Yes."

She stepped easily into my space. Feeling her body almost pressed to mine was like a dream. How many times in the last couple of weeks had I thought of something like it? Reality was better than every one of them.

Her fingers slipped through mine and her other hand rested on my shoulder. Although I hadn't done much with Whitney in the short years we were married, dancing had been one of our favorite activities.

Leslie was relaxed enough that I could easily lead her into each step, and I fell back into the movement as naturally as I ever had before.

Her shoulders came just below mine, which meant that a strand of her hair caressed my cheek with every slow wave of movement. I twirled her and she grinned, then returned just as quickly into my arms.

"You're an actual dancer," she said quietly. The hilarity of before had faded into something far more intense.

"Yes. A monkey can be trained, apparently."

She laughed again, and the sound sent a shiver through me. Holding a woman—no, Leslie—in my arms felt better than I'd remembered. The empty years seemed far away when she was right here. The future? Not so bleak, perhaps. If I let it brighten. Leslie Hill was the light I wanted on my horizon.

Stasis be damned.

The music wafted gently through the house as I led her through a simple routine. We didn't speak, and after all the quiet bustle of the day, the calm air, the simple movements, the close touch restored me. I drank in every brush of her skin against mine like a dying man.

Maybe, in some ways, I had been.

The moment the dance ended and she peered up at me, I felt the rolling stone start to fall down the hill.

Who had I been kidding? I'd been fighting my growing attraction to her out of fear, but that had been futile. Leslie tipped into my world like a gentle glass of wine, and now I'd never be the same again.

My hand lifted to her face. I pressed my palm to her cheek, my thumb gently rubbed the space below her lip. I stared at her lips, then up to her eyes. They brightened with anticipation, smoky and intense. If my suspicions were correct, this would be her first kiss since her husband.

A loaded thing.

"Leslie, can I kiss you?"

"I wish you would," she murmured.

Relief almost left me a weak man as she wrapped her arms around me, tucking herself against my body. Our lips collided into each other. The little whimper she gave at the back of her throat drove me mad. My fingers worked through her hair as her lips opened to mine.

I pulled away, breathing hard. She pressed her forehead to mine, eyes closed. I felt her hands at my back, fistfuls of my shirt in her grasp.

For several long moments she stood there, stiff, and then she relaxed. She leaned back, her fingertips touching my face. She looked so serious.

"This isn't some Christmas miracle?" she asked without any humor at all. "Do you really feel something too?"

I nodded.

She crashed back into me.

* * *

An hour later, we sat on the couch together, a blanket draped over us.

Leslie curled into my side, her stockinged feet pulled up to the cushion. She'd wrapped herself into a fleece blanket and dropped into position at my side. I kept an arm around her and watched her face light up as we watched a Christmas movie that I couldn't even name.

Mostly, I studied her.

My thoughts tumbled as the songs and movie continued, unnoticed by me. The burn of my lips. The shock of having kissed her. I couldn't muster up the gumption to ask the woman on a real date, but I did follow her around like a pathetic puppy all day and then kiss her breathless.

No, it made me breathless.

Both of us.

Thankfully, I staved off the questions and reality for later. For the first time in a while, I sat and enjoyed the warm fire, the feeling of Leslie curled up into my side. Questions of what this would mean could be dealt with in the morning.

Tonight, I was grateful to not be alone in the quiet.

Her steady, rhythmic breathing clued me in first. I glanced down as the credits started to roll to see her eyes closed. The fan of her lashes spread out against her cheek in a disarming way, and that same lock of hair had tumbled onto her forehead.

I brushed it away this time, the strands silky against my fingertips. She didn't even stir. Her body lay slack against me, giving me her weight.

If I moved, she'd wake up. If she woke up, I'd be obligated to carry her to bed, get in my cold truck, and drive up a snowy canyon road to my house an hour away. Then we'd be apart . . . for how long? Only a few days, likely, but even days felt interminable.

How ridiculous was that?

If I didn't move, she probably wouldn't wake up. That meant I wouldn't have to face the truck, the canyon, or the snow.

I tilted my head back on the couch and closed my eyes. If I didn't move, I could stay right here, with Leslie in my arms, and we'd wake up together on Christmas Day.

Like the most romantic Christmas ever.

Chapter Fifteen

LESLIE

A kink in my neck woke me the next morning.

My eyes fluttered open slowly, then popped all at once. A warm something lay beneath me. A leg? I straightened up, my eyes widening.

Holy. Sweetness.

I'd fallen asleep on Tanner.

He lounged back against the couch, his head canted to the right. He breathed softly, and quietly. I'd slumped into his lap at some point, my cheek pressed into his jeans. A giggle almost escaped me.

Moving gently, I extracted myself from his side, the fleece blanket still hooked on my shoulder. The movement brought a stir of cold air into my warm cocoon, and I shivered. The fire had banked in the night and a chilly air thinned the room. My eyes darted to a clock over the television.

8:14.

Usually, I went all-out decorating for Christmas. Swapped the clocks. New pictures. Garland. Tinsel. Stockings. Trees. Everything would be on theme for the year, which was usually just Christmas-explosion.

This year?

Only the basics. Lights. Garland. Tree. Blake didn't seem to care either way, but it felt wrong to totally forget Christmas while he was still at home. *Not decorate for a single holiday* was on my Leslie 2.0 list. Sometimes, it was just too exhausting to coordinate, pull out, put up, clean, and re-pack all on my own.

Tanner stirred slightly when I stood. I lay the blanket across him and he settled back down. A tender feeling stole over me, the kind that I'd always felt when I watched my kids sleep. The burn of our kiss followed, and I briefly touched my lips with the memory.

Christmas setting.

Elegant dancing.

Hot chocolate, warm blankets.

Christmas movie.

The night had been romance personified, and I felt it all the way to my toes. The giddiness of it. The delight.

Was this what Lizbeth always crooned over during our book clubs? I'd never understood it until now. The happy feeling that it sent all the way through my body made me feel light, and I couldn't wait for him to wake up already.

Carefully, I crept around the house. Slipped into a shower and let the steam wake me up. Put on a pair of comfortable yoga pants and a red-and-green long-sleeved shirt over a t-shirt. The whole casual vibe felt just right for Christmas because Tanner had only ever seen me in my work clothes.

With my hair in a loose ponytail on my shoulders, I slipped back out of the bathroom. He hadn't budged on the couch, which I took as a good sign. I shuffled around the kitchen, got the fire going in the fireplace, started up the coffee machine, and responded to text messages. It gave me time to think through last night.

What now?

Had we been caught up in the moment last night?

Did the kiss mean something?

Was it better than Ethan's? Definitely. Unequivocally. Tanner had been gentle and calm, everything about him warm and strong and solid. Ethan and I had been young, so it had almost felt like an attack of hormones. This? This had been perfect, from the connecting time before to the snuggle afterward.

The book club was gonna die.

I grabbed my phone off the table, Lizbeth on my mind.

Leslie: Merry Christmas! Everything going okay over there? Maverick told me I couldn't text him and check in.

Lizbeth: MERRY CHRISTMAS LESLIE!

Lizbeth: Everything is lovely. We're whipping up breakfast and there have been no wrinkles so far. What are you doing today with the boys at Ethan's? You should come over! No one should be alone on Christmas Day!

I chewed on my bottom lip. Dare I tell her about Tanner? Wrong question. Dare I *not* tell her? New-Mama Lizbeth had a scary side when the hormones of postpartum infused her.

She'd always been more intense about love and romance than most people, but now she was positively belligerent about it. If I didn't share with her a romantic moment, she'd flip.

Besides, I really wanted to tell *someone*.

I snuck a quick glance up. Tanner hadn't moved. With only a moment more of indecision, I quickly typed out a reply.

Leslie: I'm not alone. I'm . . . spending it with Tanner?

Lizbeth: WHY IS THAT A QUESTION?

Leslie: Lots to tell but we sort of had a lovely date last night and fell asleep watching a Christmas movie on the couch.

So many happy emojis followed that they filled my screen. I had to scroll to find her actual reply.

Lizbeth: WHAT? Where are my details?

Leslie: I'll tell you later, I promise. Just wanted to make sure that everything was set over there. Sounds like it is!

Lizbeth: I will hunt you down if you don't find me by tomorrow evening and tell me everything.

Leslie: Agreed!

I clicked the phone off and glanced up. The couch lay empty. A second before I almost whirled around, a firm body came up behind me. Two arms snaked around me from behind with a low growl.

"Good morning."

I shivered as his fresh stubble grazed the sensitive skin on my neck. Tanner pressed a quick kiss there, then spun me around. I melted into his still-sleepy gaze and tousled hair.

"Good morning," I whispered with a little smile. Whatever awkwardness I thought I might feel disappeared in a poof. Resistance to the inevitable fall of my heart had begun to fade as well. I put my hands on his arms.

"Sleep well?"

His crooked smile made an appearance. "Very well. You?"

"Like a warm baby."

His gaze darted to my lips, and then back. I brought my hands around his neck. "Are you going to give me a Christmas kiss or what?" I asked.

He cut off any space for a reply with his lips on mine. Last night, he'd been gentle. Today, a deeper hunger drove him. A hunger I recognized myself. Something deep and once lonely that was now thrust into the light. A fear of losing the romantic magic of waking to someone else and something else and something *warm*. The ravages of fate had already taken our first loves.

Were we marked or doomed?

No.

That wouldn't be right.

For several minutes, I kissed the fear out of him until I sensed him calm. He pulled away with a sharp intake of air, then pressed our foreheads together. The tips of my fingers raked through this stubble.

"Merry Christmas," he rumbled.

I laughed and, somewhat unwillingly, stepped out of the circle of his arms.

"Are you hungry?" I asked.

He rubbed his eyes with the heel of his hand. "Starving. Let me run to the bathroom, then I'll come help you fix something epic."

* * *

Christmas passed in a lovely blur of Tanner.

Hours of slamming together our different food traditions led into a sprawling smorgasbord of food. Tanner's time as a father had lent to more creativity in the kitchen than I'd expected. While I worked on French toast from a brioche that I kept in the freezer, he whipped up a panty-melting quiche, maple-crisped bacon, and a breakfast dish from oats and almonds I swooned over.

Once stuffed, we snuggled into more movies on the couch. Calls from the boys interrupted our time, as each of my son's wanted to make sure my Christmas wasn't lonely. Tanner's brother called, as well as Celeste.

After each round of talking, we returned back to the couch. To snuggles around Christmas movies. To make out sessions that made me hungry for more, though neither of us pressed beyond the casual.

His willingness to move slowly built a trust that felt like manna.

Throughout the day, I'd stuffed all thoughts of Maverick's family aside. The Mercedy family reunion was taken care of. Next on board would be Landon and Starla. Their upcoming wedding—which quickly approached—would be my next big focus. Not even *that* could be done on Christmas, however, so I pushed that aside, too.

Just me and Tanner in a lovely swirl of Christmas magic.

* * *

Two days later, I sat in the airport wait-and-ride to pick up Nicholas while Max and Blake chattered back-and-forth about football and a video game competition.

My head still spun with memories of Tanner. In between making calls to JJ's bake shop to request catering for Starla and Landon, texting Starla a menu of appetizers, and sourcing a store with the decoration's Starla had mentioned, I *also* thought of Tanner.

The smell of Tanner lingered in my nose. Every time I looked at the fireplace, I thought of him adding logs, stoking it up, and taking care of it. He'd fallen naturally into the house. Tidying up, managing the fire, getting more wood.

Swoony, indeed.

He'd called me both nights we were apart. We talked into the late hours, and I fell asleep thinking about him. His lips. The soft grit of his stubble, and the way his white hair highlighted his dark hair.

Tanner Beck.

My biggest surprise so far.

The sound of a car horn jerked me out of the present moment. I blinked, startled, and looked up as Max leaned halfway out of the window and shouted from the front seat.

"Nicholas Miller!"

A shaggy head of curls headed toward our SUV through the airport traffic. Nicholas was a stocky guy. Short compared to his brothers, but meaty in the shoulders and arms. My heart flopped over itself as I hopped out of the car and shouted, "Nicholas!"

That adorable head popped up. A smile worthy of a doting mother appeared there. Within seconds, Nicholas had closed the gap, wrapped his arms around me, and lifted me into the air.

"Hey Mom!"

"Let me down!" I squeaked.

"Hey, Ma!" Max cried out the window. "Look, he made it safe just like I said he would!"

Nicholas set me back on my feet, but I held him a little bit longer. His hazel eyes danced as he pulled away, a loose backpack on his shoulders stuffed to the brim.

Like his mother, Nicholas reeked of pragmatism, which is why he'd left a quarter of his wardrobe at home. When he traveled back, he didn't have to pack.

He was a brilliant child, in many respects.

"How was the flight?" I asked, gesturing to the car, which idled under a sign and the watchful eye of an airport attendant that kept giving me dirty looks for lingering in the loading zone. Nicholas headed to it with me as he pulled his backpack off, letting it drop to his hand.

"Not bad. Slept through most of it, then watched a zombie movie."

"Ideal."

He laughed. "Perfect Christmas ambience."

Max unfolded himself from the front seat, where he'd ridden after I picked him up at Ethan's house. The two of them met in a crushing man hug while they banged each other's backs. Nicholas held Max out at arms length.

"Looking good, bro."

Like Nicholas had room to talk. Working in logging the high mountains all summer and into the fall had brawned up his arms and shoulders. He was my quietest—but most intelli-gent—child. He lacked the innate competitiveness of Max, and the intensity of planning from Landon.

Blake was a more even-keeled mixture of all his brothers. Max never surprised me anymore. Nicholas always did.

Max clapped an arm on Nicholas. "Same!" he cried. "All that time in the forest was good to you, Nick."

Blake materialized out of the back seat. Nicholas exclaimed over him, wrapped him in a hug, and ground his knuckles into the top of Blake's head. Blake fought him off and the two friendly-grappled for a moment before Nicholas backed off, laughing.

"Mom!" Max glanced to me. "I'm starving and Landon says you have a new boyfriend. Let's get in the car, start the wheels toward grub, and hear what the hell he means by that."

My heart seized in my chest.

I had a *what*?

My head snapped to Blake, who stared at me with wide eyes. He shook his head back and forth.

"I didn't say anything!" he cried.

Forced to play it cool, I rolled my eyes and strolled to the drivers side.

"Get in," I said over my shoulder with intentional exasperation. "My life isn't as exciting as you're probably hoping."

My heart beat hard all the same. Christmas had erased my ability to deny that anything existed between Tanner and I. Yet, I wasn't ready to fess up to it either. Putting it into words made it all too real, and the last thing I wanted was for this to be so real that it could break.

Or so real that I could mess it up again.

When reality manifested, there was a legitimate chance that I sucked at picking men.

Maybe Ethan had been a fluke and I'd been lonely or desperate or something, but maybe not. Such a flaw would be most likely to show up in the relationship *after* my divorce. The one where I may be lonely or desperate yet again.

Tanner and I had fallen so hard into this crush that I couldn't bring myself to trust it just yet. Not until I knew myself and my position in the world better.

The boys would have to deal with that.

* * *

"Spill," Max demanded from across a table. "You gotsa a boyfriend, we hear?"

Their favorite BBQ restaurant unfolded around us with the quiet bustle of people, the chime of a cash register, and the heady smell of sauce.

"Boyfriend?" I snorted. It sounded so . . . teenager.

Max sent me a half-glare, then leaned against the seat with a hand on his stomach, his ravenous hunger satiated. For now. He'd always run like an oven. Hot all the time, and he burned through all the food I could shovel his direction in a matter of hours.

My annual Christmas dinner—which would happen closer to New Years this year—was his favorite holiday. He could eat a huge meal, then go back for seconds, thirds, and fourths for hours afterward. He'd burn it off the next day playing football.

With only the power of my Mother-magic and the smell of BBQ nearby, I'd been able to stave off the inevitability until now. Eating with the three of them gave me deep joy. Nothing made me as happy as watching my boys interact in the weird way boys did.

My only hope was that Max had eaten himself into a BBQ coma and would succumb before his brain remembered.

No such luck.

The past hour of not answering their questions hadn't prepared me for what I would say, but I did know two things.

1. A warning to Tanner would be in order.

2. Less was more.

"Spill what?" I asked not-so-innocently.

Max rolled his eyes so hard his head lolled back.

"Ma!" he cried in that unique, frustrated way that only he had. "Stop being facetious and tell us about the beau-friend already."

"Do you know what the word *facetious* means?" I asked.

Nicholas glanced over. "Wow, bro." He whistled. "College is giving you book smarts. Haven't you been hit in the head too many times for this?"

Blake chuckled, but remained buried in his phone.

Max glared at both of us.

"Not funny. I happen to have an impressive tutor." He waved a hand. "Continue with the boyfriend story, Ma."

After years of raising them, I knew when to concede. "There's no boyfriend, but there is an interest."

"Who?" Nicholas asked.

I rolled my lips. "Ah, Tanner Beck."

Max laughed. "Damnit! I was wrong."

"Maximillion!"

"Sorry." He held up two hands. "Sorry, I'll watch my language. Landon is going to rub this in my face forever."

"What were you wrong about and why are you laughing?" I asked.

Max chuckled again with a shake of his head.

"Landon told me he thought something might be happening between you and coach, but he hadn't confirmed it yet. That's all. I said he was wrong and that you'd probably never look at another man again."

How should I feel about a statement like *that*? My head couldn't quite wrap around what he meant, so I let it go.

"Blake?" I drawled.

"What?" he cried. "I didn't say anything!"

For some reason, that gave me relief.

"Tanner came over to the house when Landon was first brought Starla over," I said, "but that was the first time. Tanner had left some stuff behind when I paid him to clean the house and came back to get it. We sort of starting talking then."

"You paid someone to clean?" Max cried, because Max never spoke normally. "Ma! That's awesome. You're a next-level career-woman."

"Right. At my tiny mountain coffee shop."

"Small origins, big endings."

I rolled my eyes this time. "Onto the main point: Tanner and I are . . . interested. Let's just leave it there."

"Does it feel weird to date someone else?" Nicholas asked, gaze tapered. He hid a pair of hazel beauties behind all those lashes. I unashamedly wanted to paint his long eye-fans with mascara *just* to see what would happen.

"Little bit," I said, holding two fingers close together. "I haven't dated or anything like it since your Dad first asked me out, and don't you dare ask me what year that was!"

"Wouldn't think of it." Nicholas shook his head, hands held up. "Don't want to know. But good for you Mom. I think you should move on."

He had entirely too much gravity in his tone, but I couldn't imagine what it meant. I monitored Blake, but his expression hadn't changed. As usual, his whole attention remained riveted on his phone screen. Talking to his girlfriend across country again, I'd wager.

Only Blake had heard me talking on the phone with Tanner a few times, but nothing more than that. None of them knew that I'd spent Christmas Eve and Christmas Day with Tanner.

"Coach is cool, Mom," Max said.

"Yeah?"

"I liked him." He shrugged. "Was on point with his feed-back, not too easy on us, but wasn't a dic—"

My glare snapped to him.

"—tator," he drawled. "Coach is cool! Nicholas? What thinkest thou?" he asked, slapping a hand on Nick's thick shoulder. An expression I couldn't read flashed through Nicholas's face, but he stuffed it back.

"Time will tell," he said.

Which is exactly what I'd expected.

I snapped two fingers. "Exactly. Time *will* tell, and that's all you need to know. Now, we're going to drop the Tanner subject and move onto a topic that has actual substance. Landon's wedding."

Max tilted his head back and howled with laughter. "Oh. My. Shi—"

My glare returned.

"—iitake mushrooms!" he cried. "I forgot. Big bro is getting maaaarried!"

"Yes, he is. In less than a week at the Frolicking Moose. Preparations are steady and underway. In the meantime, we need to talk about said wedding and the decorum that I will," my eyes shot right back to Max with another snap, "expect from you."

He held up two hands in silent agreement.

"And let me assure you," I continued, "that there are no rude, four letter words that I will tolerate at this event."

Max groaned and slumped further in his seat.

"Holy fudge," he muttered, "this is going to be crazy."

Despite myself, I schooled back a laugh.

* * *

By early afternoon, the house smelled like dirty feet, the floor reverberated with the thuds and shouts of wrestling upstairs, and the living room sang a song of my people—the alternating shouts of men frustrated by a recorded sports game they watched every year at this time.

My heart had never been so happy.

We lacked only Landon and Starla, who would be coming soon.

Blake followed Max around like a puppy. He'd always been closest to Max, even though the two of them were as different as oil and water. Ever since Max had been picked up for a college football scholarship, the adoration had only increased. Smiles came faster and stronger for Blake when Max was around.

Water boiled out of a massive pot when my phone buzzed with a text. My heart leapt into my throat when I thought it might be Tanner.

Starla: We're on our way, Leslie! Should be there in an hour.

Leslie: See you soon!

I shoved my phone into the front pocket of my apron, then turned back to the boiling potatoes and flipped the burner off.

Steam billowed around me as I poured the water into the sink. Another shout, followed by a guffaw, trickled down the stairs. Plucked strains from a guitar came from the living room where Nicholas sat at the edge of the couch, messing with his old acoustic guitar. Somewhere in the cacophony sang Christmas carols—my measly attempt to keep the magic of Christmas going.

The only thing that would make this day better was Tanner.

The thought sent butterflies hurtling around my stomach so hard I'd get nauseated. Before too long, a knock came on the front door. A chord Nicholas had just started died with a *twang*. The shuffle of him heading toward the front door followed.

"Heads up," he called quietly toward the kitchen. "Coach is here."

I almost dropped a pan of buttermilk roll dough.

"What?" I cried.

"Hey coach," Nicholas called as the door swung open. "Good to see you again."

More manly back slapping followed. Before I could pull my composure back together, a flash of blonde appeared in the dining room.

"Leslie!"

Celeste appeared with a beautifully built basket that she set on the table. From where I stood, I made out a rainbow of expensive chocolates, a coffee mug that said BOSS LADY and what appeared to be a soft blanket. My heart did a triple wallop. Were those Lovers chocolates? Oh, that would need to be taken care of now. The boys would utterly raid and destroy them within twenty seconds.

I crooked my finger. "Bring that over here," I mouthed.

She half-skipped over, the basket wrapped in crinkly, clear cellophane safe in her clutches. I set aside the dough to let it raise in the background and set my hands on my hips.

"First of all," I said to Celeste, "you look lovely, as always."

A comfortable pair of sweats ran to the floor, complete with a fitting shirt under a too-short sweatshirt. She grinned.

"Thanks. We're treating today as an extension of Christmas since I just returned from my Mom's, so I kept on my comfy clothes."

"You're the only woman I've ever met that pulls off pajamas in such an impressive way."

She beamed. "Not true, you should see my Mom. Anyway, we brought you this Christmas basket. Dad made the sugar cookies—he's that good. I think he and JJ should team up for his next company if he lets the cleaning business go when I'm gone."

I blinked, startled at her casual mention. Wait, what? Tanner planned to sell his business?

Was that a for-sure thing?

My mind spun with the implications of such a statement. First of all, it didn't really matter to me if he did let the cleaning business go. Except . . . if Celeste was off to college and he didn't have the cleaning business here, exactly how much would he be in Pineville?

Second, that seemed a big thing that I knew nothing about. A reminder that Tanner and I still had a long way to go. Being almost-fifty meant there was more life to catch up on, not less.

A rush of panic threatened to overtake me, but I tamped it down. No. I would *not* think myself into a tizzy when all my boys would be home. Nope. That spell of apoplexy would come later when I had absolutely nothing else to stress over.

For now, I'd play this casually.

Tanner and I hadn't discussed what our little Christmas adventure would look like once our kids all returned. Had I even told him that my Christmas present was to fly the boys home?

Crap. I'd probably end up playing this awkwardly.

A broad-shouldered figure moved into the room behind Nicholas. I pretended rapt attention to Celeste, who jabbered away about Christmas presents and this guy that asked her out and how she found a thong under a pillow while cleaning a house.

Her voice made it easier to act like I didn't see Tanner back there, because then I'd totally lose my composure. He'd be able to see just how much I wanted to see him, and I wouldn't be able to play this off.

Deep down, I prayed he'd just roll with it.

"Come on in," Nicholas said. "I'll grab Max. He said he wanted to see you while he was home."

Nicholas disappeared up the stairs, taking them two at a time. That left Tanner back there, lingering like a ghost while Celeste finished jabbering. Before I could comment on a really expensive spa she had booked with her Mom or the new car that her step father promised her, she finished with a breathy, "Is Blake here?"

"Upstairs."

"Can I go see him?"

"Sure."

"Thanks!"

Within moments, she'd disappeared up the stairs as well. Unable to help myself now that we were alone, my gaze shifted to Tanner. He stood against the wall, one shoulder propped up, and watched me with a carefully neutral expression. Likely the same cautious one that I had on my face.

My lips twitched in a soft of amusement. This entire thing was so ridiculous.

A cautious smile appeared on his face. I had to stop myself from rushing into his arms. The way he leaned against the wall, and the hunger that showed on his face, made me want to throw myself back into his kiss and never walk away.

"I haven't told the boys," I said quickly. "It's not that I don't want to, I just—"

He held up a hand. "Celeste either. Let's just play this as friends."

Relief melted through me like a wave. "Really? You're not, like, offended or annoyed or hurt or something like that?"

"No. I didn't know they'd be here or we wouldn't have interrupted, anyway. Celeste wanted to bring you the basket and I . . . well, I wanted to see you again."

I glanced at the basket again. Inside the bag waited a plate of delicious sugar cookies, decorated with white frosting expertly swirled with red. Amongst them was a gift card and a few other things.

"Thank you for the basket. It looks so fun. Are those Lovers chocolates?"

He grinned. "They are."

"For me?"

"Definitely not for those goofballs." He motioned upstairs with a jerk of his head and a laugh that nearly unseated my control. I slipped my hand in between the crinkly cellophane, whisked the chocolates out, and slipped them into my other pocket.

"Consider them safe."

He winked.

My heart stopped.

Feet banging down the stairs sent him turning around to

face the descending hoard. I turned back to the stovetop, my back already to them by the time Max and "Coach" greeted each other in the same neanderthal-like way.

The two of them chattered like squirrels, tossing football vocabulary and questions back and forth that I couldn't hope to answer.

Meanwhile, dinner bubbled away on the stove, Christmas sang in the background, and my full heart sang a happy song.

Chapter Sixteen

TANNER

Celeste and I stepped into freezing air that night, the pinch of cold tight on my cheeks.

I stopped, closed my eyes, and drew in a deep breath. Eight hours of rambunctious boys, hilarious board games, and way too much food lay behind us. The most wonderful eight hours I'd had in years.

Celeste's breath puffed out in front of her like a fog as she moved ahead of me toward the truck.

"Welp," she cried, "that was unexpectedly amazing and maybe the best Christmas party that I've ever been to."

"Same."

She sent a wry glance my way as she climbed into the truck. It groaned from the cold as we climbed in and shut the doors, the slam echoing as they closed together.

"Leslie was attentive to you tonight," she sang.

Like the boys, Celeste was intentionally in the dark about what had happened between me and Leslie over Christmas Day. After I'd left Leslie's house on Christmas evening, I'd returned home, picked up Celeste the next day, and we'd spent time together until today, two days later.

Now that I'd seen Leslie again, however, I couldn't get her out of my head.

Her *or* those hot kisses.

I shook my head to clear those thoughts and jammed the keys into the ignition, ignoring Celeste's delighted titter of amusement. Right now, I didn't want to know what such a laugh meant. I just wanted to get home, fall asleep for ten hours, and wake up ready to tackle this whole I-really-like-Leslie thing.

Or did we need to yet?

My mind spun over the last few hours as Celeste and I quietly drove through sleepy little Pineville and toward the canyon. I still had an hour of driving ahead of me, and I was glad of it. Something about tires on pavement made it easier to think. Besides, Celeste seemed contemplative herself, so we left each other to our thoughts.

Seeing Leslie alone on Christmas Day, and in her element as a single woman—the life she'd inevitably live after Blake left the house—was a whole new side of her. The side with her boys all under her care? Well, that had changed her even more.

The joking-but-still-doting mother fit her well. She somehow tempered the line of concerned, but not overzealous, with a casual finesse. I imagined a rampantly anxious mother lived underneath her calm expression, but she'd never revealed a glimpse of it. Her boys seemed to feel free to live their lives how they wanted.

No small feat.

My appreciation for Leslie had only grown tonight, particularly the quick way she allowed Celeste and I to be pulled into the party for a second time. Landon and Starla had arrived with Starla appearing much less green than the last time I saw her.

She'd given me an extra long hug with a whispered *thank you so much*.

"Dad?"

I startled back to life with a shake of my head. "Sorry," I murmured, "what?"

Celeste lifted one eyebrow, assessing me with a critical gaze. "You all right?"

"Yep. Sorry. What did you say?"

"I just wanted to know how you felt about tonight."

"Great."

"Great?"

"Yeah, it went really well."

She let out a long breath. The heater had started to catch up, removing the cold tinge from the air. Her breath didn't show anymore, and the backs of my thighs warmed from the seat heater.

"What about you?" I asked.

"Quite fun."

"You sound surprised."

"I was. Four barely-post-adolescent males? No thanks. But it was fine. Max is really funny, I loved Nicholas on the guitar —smoking hot on any man—and Landon and Starla were adorable together."

My teeth ground together at the words *smoking hot on any man.* The sentiment wasn't new. Celeste had never been shy about admiring boys before, but it still set my nerves on fire every time. One day, she wouldn't be under my protection and she might say something like that and . . .

I forced that thought to slow.

"Plus," I added, "Leslie is an amazing cook."

"Yes." She groaned. "I'm going to gain thirty pounds, but it was so worth it."

I rolled my eyes. Not a chance. Celeste moved on—she'd never focused much on that kind of stuff anyway, thank heavens.

"Look, I'm just going to be straight." She canted herself in the seat so she could look right at me. I met her gaze for a brief moment, then looked back to the road. Never had I felt the need to cower to my daughter, but if there was ever a time to be a little afraid of what she might say, this was it.

"Then be straight," I said.

The road illuminated as my blinker flipped on to change lanes. I was very grateful I had driving as my focus.

"I think Leslie is interested."

I coughed to hide my laughter.

"What?" she cried. "She was definitely trying not to stare at you all night, and she very subtly kept you mostly in her line of sight, unless it really couldn't be avoided." Her finger poked my shoulder. "So if you're worried that she'll say no to going on a date, tonight she erased any of that. The two of you would be great together."

"I agree."

Her mouth dropped open. "What?"

"We already went on a date. Well . . . sort of." Rage clouded her pretty features. Before she could explode, I continued. "I helped her on Christmas Eve while you were with your Mom."

"And?" she cried.

"And it was fun."

"That's all you're going to tell me?" Her voice would have riddled me with holes if it had been any sharper. "In the last fifty-something hours I've been home, you couldn't possibly think to mention it?"

I shrugged.

She growled.

"So?" she finally drawled, sweeping a hand in front of her. "Tell me how it was. Did you enjoy it? How many hours were you together? Did Leslie give you any signs?"

"Yes, pretty much all day, and what are signs?"

Celeste balled her hands into fists. "Dad, c'mon! Don't be a neanderthal. Did she give any signs of liking you?"

"Celeste, I have no idea what signs you're talking about."

I intentionally kept my voice low and modulated. Not just to keep her from *really* losing it, but to skirt around the fact that Leslie had definitely given me some signs of interest. Still, it wasn't time to reveal that to Celeste. Thankfully, Leslie and I had been on the exact same page there.

"After spending that time with her on Christmas Eve, I think she'd go on a date with me," I said, just to tilt the topic a bit. "Actually, I still think Christmas Eve should count."

Celeste sliced a hand through the air. "No dice, Dad. Doesn't count. You need to take her on a romantic date! You're good at those."

"I'm adequate."

"Just *ask* already!"

"I will."

"When?"

Ah, she'd found my weak spot. While I had confidence that I would ask Leslie out on an official date, the problem was knowing *when* to do it. I swallowed, simultaneous mental paths popping up in my mind. Had to be careful here.

If I said the wrong thing . . .

"Now is not the time," I said with a finger jabbing her way. "With her boys here, New Years in a few days, and a wedding around the corner, the last thing she needs is a date from me."

Celeste folded her arms across her chest. "Fine, I'll agree with that, but tell me when you're going to ask her out."

"What is this?" I cried. "Are you my life coach?"

She blew a raspberry. "You totally couldn't afford me. Mom is a life coach and makes like ten thousand dollars a month. I've got it in my blood. Anyway, you have a goal, you have to set a date." She had the gall to look annoyed. "Remember? We went through this with my college applications."

I sent her a sour glare. She beamed. Of course she'd use my lecture on goal setting against me now. Appropriately too, which only made it that much more galling. The fact that I didn't want to set a date for asking Leslie on a date was telling, too.

Why did I skirt it?

I frowned and wrestled over the question for several long moments. Celeste let it ride, but her eyes never left my profile. She watched me squirm my way into the truth.

And the truth wasn't pretty.

"I don't want to set that definite of a goal yet," I finally admitted with a hard breath. "Because . . . because I'm not really sure I'm ready for this."

"For a girlfriend?"

"For Leslie Hill."

"What's wrong with her?"

"Nothing."

"So . . . this doesn't make any sense."

No, I wanted to say, *I'm not ready to crash my bachelor-style life into the mountain that is Leslie Hill and never recover myself.*

Life with Leslie was something I wouldn't recover from soon. Sure, the metaphorical stone of me liking her was already rolling down the hill—and gaining momentum. Kissing her on Christmas had drawn a line in the sand from which there was no recovery.

Yet, on the other side, an equally frightening quietness and loneliness awaited.

"I want to make sure that I'm not dating Leslie because I don't want to be alone," I finally admitted. I did a quick glance at her eyes, back to the road, then back to her again. The headlights cut a beam right in front of the truck, illuminating an empty canyon.

Celeste's face wrinkled. "What do you mean?"

I sighed. How honest should I be? Celeste was too intelligent to pander with, but I also didn't want to unintentionally give her things to worry about.

She was still a kid.

"You're leaving to go to college soon and that is great. It's absolutely what you should be doing and I'm 100% supportive." I held out a hand to drive the point home. "You're on the right path. But it will mean a very quiet house and . . . I'm not looking forward to missing you."

She melted a little. "I know. I'm worried about you, too."

"What?"

She shrugged and looked entirely too much like me.

"Dad, you're a mess sometimes. Yeah, you pulled your life together and raised me without Mom being around all that much in the beginning, and then you did the majority of caring for me. You clean houses like a pro, you whip up desserts like it's your hobby—which, okay, it is your hobby—but that's with me there. I'm worried that when I'm gone, you'll struggle."

Well, damn if she didn't constantly surprise me.

"That's quite mature of you."

She smiled.

"I'll be fine," I insisted. "I promise. I just need some time to figure out what it's really going to look like. Okay?"

"Okay."

She leaned back against the seat with a sigh, and we drove the rest of the way home in silence.

* * *

Life resumed from the quiet Christmas holiday.

Celeste made herself scarce with her friends, a new housekeeper joined the team, and I set him to work in the company.

At night, I talked to Leslie for too long while she hid in her bedroom, away from the rambunctious sound of boys in the background.

On the 28th of December, a text message interrupted my last few minutes of sleep.

Landon: Any chance you have a few minutes to spare?

Underneath the calm words, I sensed hesitation. Or maybe it was the fact that he'd sent the text at 6:30 in the morning. I grumbled under my breath, but rolled over, turned on my lamp, and sat up so I didn't fall asleep. Forget texting. I hit the phone icon and called.

Landon answered with a harried breath a few moments later. "Hey coach."

"What's up?"

"I need help."

"Everything okay?"

"No." His firm tone, quick words, and the sound of moving in the background had me sitting up straighter. "Can you come over now?"

I stood up and reached for my pants.

"On my way."

* * *

Half an hour later, Landon pulled open the door of their new apartment. The sound of retching rolled out from behind him.

Bags darkened his eyes, like he hadn't slept all night. His hair lay askew. A long-sleeved white button down, and a half tied-tie, completed his zombie-like ensemble.

"You look like death," I said.

"I need help."

I stepped inside as he rushed around. "What's going on?"

"I'm sorry to bother you, coach, I just didn't have anywhere to turn. Mrs. Donovan next door is still asleep and she's so old, I don't want to wake her up. Celeste needs a ride to the doctor's office to get a hold of her nausea and vomiting, but I've got a meeting at the new job that I can't miss. She's retching so much, she can't drive. She's so weak, too. I already had a training meeting that I had to step out on to help her right before Christmas, and if they fire me . . ."

His words lingered in the air, fragile, as he snatched a pair of keys off the floor. They still didn't have any furniture.

"Go to work. I'll take care of her."

He paused, maybe for the first time in hours. "Really?"

"Yeah, with one caveat."

His shoulders tensed under my palm. "You want me to tell my mom."

"It's time, Landon," I said gently. "You can't do this alone. I know the pressure you must feel to take care of her and be all the things for your new wife, but you can't. You never will. The sooner you accept that, the more you *can* take care of her. Your pride doesn't matter as much as her health."

His nostrils flared and lips pinched together. He looked so much like Leslie in that moment I had to blink to clear the picture.

Finally, after what felt like an eternity, he nodded once.

"Okay. I . . . it's not how we wanted to do it, but you're right. We're going to lose my job and insurance and . . . it's not worth it."

"You're doing great. Now it's time to let people help. More than just getting a safer apartment, okay?"

"Okay. I have to go. I'm almost late. I'll call my Mom on the way in, but I won't have time to explain everything."

I sucked in a sharp, quiet breath. From the moment I'd stepped into their apartment, I'd known exactly what would happen: I'd tell Landon to tell Leslie. He would. Leslie would finally learn that I knew the whole truth all along.

What would the coming confrontation mean? Leslie wasn't going to be happy about my secret-keeping. Our budding *something* might just take a total crash and burn.

I ruminated over the obvious path for a few moments. I could not involve Leslie, handle this with Landon, and hope he didn't lose his job in the meantime.

No, that path was unacceptable.

Leslie in the dark no longer felt sustainable. If it had reached this level with Celeste, I'd want to know.

Potential-angry-Leslie or not, it was still the right thing to do.

Resolved, I turned Landon toward the door and shoved him gently forward. "Go. I'll get Starla to the doctor and this place cleaned up. Then I'll call your Mom and have her come up here. We can figure something out."

"I can come home for lunch. I'll be here from 12:30-1:15, then at 5:00."

"Go!"

"Thanks coach!"

He disappeared down the metal stairs with a hustle that I hadn't seen from him since the championship game he'd won. I glanced around, stacked my hands on my hips, and let out a giant sigh.

A quiet voice came from just behind me.

"I'm sorry to cause you trouble again."

I whirled around to see Starla leaning against the wall. She folded both arms over her middle, looking as weary as Landon. Based on their mutual appearances, neither of them had been sleeping much.

"Hey," I said.

She frowned. "This is exactly what we wanted to avoid," she croaked, then swallowed hard. She tucked a stray piece of hair behind her eyes, which looked pained and confused and one hundred shades of stressed. I tried to imagine Celeste in this position and couldn't handle the emotions it stirred up in me.

Despite Starla's desperate appearance, I still sensed a pillar of strength in her. The same sort of thing that would have drawn a guy like Landon to her side, a mere moth to a flame.

"You don't want any family to help?" I asked.

"I don't want to be a burden."

"Is that what you think you are?"

"I could be." She tilted her head against the wall, as if even that tired her. Any question of whether she'd be able to drive herself dissipated. "I just . . . I didn't want this to be how his family met me. I'm in this marriage with Landon forever, the last thing I want is them remembering sick little Starla."

"You're not giving the Millers enough credit."

She blinked, then sighed. "Maybe not."

"Let's get you to your appointment," I said gently. "Then we'll come back, I'll grab some food to stock you up, clean the place, and you can rest. We'll take the next step as it happens, all right?"

Tears filled her eyes like misty clouds.

"Thank you."

I held out an arm. "Your chariot awaits, Miss Starla."

While escorting her weakened steps down the creaky metal stairs, my mind drifted back to Leslie. Despite all the thrills and excitement she normally stirred up in me, right now, the only thing I conjured was dread.

Leslie Hill was going to be hurt, and that was on me.

Chapter Seventeen

⁓

LESLIE

My heart raced the entire time I drove up the canyon to Jackson City.

Landon's voice rang in my ears, bleak around the edges and hollow. He'd called while I was away from my phone and left a voicemail. An hour later, I finally listened. Another hour passed while I extricated myself from appointments at work, stopped at home, and headed on my way up.

"Everything is fine, Mom," Landon's voicemail said, "but I need some help with taking care of Starla. Tanner is with her now, so she's fine. I just . . . I think it's time we explain everything. Get here as soon as you can safely do so?"

Whatever that meant, it felt as if all the burning questions I'd had for weeks had just settled into something calm. Something that waited.

Maybe now we'd get some answers.

Where *here* ended up being was an apartment building on the south side of Jackson City, not far from the canyon. I hurried up three flights of stairs to the top floor, as Landon had directed. My mother's instinct told me that both of them lived here now.

My entire body felt like I'd flushed it with ice water as I lifted my hand and knocked on the door. Three seconds later, Tanner opened it. An unreadable expression filled his face when he saw me, hesitated, then pulled the door open and indicated I should step inside. I obeyed, eyes darting around.

"Come in," he said quietly. "We just returned."

A mostly-empty space greeted me. One rug lay on the floor between a brown carpet in the living room and a white-tiled kitchen. Three large pillows cluttered the ground, an old grayish sofa with a single drape of garland over it, and a half-ripped picture of an old Santa Claus with rosy cheeks filled the room.

The smell of window cleaner lingered in the air, and I recognized Tanner's signature of a clean house.

"Where's Landon?" I asked when the door closed. "Starla?"

"Starla is laying down. The trip to the doctor and back really tired her out."

I studied him, more concerned about the tense way he held his shoulders than the cryptic call Landon had given me.

"What's going on?" I asked.

Tanner nodded toward the couch. "This shouldn't come from me, but Landon's gotten himself into a situation he can't get out of on his own. I've been . . . helping him, to use a loose term. Today, I insisted we get you involved."

My arms tensed, which made my neck rigid. Whatever came next wouldn't be good. I licked my lips and steadied myself mentally.

"Okay," I said.

Tanner hesitated, then let out a long breath. "I don't know many details, but this is what I do know: Starla was diagnosed with non-Hodgkin's lymphoma a few weeks ago, right after the time they officially began to date. They've been diagnosing her exact stage and the aggressiveness of the cancer for the last few weeks. She's had to go in and out of different doctors to make it happen. They've figured it out and plan to start chemo on January 3rd."

He stopped talking, studying me as the puzzle pieces finally slotted into place. The abrupt change in wedding date. Her pale appearance. The hesitant way she interacted with me at first, and her fear of me thinking she was pregnant.

Chemotherapy, okay. That wouldn't be fun, but why get married so quickly? It dawned on me.

"Insurance?" I whispered.

"Yes, but no." Tanner ran a hand through his hair. "That's what I thought at first too. I . . . from what he's told me, they fell in love at first sight. She'd started to not feel well before they met. As they dated he encouraged her to see a doctor and this whole thing began. Yes, she needs his insurance but . . . I really believe it's more than that for them."

"So he quit medical school." I lowered to the folding chair just behind me. "And now he's working?"

Tanner nodded.

"They moved into this apartment a few weeks ago. Before that, they were in a different one, on the other side of town. My friend, Mrs. Donovan, lives next door. She's been able to help Starla."

"You saw the other apartment?"

He nodded. His gaze didn't waver from mine, but I sensed tension build between us. If he'd been to the other apartment *and* this one, that suggested a timeline. And timeline meant he'd known the truth for much longer than me.

The quiet must have been too much, because he kept explaining.

"I'm going to hazard a guess that they haven't been able to afford any furniture." He waved a vague hand toward the kitchenette area. "I stocked them with food last time, and was going to go again once I returned from the office with Starla.

Things are pretty lean for them, I think. Landon doesn't give a lot of details. I think he's having a hard time."

I ground my jaw together. Curse Landon and his blasted pride.

"Starla didn't want to tell me?" I guessed as I gazed around, unable to look right at him. No, then he'd see the building frustration. My child was in need and Tanner knew it. He'd deliberately withheld that information during the dozens of hours of phone calls that lay between then and now.

The opportunities to tell me were endless.

He didn't.

"She didn't want her first impression on the whole family to be her sickness," Tanner murmured. "She wanted to enjoy Christmas, the wedding, and meet everyone without the diagnosis hanging over everything. What they feel is real. They don't want people to think that their marriage only happened because she needed some extra support."

Unable to fight the building tension in my chest, I exploded to my feet and began to pace.

"Her family?" I asked.

He shrugged. "All Landon has said is that her family isn't in the picture, and it's better that way. She has no one else except two roommates that genuinely care about her, but are really busy with their own lives. They couldn't give the support she needs, and she can't work in this state. Not while undergoing chemo," he added, "and the radiation that will follow."

Two decades of raising pillars of testosterone taught me how to hold my tongue and think a situation through. I leaned on that experience now. I pressed my lips together as an added measure so I didn't lash out at Tanner, although maybe he deserved that too.

None of this felt good, right, or easy.

While my mind spun out over the fact that Landon had

been hiding all of this from me, I couldn't set aside Tanner's responsibility in all of this.

All this time he'd known the secret.

He'd been helping my son and didn't breathe a word of it to me. I couldn't tell which betrayal felt greater. Landon's lack of trust and openness with me, or Tanner's.

In the meantime, my heart went out to Starla. Estranged from her family and on her own with such a scary diagnosis. Any young-twenty-something might have done the same thing. Didn't make it the correct path, but certainly made sense in light of their age.

Two full minutes passed before I could summon up a word.

"I'd like to talk to Starla."

Tanner lifted a wary eyebrow. "And say?" he asked. A sense of protectiveness lay in that tone, and my cup boiled over.

"That is not your business," I snapped with a step toward him. "I think you've done enough. Thank you for encouraging Landon to call me. Thank you for helping him when he wouldn't let me, and thank you for buying them food. But now I need you to go."

"Les, she's in a really vulnerable—"

I held up two hands when he stepped toward me.

"Don't come near me."

A wounded look crossed his face, but I didn't care. He'd given me a chance to vent all the bubbling helplessness I'd been dealing with for *weeks* while he went around my back, parenting my kid.

With fury in my voice I said, "If you really think I'm going to take out anything on that sick girl in there, you don't know me at all. You've offended me with that insinuation and I don't want to talk to you right now. Please go."

A thousand things appeared in his gaze all at once. One could almost call the look soulful until it passed.

The mixture of frustrated, confused, aggravated, and loss startled me. How could such a large man still seem like such a little boy? He blinked it away and shuffled back a step.

"Okay."

Without another word, I brushed past him and into the other room. The door closed behind him only a few seconds later.

* * *

At 5:15 sharp, the front door opened.

Landon hurried inside, then skidded to a stop. The anxiety in his expression dropped the moment he clapped eyes on Starla.

She sat upright on a different, gently-used couch the color of evergreen. Pillows propped behind her. A used coffee table held a cup of broth, one of tea, and a plate of soda crackers and toast. Starla's pale expression had a little more color to it after a change in nausea medication and a long nap.

"Hey," she murmured to Landon. She held out a steady hand with a little smile.

Landon rushed to her side and dropped to his knees in front of her. I faded back into the kitchen to give them a moment.

The swirling relief and fear in his expression tugged at my heart. What mother ever wanted to see heartfelt anguish on their child's face?

A riot of emotions rolled around my body already. They worsened at the sight of his utter adoration. The painful love returned in her gaze. Landon looked as if he'd been through agony all day, waiting to get home.

In the interim between kicking Tanner out and Landon returning home, Starla and I had spoken in bursts. While Starla napped, I'd called a local friend and asked her to bring over some gently-used furniture, accepting basic descriptions as they told me about them. I ran to the Bed and Bath store to stock up on a few things. After the couch arrived and settled Starla onto it, she'd opened up.

Her whole story came out, from an unstable home and awkward family life that she hadn't returned to since graduating high school, to the onset of symptoms. Her shock over the diagnosis as she spoke about it was still apparent in her tone.

"I don't know what to think," she'd murmured at one point, her brow heavy. "I'm afraid for what it might take to treat it, but more afraid of how it'll affect Landon. I already feel like a burden to him . . ."

Now that all the information had been laid out, I didn't know what to do with it. My simmering frustration with Tanner had abated a little.

He'd been heroically supportive considering all facets. The apartment. Cleaning. Stocking food. He'd also dropped off some clothes for Landon and checked in through text messages every couple of days. I couldn't make sense of my gratitude for his help toward my son when it coupled with my irritation that he'd kept all those secrets.

Landon shuffled into the kitchen and broke apart my thoughts. He didn't stop at the fridge the way I expected, he just walked right over to me and pulled me into his arms.

"I'm sorry." His voice broke. "Tanner was right. I was being a proud idiot and didn't want to take help. Didn't want you to think badly of Starla or that I'd bitten off more than I could chew. I wanted to prove I could do this. That my career change and quick wedding weren't related. I'm sorry, Mom. I don't think I can do this alone."

I wrapped my arms around him and pulled him close. A muted cry followed, then calmed. He gripped me hard for almost a full minute before he finally pulled back. A quick swipe of his thumbs cleared the moisture from his cheeks.

I grabbed his wrists.

"I know how much you love her," I said, "and I see how real it is. I trust you, Landon Miller. Now, please give me the same courtesy in the future?"

His nostrils flared as he nodded, blinking away the last of the emotion. His hands shook as he wiped his cheeks off again. A distressed, square table stood in the corner of the kitchen now, surrounded by four sturdy chairs. Next to it, a broom, a mop, a vacuum, and a few other necessities stood against the wall in a pile. He stared at all of it, nostrils flared.

"The furniture," he said, his voice husky. He gestured to it, "Did you?"

"I did."

"Thank you. We'll—"

I held up a hand. "If you offer to pay me back, I will personally cut off your legs."

He softened. "Thanks, Mom."

"A few other little things will arrive tomorrow. A TV and recliner." I gestured to a folding card table and two rickety chairs that looked like they'd been scrounged up near a garbage pile. "Please give those away?"

He laughed. "Of course."

"Also, I spoke with the nurse from the clinic where Starla is being seen and got copies of all her appointment times. I will be up here to take her to her appointments. If I can't, I will find someone to come and get her and take her home."

He opened his mouth to protest, the refusal building in his eyes, but I cut him off with my sternest glare. His mouth closed.

"Consider it my wedding present, if you will," I said in a conciliatory tone.

"Starla told me you refused the money that we have to pay

for the wedding," he said. "I think paying for all the catering, the decorations, the Frolicking Moose rental, and my tux is plenty of a wedding gift."

"Your father is paying for half of it," I added as an aside, because Ethan had already sent the money. "Either way, I'm here for both of you."

All the blood drained from his face.

"The wedding," he whispered. "I almost forgot. We can't have the wedding when she feels like this! It's in like three days!"

I rolled my eyes. "Landon, you've always been my most dramatic son, and you maintain that title even today. Please, invest a little faith in your mother. Starla is a part of the family now, and we take care of family. Starla asked the doctor about it with Tanner today. The doctor gave her a sufficient prescription so that she can have a better day then, and almost everything is already lined up. We're going to have that wedding, and it's going to be one you will never forget."

* * *

That night, I collapsed on my bed.

With Blake, Nicholas, and Max gone to a shoot 'em up movie at the theater in Jackson City, and then to stop and see Landon and Starla for a few minutes, I had the house to myself for the first time in a while.

For what felt like hours, I kept my face pressed into the blankets and drew in deep breaths of a light, clean cotton. It only made me think more of Tanner, so I turned my face to the side and stared at my dark room.

This situation was beyond me.

Desperate, I dialed the only person that could help me talk out of this disaster. Within two rings, a perky voice answered the other line.

"Leslie!" Lizbeth called. "Hello, my favorite. What's up?"

I rolled onto my back. "Lizbeth, I desperately need your optimism."

Her voice dropped. "I'm here. Spill."

"You have a few minutes?"

"I have *all* the minutes. Baby girl just fell asleep and I'm relaxing with a rom-com I've seen eight billion times."

Almost like a robot, I let the story flow out. Tanner, our time together at Christmas, Landon and Starla, and the crash of finding out the truth. Her quiet exclamations, calm murmurs, and gentle questions soothed the story out of me. By the time I got around to what happened today, my throat felt raspy.

"So." I let out a hard breath. "That's the story."

"Sweet baby pineapple," Lizbeth breathed. "Your life is a walking romance novel. You see it, right?"

With a scowl, I muttered. "I see it."

"Okay!" Her voice perked up. "All romance ever wants is acknowledgment. Moving on. How are you feeling toward Tanner?"

"I don't know! That's what you're supposed to tell me. How am I supposed to feel about Tanner?"

She scoffed. "I can't *tell* you what to feel, Leslie. Nor can I tell you what to do. But I can listen and guide, and Imma guide you right into the place of *oh my gosh, look at how much he did for your kid while you weren't there.* How about them apples?"

My nose wrinkled. "I don't like your apples."

"You never do."

"Right, Tanner was very helpful to Landon. I am truly grateful for that. But he should have told me."

"From what I gather and sort of assume, Landon asked him not to say anything. What would you have done if the situation was reversed? You love Celeste. You'd do anything to help her in a situation like that."

I drew in a breath to reply, then paused. Reversed situation certainly gave me a moment of pause. Would I hold Celeste's secret? Likely, as long as she wasn't on death's door and was mostly safe.

"I'd do what he did," I muttered. "I'd help her however I could within the boundaries she set."

"Right, because that whole situation is one that needs to come from your son, right? It wasn't Tanner's place. So he did the best he could. Super hot, if you ask me. I'm just sayin'."

I rolled my eyes. Her reminder of Tanner's attractiveness certainly didn't help, but I set that aside for now.

"I was angry with Tanner," I admitted quietly. "Landon too, but I snapped at Tanner and asked him to leave and sort of took the whole situation out on him." My eyes squeezed tightly shut. "Oh, crap, Lizbeth! I suck at this!"

"C'mon, Les! Any woman would have done the same. Situations like that are intense. Whattaya do?"

I frowned. "You can't be serious."

"I am. I've certainly done similar things to JJ without meaning to. I just reacted. I'll bet Tanner is blaming himself because he seems like that kind of guy. If you're asking whether I think you've lost your chance," she drawled, which I absolutely was but hadn't exactly put into words, "then my answer is no. I think you've been given an opportunity to see how this guy works through conflict. That's a pretty cool thing."

"Yeah," I murmured. "It is."

"You know that more than anyone," she added quietly, "because that's when you knew when things were over with Ethan, remember?"

A moment of silence passed between us.

"I remember," I whispered.

"But?" Lizbeth drawled.

I dropped down to the floor and propped my back against the bed. My head fell back.

"But I . . . I just don't know what to do next. Do I call and apologize? Do I wait? Do I let him come to me?"

"Don't do anything tonight. Go to bed. Sounds like it was an exhausting day and you have a book club at the Frolicking Moose tomorrow, then the wedding two days after that. This can be broached later."

"Right. Sleep."

"March into your bathroom," she demanded, "wash your face, brush your teeth, and climb into bed. Lizbeth's orders. Just because you're living a romance novel doesn't mean you have to fall to pieces."

"Got it. Thank you."

I could feel her smile over the phone.

"I always got you, Leslie. I, for one, am happy to hear how you've changed course on your romance belief systems. Well done, my friend. Romance approves and will send its mystical powers your way."

Chapter Eighteen

TANNER

"I messed up."

Celeste peered at me from over the counter, a slice of pizza in her hand. Her gaze tapered.

"What do you mean?"

"With Leslie."

I shoved the greasy box of pepperoni pizza away from me and dropped my head into my hands with a groan. Yesterday had been replaying through my mind over and over again. I should have handled it differently. That much was blatantly obvious.

But how?

"What happened?" Celeste asked, mouth full of pizza. I shook my head.

"I *totally* messed up."

She poked me with the end of a fork. "Details, please! Can't help you until I know what I'm dealing with."

Reluctantly, I straightened up and spilled everything. Landon. Starla. Their hidden life and new apartment and awful diagnosis and Leslie's reaction to all. Celeste grew steadily more concerned in my retelling until she finally set the pizza aside and left it to grow cold on top of the box.

"Whoa," she whispered when I finished.

"Yeah."

I ran a hand over my face, still bleary from the long day yesterday.

After leaving Starla in Leslie's capable hands, I had advertising sources to follow up on and another house to clean in a different part of Jackson City. I had to turn away work without Yessica for a while, which led to low income. Another worker left and I hadn't been able to find another replacement that could drive to all the different locations.

In a word, business was hard over the holidays.

While Celeste struggled to find something to say—at least she hadn't started to chastise me right away—I spun over the problem.

What should I do next? Leslie clearly needed some space or time. Both, probably. That's what I'd want. When I twisted this situation around to try to see it from her perspective, I understood it. If Celeste had done all of those things without me, I would have been pissed too.

Which was the hard part.

"I think you start with apologizing," Celeste finally said, her voice firm. "Really, at this point, that's all you can do. Yeah, you kept secrets from her, but you were also actively helping. If they had been in true danger, you would have let her know. But you respected that Landon is an adult and you kept an eye on him. I think she'll see that."

I peered at her through my splayed fingers.

"You think so?"

"I hope so. Leslie is . . . sensible, if nothing else."

My forehead ruffled. "Sensible, yes. But bubbling under all that sensibility is a woman with a lot of emotions. I'm worried that trust is broken and can't be regained. Sure, she'll probably forgive me, but what will that look like on the other side?"

Celeste reached over and squeezed my arm. "You really like her, don't you?"

"Yeah."

Until she'd asked the question, I hadn't let myself question the strength of my feelings. At that moment, I couldn't have stopped myself if I wanted to. There was no denying what I felt about Leslie anymore. That stone had long been running down the mountainside, gaining steam.

Now, it might just crash, crack, and die.

My fingers itched to grab my phone and call her. Text her, even, although we didn't do a lot of that. I preferred to hear her voice. But I didn't.

Because each time that I almost called, I heard the hardness in her tone all over again. I didn't want to hear that tone directed toward me twice.

Besides, she had a wedding to plan, prepare, and execute. Landon and Starla couldn't do much to help and all her boys were home. The next couple of days would be the worst possible time to broach this. I could give her space, but it would suck for a while.

Two more days. I could make it two more days. Then I'd show up at the wedding and clear the air at the end. The unfortunate truth was clear: Leslie Hill didn't need me.

But maybe I needed her.

Chapter Nineteen

LESLIE

The day of the wedding dawned with a crystal blue sky.

Although cold air settled onto Pineville like a crisp blanket, not even the chill could wipe away my optimistic mood. My son would marry a wonderful woman today. Their secrets were out and all my boys were here.

Plus, I didn't have to listen to Ethan complain about wearing a dress shirt.

He was someone else's complainer now.

After donning a gentle black skirt with a flattering, navy-blue top, I wrapped an apron around myself and set to work on a big breakfast that would get everyone through the morning.

The catharsis and familiarity of making a meal for my sons banished all the cobwebs left over from Tanner.

Tanner whom I *still* missed.

The fact that I hadn't heard from him wasn't making me feel any better about this situation, either. Lizbeth's conversation still worked through my subconscious.

Somehow, there had to be a path to apologizing that didn't leave both of us in an awkward position. I'd jumped the gun on being angry with him, and after all he'd done for both of them, I wouldn't fault him for being ticked at me in return. I should have given him more of a chance to explain. He hadn't spoken for himself. He'd answered my questions about Landon and Starla and then respected my request for him to leave.

That hadn't been fair to him.

The shuffle of feet coming down the stairs drew my gaze away from the bubbling butter on a griddle ready for pancake batter. Nicholas, still sleepy-eyed, headed toward the kitchen. He sat on one of the stools at the counter.

"Hey, Mom."

"Hey kiddo." I eyed him in between dropping batter on the griddle. Never mind that he was an adult now, he'd always be my kiddo. "How did you sleep?"

"Good."

"You ready for the wedding today?"

He shrugged. "Sure. Seems pretty simple. Show up at the Frolicking Moose at 3:00, watch them get married, eat a lot after."

I laughed. "That about sums it up."

My hilarity was short-lived. By the time I'd flipped the bubbling pancakes, he'd worked through the remaining sleepiness and asked, "Are *you* ready for the wedding today?"

Trust Nicholas, my most in-tune and introspective child, to ask the walloping question. I drew in a breath, not certain how to answer that. On some level, absolutely. This was a hurdle that could easily be overcome, and usher a new phase of life to my oldest. It'd take a lot off my plate, and give everyone a reason to be happy in the New Year.

On the other hand . . .

"I think so," I replied. "It's certainly strange marrying my oldest off, but . . . had to happen sometime, right?"

"Right."

"How did Christmas go?" I asked. "Did you spend it with your friend since you didn't go to your Dad's? What is her name? Stacey?"

Nicholas' lips tightened into a thin line. "Not really."

He looked down, the curls at the base of his neck giving me a little pang. They reminded me so much of him as a little boy.

"Did you spend the day alone?" I asked as I lifted up one of the pancakes and inspected the underside. The forced nonchalance probably didn't fool him.

He shook his head. I paused, glanced at him, and dropped the pancake.

"So what did you do?"

His nostrils flared. "Don't want to talk about it, okay?"

"Really?"

"Really." He shrugged. "Things with Stacey just didn't work out and I dealt with it."

"But you've liked her for—"

"I know."

His clipped tone startled me, but I let it pass. A wounded Nicholas was an angry Nicholas. It tilted my head to the side. On instinct, I pushed my luck.

"What happened between you and your Dad?" I asked quietly.

Nicholas opened his mouth, closed it, and eventually said, "We had a falling out and I'd rather not go into details."

"Okay."

Something fractured between Nicholas and his father ever since the divorce, but I hadn't been able to peg down what. Blake claimed not to know, and any questioning of Nicholas led to stony-walled silence.

Whatever happened had driven a deep wedge and I wished I could heal it. Something similar seemed to happen with Stacey, and I couldn't help but wonder if it had something to do with Nicholas's propensity to shove everyone away from him as fast as he could.

Turned out, however, it was my turn to get grilled.

"I heard you got in a fight with Coach." He leaned forward slightly. "What happened?"

"Said who?" I asked.

Nicholas shrugged. He didn't look away, even though I kept the majority of my focus on the pancakes. Unnecessarily, perhaps. No batch of pancakes had ever been this critical.

Whomever gave him his information, he wouldn't give them up. He would have made a great reporter with his natural intelligence, hot pursuit of the truth, and ability to keep everything locked inside.

"Fight is a strong word," I replied. "Misunderstanding might be better."

"Have you talked with him about it?"

"Not yet."

When no further response came, I glanced up. Nicholas stared, unseeing, at the griddle where the pancakes browned. I flipped them on top of each other in a growing stack, then plopped it on an empty, waiting plate. More circles appeared on the griddle as I poured the next batch, and the routine soothed me.

My frustration, though I'd directed it at Tanner, had really been geared more toward my lack of control. A deeper issue was at work here.

My boys were growing up.

Separating myself as their sole help in times of distress hadn't come easily. Landon also hadn't experienced the true toils of adulthood before now. Not being the first person Landon turned to had hurt my feelings, but it was also a part of life.

Sure, he'd had some mishaps and broken-hearted moments in college, but nothing *truly* deep, like what he and

Starla would face now. Landon and Starla already had a depth of love that I'd never seen.

I was honest enough with myself to accept that I couldn't be everything for all my boys, nor could I remain their number one forever. The realization didn't come easy, but felt right when I let it in.

Now, I had to find the words to say it all to Tanner without breaking my chances.

My hasty reaction and frustration toward him may have cost me more than I wanted to give up. I already missed him.

How could that be?

"How is logging?" I asked. Nicholas blinked out of his thoughts, then leaned his head onto his hand.

"Fine. Busy."

"Tiring?"

"That too."

"How much longer are you going to do what's ranked as the most dangerous job in the country?"

I tried to infuse as much meaning into the question as I could manage. Nicholas's lips twitched, but he let the subtle jab go.

He shrugged. "Not super sure. I'm making $50,000 a year right now. Since I'm sharing a place with some other guys for really cheap rent, I think I'll work another year or two and save up."

"For what?"

He opened his mouth, but shut it again. Something big lay in his eyes—a plan. Just what that plan would entail, however, I had no idea.

"Something," he finally said, and left it at that.

Blake and Max came thudding down the stairs, saving him from the questioning about to follow. The carefully-curated stack of pancakes quickly disappeared, victim to their ravenous forks, and I hustled to keep up with their larger-than-life appetites.

Today, I'd need their cooperation and help, and that came more easily on the heels of a full stomach.

I pointed my spatula at Max.

"You and Blake are on look-out duty. Okay? Make sure no one is looking left out or stuck in a weird conversation and in need of help."

Both of them nodded. I gestured to Nicholas next.

"You're on Landon and Starla duty. If they need something, you get it. Keep them hydrated."

He chugged a glass of milk. "Got it."

"The three of you will clean up the breakfast dishes, please, then head up stairs and get ready to go. I will be leaving in an hour for the Frolicking Moose."

"An hour?" Blake cried. "But the ceremony isn't until 3:00. Why are we going at 10:00? That's five hours early! I'm going to miss a game with Missy."

"Because we have things we need to set up and errands that I need to run." I popped him gently on the arm with the spatula. "That's where I need your help, all right? You can separate yourself from your girlfriend for at least that long."

With a muttered groan, he turned to go back upstairs. Max finished stuffing the last of his tenth pancake into his mouth, then gave me a thumbs up.

"Perfect, Ma!"

Seconds later, the two of them disappeared. Nicholas stood, gathered the plates, and walked over to the sink. Of course, his two brothers had already forgotten my dictate to clean up, then change. While Nicholas plugged the sink and ran the hot water, I gathered all the dirty plates.

"I like coach, Mom."

I paused, my hand halfway to the sink. Nicholas kept his back to me, but I could sense the power in his words. A dozen questions streamed through my mind, but I couldn't bring myself to ask any of them.

An endorsement from Nicholas was a powerful thing to have. He didn't give friendship or approval lightly.

"I know," I finally said.

"So what happened?"

"We . . . didn't really react to Landon's situation in the best way."

"Oh."

The silence that followed felt heavy and weighted. I wasn't sure what else to say because I hadn't worked through all of it myself yet. Landon and Starla must have told them after my visit.

"Were you going to ask him to come to the wedding with you?" Nicholas asked, breaking apart my thoughts.

"Ah . . . I don't know." I frowned. "I hadn't thought about it yet."

"You didn't?"

"No."

Nicholas turned around and wrapped me in a hug. "You'll never be alone, Mom. We've always got your back."

Tears brimmed in my eyes as I returned the embrace, then he let go and turned back to the dishes.

I let my heart drop to my feet and flop around. No matter what happened with me and Tanner, I still had the best kids on the planet.

* * *

A flurry of activity met us at the Frolicking Moose.

Thanks to the busy skiing tourist season, Maverick agreed that we could close the dining area to prepare for the wedding, but keep the drive-through open. Wedding â la coffee shop was never something I had imagined for my boys, but they always surprised me.

Dahlia buzzed behind the counter at the drive-through, bundled up with what looked like four long shirts, a pair of yoga pants under sweats, and fingerless gloves that weren't up to dress code. She did, however, have a frosty white hat on top of her head, which gave a wintry feel to her aesthetic. Outside, whirls of snow spun around in spirals.

"Aloha boss lady and wedding party!" Dahlia called to us, but turned back to a customer at the window.

Blake, Nicholas, and Max shuffled in behind me, carrying boxes of various sizes. Garlands, Christmas lights, wrapped presents in shiny silver-and-red foil filled their arms. There would be several more trips for them, but at least it would keep them busy and out of trouble. Even as adults, mischief found them.

Or I should say *especially* as adults.

"Landon is supposed to meet us here," I murmured as I crossed through the shop and into the back room, where the ceremony would happen.

Several days of final preparation—mostly last night— meant we were 60% of the way there. Five hours would be just long enough to doll up this place, get ready ourselves, receive the bride and groom, and coordinate the growing chaos as family arrived from out of town.

Hopefully, Tanner would show up for the wedding and I could talk to him after. Maybe it was for the better, anyway. Now that I'd snapped at him, and he'd held things from me, neither of us were under obligation to fix it before we were ready. Except, I was *so* ready to fix whatever we had.

At this rate, I'd be lucky if I had a chance.

The boys finished unloading all of the boxes, and I organized them into piles according to what needed to be completed first. Dahlia slipped into the back, caught my eye, and crooked a finger. Startled by her worried expression, I set aside another coil of lights and followed her to the counter.

She slipped behind it and stood at the window. A steady line of cars lined up outside. In the corner, Bastian typed away at his computer, brow furrowed into lines. Whatever he did with such intensity, I'd never know.

"Your girl is upstairs." Dahlia pointed up. "She didn't look good. They showed up a few minutes before you. Landon asked if they could go up there for a moment."

"Thank you."

Cold, snowy air pelted my cheeks when I stepped back outside, hooked around the side of the Frolicking Moose, and into the back. A door there led to the loft. I pulled open the door and stepped inside.

A few steps up a spiral staircase later and I heard a quiet sob. With quick, pattering steps I made it all the way up and slipped inside the canted door.

Landon and Starla sat against the far wall. Today, she didn't appear pale or sick, which might be a short-lived miracle or miraculous makeup work. Instead, tear streaks tracked down her face.

The two of them sat side-by-side, hands linked. He murmured something and she laughed under her breath. Seeing no one in imminent danger, I slowed.

Both of them looked up at the same time. Starla's eyes swam with tears again. Relief crossed Landon's face.

"Hey," I said.

"Gratitude," Starla quickly said. She motioned to her face with a swirl of her hand and a half-laugh, half-sob. "I saw the room downstairs and I just . . . I can't believe what you've done for me. For us. There's so much glitter!"

Landon squeezed her hand a little tighter as I advanced into the room.

"Honey, you haven't seen anything yet," I said with a smile.

I lowered onto the ground next to them, pressed my back to the wall near her, and sighed. For almost a full minute, the quiet descended around us. Chaos would fill the rest of the day, so I took the moment to enjoy the stillness with the two stars.

I reached over, grabbed Starla's free hand, dotted with tears, and asked the question that had bothered me all along.

"You're already married, aren't you?"

Landon sighed and tipped his head back.

"Yes."

"We went to a justice of the peace," she whispered, gaze downcast. "In the courthouse."

"Insurance?"

They both nodded. I squeezed Starla's hand. "Good for you."

Her head jerked up, brow furrowed in silent question. I smiled and said, "You needed to get it done to get on his insurance for treatment, and I think that was wise."

"You're not upset?" she whispered.

"Nah." I tossed my hands in the air. "What's a wedding, anyway? A time for everyone else to celebrate the union of two lives. Whether that happens as a party, an actual ceremony, or whatever else, doesn't matter. Still, I think the boys will enjoy being part of it, so I say let's keep it a secret and proceed as planned."

Starla wiped the tears off her cheeks with the back of her hand. She didn't look at me when she murmured, "Thank you, Leslie."

"It's my pleasure."

Her teeth dug into her lower lip before she blurted out, "My mother and father divorced when I was eight. I lived with my Mom and we were so close. So close."

Tears thickened her voice again. She stared straight ahead, but her voice had strength in it as she continued. I sat back to give her space to speak.

"Then she died in the middle of what should have been a pretty routine surgery and they found she'd had an underlying, undiagnosed heart issue they weren't aware of. I was seventeen. My father had moved on, found another wife, and had more children. We weren't in contact. He reached out to me on her death but I didn't answer the calls. We haven't spoken since my tenth birthday, which was the last time he called."

Landon, whether on purpose or not, had pulled her closer —if possible—and tightened the arm around her shoulder. Pride swelled in me for him. My son was a good man. In all this mess, he'd only wanted to make the love of his life happy.

I could easily forgive that.

"So," Starla whispered, clearing her throat, "with the help of friends, I found my way to the preschool where I worked and have been figuring out my life ever since. It's been hard. Money has been a struggle, and sometimes I thought I'd be so lonely I would die."

Her face lifted to look right at Landon. She reached up, a trembling hand pressed to his face.

"Then I met your son."

Her words sent a shiver through me and I had to bite back my own sob. Starla blinked away tears, but they tracked down her face anyway.

Landon stared at her with an adoration I'd never thought possible. An adoration straight from the romance novels Lizbeth constantly shoved under my face. The ones I pretended to hate but secretly craved. The ones I'd never really believed in . . .

. . . until I saw that expression on my son's face.

Not Lizbeth, not romance novels, not any number of

Tanner's kisses could have convinced me more than the unconditional love that washed between them. Tears pricked my eyes. Had I actually witnessed a Christmas miracle?

Sure felt like it.

"Now," Starla cleared her throat, "I have a family and a beautiful wedding, and a diagnosis that I don't have to deal with on my own. I'm just so grateful."

I touched her shoulder. She turned. "Starla, I didn't know your mother, but I have a feeling that she's right here with you already. Can I give you a hug for her?"

Tears dropped down her cheek, thick yet bright. She fell into my arms.

"You absolutely have a family now," I murmured, looking to Landon over the top of her head.

He blinked, eyes red, and nodded.

"And this family is loud," I continued, "often obnoxious, and we are here for *everything*. There is no bill so large, no diagnosis so deep, no treatment so difficult that it could scare us away. You, Landon, and the entire Miller family will get through this together, all right?"

She nodded against my shoulder, her sobs deep and wracking. I stroked her hair back from her face.

"As you so deeply wanted, your secret is safe, and this is on track to be the happiest day of your life—the way it should be for any bride and groom."

Half a minute later, with a bolstering sniffle, she pulled out of my arms. An embarrassed chuckle followed while she mopped her face up.

"I swear, my life isn't always this dramatic."

"We all are," I said with a wave. "Now, shall we fix up your makeup for your wedding?"

Chapter Twenty

TANNER

"Don't care how many times you tell me you're not," Celeste called from the other room. "You're definitely going to the wedding."

I grumbled from the depths of my closet in response.

Grumpiness aside, I stood in the back right corner, where my suit had been sitting in a plastic bag for too many years. It was a bit tight through the shoulders and arms, but it would do for now.

"Not," I shouted back, even as I adjusted my tie.

Of course I wanted to go to Landon's wedding. Not only was I committed to seeing this through, but I needed to clap eyes on Leslie.

We'd been avoiding each other since she kicked me out of Landon's apartment. While I contemplated all the ways I could tell her that I'd been a schmuck, she'd been dealing with a wedding, a secret, and a sick daughter-in-law. I wanted to help her.

But I didn't know how.

Celeste appeared in my closet, an argument clearly poised on her tongue, then fell silent when she saw me. A bemused expression followed. I grinned and spread my hands. "Well? Does your old man clean up okay?"

She advanced inside, messed with my tie, brushed off my shoulders, then smiled. "Better than okay, Dad. You're a silver fox."

"Did you just call me a fox?"

"No." She stepped back a twinkle in her eye. "A silver fox. It's a romance book thing. I heard Dahlia call you that the other day, and Lizbeth gave an emphatic agreement. It's a good thing," she quickly clarified. "It means you're attractive for your age."

"For my age," I muttered. "Why did that have to be tacked on?"

"Ready to go?"

Her brightness didn't distract me from the comment, but I did let it slide. No, I wasn't ready to go. But then, I'd never be ready to face Leslie and the possibility that she wanted nothing to do with me.

"You look lovely." I eyed her dress, but found no fatherly-faults with it. She'd chosen a Christmas-y type. Long sleeves and a skirt to the knees, all in red with a black belt buckle across the front. Cute and, I would have imagined, very in fashion. That was her mother's influence, not mine.

"Thanks." She twirled a little, displaying her favorite boots with fuzzy tops. Golden curls winked in the light as she moved. "I even curled my hair."

"It's beautiful."

"I know. Shall we go?"

How she managed to compliment herself without sounding like an arrogant brat, I'd never know. Celeste had always had that uncanny ability to own herself, even at a young age. At moments like this, I couldn't be more proud to be her father. I stuck out my arm. She smiled and linked hers through it.

"Now," she said with determination. "Let's go grovel to Leslie and watch a wedding. In that order."

* * *

The parking lot of the Frolicking Moose bustled with life.

Cars filled up every spot, spilling onto the road, across the street at the grocery store, and down the row, near the hardware center and the medical clinic. All of Pineville had watched Landon grow up, and like they always did, all of Pineville wanted to be part of the party.

The Frolicking Moose bustled inside. Jingle bells. Tinsel. Twinkle lights. Peppy Christmas music played in the background while a conglomeration of visitors milled around. The moment we stepped into the madness, a bevy of old students gave a collective shout, then surrounded me. Their thunderous claps on the back followed.

Just as quickly, Celeste disappeared, plunging deeper into the madness.

Above all the warm camaraderie, my gaze didn't stop searching for one particular blonde head of hair with dark roots, probably wearing something black and snazzy, with a twinkle in her eye and quick smile.

To my dismay, I couldn't peg Leslie anywhere. Nicholas stood nearby, and Max and Blake buzzed through the room.

While a rock-and-roll version of Jingle Bells played in the background, I managed to extricate from a rowdy conversation between a couple of former football students and sidle toward the back of the room.

A door existed back there that led to an outside porch, and I had a feeling Leslie would be somewhere bustling in between the two. She wasn't the sit-around-and-chat type, not while a party happened.

Following the hunch led me to a less densely-packed area

of the place, where I recognized Lizbeth and her younger sister, Ellie, busy near a punch table. As expected, Leslie lingered not far away, dictating orders rapid-style while she arranged cookies on a platter.

I stopped to watch her, my chest tight.

Lizbeth glanced up and paused. A waterfall of red hair fell over one shoulder. Strapped to her chest was a small baby with equally bright hair on top. The baby slept, cradled close to Mom. Ellie, sensing her sister's change in pace, glanced up. She looked at Lizbeth, then me, then Leslie. Her expression darkened slightly.

Uh oh.

The words began to churn in my head before I could talk myself out of it. *Leslie, can we talk? I need to apologize* or *how are you this beautiful?*

Before Leslie could turn around, a hand hit my shoulder.

"Coach," Max said. I sensed more than saw a couple other bodies with him as he spun me around and faced me back the way I came. "Let's talk."

* * *

The four Miller boys surrounded me outside.

Their breaths came in clouds around them as they half-circled me. The cool air on my cheeks felt good compared to the oppressive feeling of too many people in one place inside. Landon had taken his black jacket off. A perfectly pressed tuxedo stretched across his shoulders. All burdens aside, the kid looked undeniably happy.

Stern, too.

Max, Blake, and Nicholas were in various, but similar, states of disrepair. They'd probably been here all morning helping their mother—something I wished I had done. Now, however, they had the bright eyes of people that had been enjoying themselves. Minus the overtly somber expression.

I'd been anticipating something like this, but it had come sooner than expected.

"So, coach," Landon drawled, arms folded across his chest. "You and our Mom, huh?"

I eyed him. There were so many approaches I could take to responding to that. Obviously these boys wanted to hold the power in this conversation. They were sticking up for their mother—and good for them.

But that's not how this would go down.

"Is that how you want to swing this, Landon?" I lifted one eyebrow. "You know I could beat the crap out of you still?"

Five seconds passed before the veneer cracked. He broke into a smile and laughed, arms dropping to his side.

"Nah, just kidding, coach!"

I laughed and the weird air fractured.

"But seriously," Max cut in. "What's going on with you and Ma? We get veto passes on any man in her life that isn't one of us."

Blake nodded, but his eyes darted to Max first, then back to me. He followed his older brother's lead here. Nicholas remained quiet, watching me. I met his gaze.

"I like your Mom," I said. "I like her a lot. She's funny, compassionate, able to do everything, I think, and happens to really care about you four schmucks."

All of them grinned.

"Are you going to have a problem with it if I make a move?" I asked.

Max's nose scrunched. "Ew."

I rolled my eyes. "Not like *that,* you idiot."

"If you're asking for permission to date our Mom," Landon said, jabbing an elbow in Max's ribcage, "then yes, we grant it."

"Wasn't," I countered, "because she doesn't need it and neither do I, but for your approval, thank you."

"Do you like her?" Blake asked. For being seventeen, he had a surprising poker face. I couldn't even tell if my interest in his Mom grossed or weirded him out. Then again, maybe Celeste had been talking to him.

"I like her a lot."

"Enough to marry her?" Landon asked.

"That's not on the table right now, but I don't have plans to go anywhere anytime soon."

"Then what *is* on the table?" Nicholas asked.

"An official first date, for one. I've been meaning to ask her out forever but it hasn't happened yet. After I woo her with romance, a second date, if she'll have me. Then a third. I'll keep cleaning her house, but at some point I probably won't charge her anymore."

"Dude," Max cried. "*You're* the one that cleaned the house! I called it!" He high-fived Nicholas. "I totally called it. I thought you had people that worked for you. It was never that clean, for the record. I mean, there's no dust."

I nodded, lips pursed to control my smile.

"Okay, so let's say you break her heart," Landon said, then pointed between the four of them. "Who gets to deal with you after that? Oh, right. *All of us.*"

I held up two hands. "Heartbreak is not on my list."

"Better not be," Max mumbled.

"Mom likes you," Blake said, then shrugged when his brothers looked at him. "What? She does. I heard them talking on the phone a few times. She giggled. It was super weird. Plus, she talks to Lizbeth about him."

I grinned. "Yeah?" I asked. "What did she say?"

"Fine," Nicholas broke in, "We'll give our blessing but . . . only after you grovel about the whole thing with Landon."

I sighed. "Yes, there will be groveling involved. Flowers,

too. Another round of expensive chocolates, if that's her thing, but more likely another Irving Berlin movie, or something. I haven't had a chance to gauge her on this yet."

"Groveling?" Blake asked. "What thing with Landon?"

"Coach helped me with a few things," Landon said before I could. His gaze remained on mine. "He didn't tell Mom about me and Starla because I asked him not to. Then Mom found out and was mad. It's all on me." Landon spoke right to me then. "I'm sorry, Coach. I'll help you get her back."

"Knucklehead," I muttered, then smiled. "The last thing I need is *you* getting a woman for me. Please, don't bother. Your mother will decide if I receive redemption or not, all right?"

"Redemption depends on how well you grovel."

The feminine voice came from behind me. As one, the wall of testosterone grinned. Max tilted his head back and started to laugh. I whirled around to find Leslie standing back there, a vision in a black dress, the way I'd expected.

She wore her hair down around her shoulders, but pulled away from her face at the top. Her eyes looked wide, and a bit darker than usual, with thick lashes and a wary expression. Her tasteful black-and-silver dress glided to the ground, hinting at a pair of heels.

As far as mother-of-the-brides went, she was the most stunning I'd ever met. Words failed me. Staring at her in the falling snow, her cheeks heightened with color. Low wolf whistles and long drawls of "oooh, he's in trouble now!" rang behind me.

How long had she been standing there?

"Miller boys," she called without taking her gaze off of mine. "Go inside. It's twenty minutes until the ceremony begins. Landon, find your bride. The rest of you go straighten up and get into your places. I'll be there in just a minute."

Chapter Twenty-One

LESLIE

The moment the door closed behind my sons, the pressured, days-old words came out of me.

"I'm sorry."

Confusion registered first on Tanner's face. He tilted his head to the side, gaze tapered.

"What?"

"I overreacted. I'm sorry. I'm sorry that I snapped at you, made you leave Landon's, didn't call you after, and that it's taken me so long to apologize. I wanted to, I promise. I just . . . I wasn't sure and—"

His eyes widened. "Leslie," he said quietly, "you have nothing to apologize for. I'm the one that should be saying it first."

We fell to an impasse for a full ten seconds. He wanted to apologize first? Did he need to? The past few days had been a rolling question in my mind of whether we both held guilt, or just me.

Apparently, he'd had something of the same battle.

"No, you helped Landon," I said. "You . . . you respected my son and his adult life. I get it. Starla and Landon explained everything. Once I stepped out of my need-to-control-and-make-safety-haze, I learned that you'd actually been helping my son all along. If there was anyone else I would have wanted to be there for him when I couldn't be, it's you."

The intensity of his expression softened slightly.

"Please," he said, still as silky as ever, "don't apologize. You were a concerned mother and I hated every moment of that secret. But—"

"—it was the right thing to do," I finished softly.

Tanner drew in a deep breath, his shoulders expanding. Snow collected in tiny piles, and I wanted to step forward and sweep the flurries off. Wanted to get one step closer to the broad shoulders that had held me so closely and effortlessly at the same time only a few short days ago. My lips burned with the memory.

"I did want to tell you," he said quickly, as if afraid I wouldn't give him a chance to say it when all this finally landed. "I just . . . I also wanted to respect Landon's position. I know how it feels to be a young man with a wife that you want to take care of, and a world you feel like you have to answer to."

My eyebrows lifted, a vague sign of the shock that still permeated my mind. My oldest son was about to be married. He had shucked off his planned path to tread on a totally new one. In comparison, the other kids seemed more stable. Never thought that would happen. Then again, life threw curveballs all the time.

Wonderful curveballs.

Tanner reached out and trapped my wrist in his hand. The gentle pressure of his fingers against the sensitive skin sent a little thrill through me. I forced myself to look back into his eyes.

"I am sorry, Leslie, even if you don't think I need to apologize."

My lips twitched. "Unnecessary forgiveness given."

He smiled. With a tug, he pulled me a little closer. We only touched where his fingers encircled my wrist, but the breathless feeling of being near him went all the way through my lungs.

"If nothing else, we've proven that we *can* fight," he murmured.

I drew closer to him on my own, pulled by a musky scent. The heat of his arms. The emptiness of the days without him that reverberated through the air between us. I pulled in a little breath.

"Fighting isn't always a bad thing," I murmured.

The subtle reminder of our previous conversation sent me for a whirl. Not only did it feel *so good* to be heard again, but to understand the truth in what he said. Yes, we had a fight. A short one, and hardly a fight. More a strong disagreement. Those weren't the worst thing.

Coming back together?

The best.

He closed the distance between us. His arms wrapped around me as I tilted my head back to stare into his eyes. The feeling of his thumb tracing along the back of my rib cage sent a shiver through me.

Snow drifted lazily around us. The sound of Christmas music pealed from inside, along with laughter. The Frolicking Moose was packed with all the people I cared the most about. All of Pineville had come to show their love and support. Yet now that Tanner and I had reconciled, I couldn't wait for all of it to be over.

"It's New Year's Eve tonight," I whispered. My gaze dropped to his lips, then back to his eyes. A stormy look had grown there, and I felt giddy at his hunger.

"Oh?" he drawled.

"I hear that it's really bad luck to start a new year out without a kiss."

"I've heard that too."

His arms tightened around me. I tamped down the rush of near-giggly-hysteria. "Max and Nicholas have friends in town. Apparently, they're going to go meet up with them to celebrate the new year and Blake is tagging along. Seems like I'll be all alone tonight."

"Well." He leaned back a little. "We can't have that, can we? The mother of the groom shouldn't celebrate her son's nuptials alone."

I smiled. "Not at all."

He lowered until our faces were so close our breath mingled. A moment away from my lips, he stopped.

"Before we do anything else," he murmured, his breath a warm caress on my cheek. "May I ask you something I've wanted to ask you since we first started this whole adventure?"

"What's that?"

"Leslie Hill, will you go on a date with me?"

"I don't know," I drawled, my hands finding their way to his neck. "What do you have planned?"

The tips of my fingers rubbed against the smooth skin beneath his jaw. I missed the stubble from Christmas morning. He shivered when I wrapped my arms all the way around his neck.

"The most romantic date you'll ever have."

"Christmas was pretty romantic."

"Ah, but it wasn't a date."

My lips twitched. "Fair, but that's still a heavy promise."

"Is it?" That intriguing eyebrow lifted. I pulled closer to him. His gaze darted to my lips. Our breath kissed, so close I could feel his heartbeat against mine. "My daughter has been helping me. She's taught me the way of the romantic."

"Kissing me under the snow?" I murmured. "I think you've got romance down."

Our lips collided, magnets that could no longer be denied. His warm hands splayed against my back and slid higher, holding me close as he tipped me back. My hair fell away from my neck in a cascade, allowing a cool breath of air to calm my frazzled skin.

When his lips slanted over mine, hungry and eager and happy, I felt something settle all the way into my bones.

Romance.

Just like I had all along.

* * *

The ceremony came together with utter perfection.

Landon returned to Starla's side after his attempt to act like the man of the house and hadn't left. Her energy remained high despite the constant flow of people to meet and greet. I watched her closely, like a new mama with a baby bird ready to leave the nest. She sent me warm looks of gratitude with every new iced coffee or treat I brought her way to keep her energy high.

By the time they officially tied the knot in front of half of Pineville, the gentle fall of snow had turned into a whopper of a storm. Slush turned to ice on the roads. Snow trucks hissed by, plowing mounds into mountains on the street corners.

The general ambience of the party waned as people made their way home, eager to return before the descending blizzard trapped them at the coffee shop.

Landon and Starla slipped away first, heading to a cozy little cabin tucked not too far away for their honeymoon. I'd packed a bag of her prescriptions, anti-nausea meds, some over-the-counter pain medicine, and a few other mom touches that I'd shoved into her hands as they left.

She'd wrapped her thin arms around me, promised to see me soon, and started her new life with my son.

I'd probably like her better than him within a year.

Dahlia, Katelyn, my boys, and Lizbeth helped me pick up the worst of the garbage around the shop. In the quiet aftermath of the party, my nerves soothed. Tanner kept drawing my gaze from the other side of the room, where he cleaned up with professional efficiency.

When the song shifted to one we had danced to on Christmas Eve, he looked up, caught my gaze. His expression softened, then he winked.

My heart smoldered.

"Storm is growing too fast," I said to Dahlia, then glanced to Bastian, who gathered the last of the empty cups set aside. "Get back to your RV before you can't see, all right? I'll come back early and clean before customers arrive in the morning."

Dahlia hesitated, then nodded. "Thanks, boss lady. I've been nervous about getting back. Jayson's grandmother's ranch where we're parking the RV this winter is so far from here and a little treacherous when snow falls."

"Go and be safe. Text me when you get there."

Bastian sent me a nod and held out his hand for Dahlia. She accepted, and the two of them dodged into the storm, jackets zipped tight and hoods up.

I sent Blake, Nicholas, and Max on their way to their local friends, thankfully not far from our house. Blake coaxed Celeste into joining them. They'd have no problem getting home afterward, or in the morning after they finished playing video games all night.

Finally.

Tanner and I remained alone in the Frolicking Moose.

Through a maze of chairs, glittering streamers, and lines of tinsel, Tanner crossed the room and pulled me into his arms. Christmas music played gently in the background. I closed my eyes and leaned against him, content to let him take my weight for a bit. He hummed, swaying us back and forth.

When he linked his fingers through mine and stepped back to slide an arm around my waist, I instantly fell into step.

"The mother of the groom," he murmured, "should get to dance at her son's wedding."

"Landon is a terrible dancer."

"Then let me sweep you off your feet."

"Is this the romantic date you dreamed up?" I asked, casting a wry glance at the empty sheet cake tray on the other side of the room, a demolished wedding cake stand that once held a 5-tiered beauty made of marbled pink roses from JJ's bakery. All sugar had disappeared from the Frolicking Moose, and I could attribute 75% of the responsibility to my three youngest offspring.

At least they wouldn't burn that energy off at my house tonight.

"No." Tanner scoffed. "Our first date is happening tonight after all of this. See?" He nodded toward the front of the shop, where brown paper bags sat on the ground near the door. "I've already been to the grocery store for everything we'll need."

"Oooh? So efficient."

He winked. "I had sufficient motivation."

"I can't wait."

"Good." He frowned at the door, where wind blasted by. "We should get going. Celeste will be safe with Max and Nicholas . . . right?"

"I wouldn't go so far as to say that," I murmured as I slipped into my coat, "but I will say that my old-soul son Blake is the best driver I've ever met, and he's down-to-earth, just like me. So she's safe with Blake and Nicholas will temper Max."

He paused. "I meant in general."

"Oh. Um, yes."

Only slightly mollified, he took my hand and we stepped outside.

After I locked the Frolicking Moose behind me, Tanner wrapped an arm around my shoulders and we plunged into the storm together. Sort of like I left my old life behind me.

Now, it was time to walk into something better.

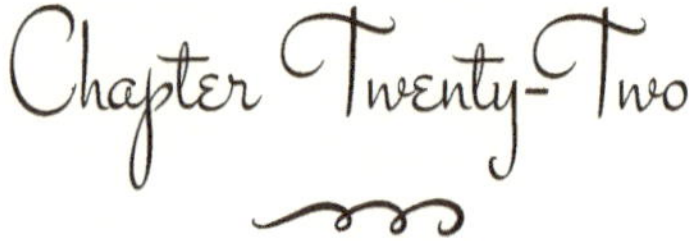

Chapter Twenty-Two

TANNER

Leslie stared at me in utter disbelief later that night.

"You're kidding. You want me to do what?"

The wedding had roughed her up a bit. Mascara gathered under her eyes, which looked drawn from a long day, and her stomach growled. I didn't recall seeing her eat anything all day. Now, her home felt frigid cold because I didn't have the forethought to come back early to start a fire.

Outside, the blizzard whitened into a literal frenzy.

I pointed past the kitchen and to her room, as serious as I had ever been. "Go get into the pair of much-too-big sweats that I saw on the floor the other day. Then some other shirt that's really comfortable. Then come out here. The date will be ready."

She eyed me, clearly at a loss, but was too tired to fight. Something I'd also banked on.

With a sigh she muttered, "Fine. But how anything can be the height of romance in those nasty old sweats, I'll never figure out."

I grinned and headed for the brown paper bags.

"Trust and faith," I called. "Trust and faith."

Her door shut on another muttering, and I chuckled to myself. Ten minutes later, I emerged from the guest bathroom wearing my most comfortable workout pants and my favorite ratty old shirt.

Leslie stepped into the kitchen and I burst out laughing. "Well?"

She spread her arms and I doubled over. Not only had she donned the requested sweats, but a ridiculously large tie-dye shirt that hit her mid thigh. She'd pulled her hair up into a way-too-high ponytail that sent her locks almost onto her forehead, and she'd wiped the makeup off her face. On her feet were a pair of slippers that had seen better days. Eyes wet from laughing, I motioned to the slippers.

"What *are* those?"

She held one up, twirling it in a circle around her finger. "They used to be monsters. A Christmas present from five-year-old Max, thank you."

"You've had those for fifteen years?"

She smirked. "Mom-power. They happen to be quite comfortable, thank you very much. The monster face has rubbed of and the soles are threadbare and cracked, but it doesn't really matter. I love them."

I rolled my lips to quell the next laugh. She looked ridiculous—and perfect. I motioned between us.

"Stage one of the most romantic date is complete. We're in comfortable clothes. That's very romantic."

She held up a hand in silent capitulation. Meanwhile, I pointed her to the dining room, where several things waited on top of the table.

"Is this dinner?" she asked as she approached.

"If you want it to be." I came up behind her and put my hands on her shoulders. "Any romantic date has wine, right? I figured that would be a necessity, and Celeste tells me that's your favorite."

Leslie grinned when I motioned to a bottle of red across the way. "Well played, sir," she drawled. "And the tub of ice cream next to it?"

"Max said your favorite was mint chocolate chip." I fake-gagged. "Gross, but because I care about you, I'll deal. You will get that entire tub to yourself."

"Best date ever. Which is why there's a Moose Tracks next to it, I assume?" The tenor of her voice made me think she held back a laugh, but I still stood behind her and couldn't be sure.

"You got it, baby."

"And the rotisserie chicken, container of mashed potatoes, and coleslaw all sitting next to the ice cream?"

"I'm starving," I said, "and I take clean up very seriously. Do you see this entire spread? Each of us will only need one fork, and one spoon while we watch your favorite Christmas movie—which is A Miracle on 34th Street—because that's what Blake told me. Also, I put a blanket next to all of it because once we're done eating, we'll snuggle on the couch."

Leslie opened her mouth to say something, but stopped. She closed her mouth, opened it again, but nothing came out.

"Well?"

She sighed. "You're right. Sweats, being comfortable, a glass of wine, no-clean-up-dinner, my favorite ice cream, the best movie in the whole world, and snuggling with you is *the* most romantic date I've ever been on."

I stepped back, arms held high, then bowed.

"Don't tell Lizbeth, but I concede. Romance pretty much rocks."

I smashed a quick kiss on her, but she wound her arms around me and all thoughts of quick dissolved. Minutes later, her protesting stomach urged me to push her away. I broke the kiss and sent her a look of promise.

Leslie sent me a smoky smile, then held up a spoon.

"Shall we begin with the ice cream?"

THE END

Authors Note

Ever since the first moment that Leslie appeared in LOVESICK with our beloved Lizbeth, I've wanted to tell her story.

She gave me the unique opportunity to unleash my inner mom (so few of my characters give me that chance!) and the wit that having children follows.

Also, who doesn't love a silver fox story?!

I hope you enjoyed Leslie and Tanner's story. I know that I had a huge blast doing it, and they pushed me right into the Christmas spirit.

As always, I want to send out a huge *thank you* to my team for all they do for me, my family for enduring my weird habits (yes, a lot of people write strange post-it note messages to themselves and color code them on the wall, thank you *very* much!) and to my readers for sticking with me through a busy writing year.

You are all the reason I love this work so much, and you make the books worth it.

MUAH!

Protect Me

A SNEAK PEEK FROM BOOK 9

KATELYN

A pair of glaring red lights jerked in front of my car, nearly clipping my front bumper. On reflex, I stomped on my brakes.

My car skidded to a stop seconds before it would have slammed into an obnoxiously lifted truck with chrome rims. With a hitch that size, it would have completely totaled my front end. With a belch of black smoke, the truck scampered down the mountain highway again, oblivious

"Jerk face!" Knuckles white on the steering wheel, I loosened my clenched jaw. "May you get fined and not be able to pay the bill, you arrogant, slimy newt!"

Not that it mattered.

The ring of my phone echoed through my car, distracting me from my rage. With a deep exhale, I hit the *accept* button on my car dashboard. The dulcet tone of my best friend, Vinita, followed.

"Kaaaaaatelyn!"

"Hey," I breathed, relieved to hear her voice. "Please tell me something happy about you and Zayne. How are baby preparations going?"

Concern laced her tone. "Uh oh. What's going on?"

My nostrils flared as I hesitated to respond. Vinita was only a few short months away from delivering a set of twins: a boy and a girl. Not being at her side during this momentous time in her life was hard enough, but dealing with the breaking down of my day made everything seem worse.

"Talk to me," Vinita said when my silence continued. Realizing I wouldn't be able to squirrel out of it, I gave in.

"It's just . . . today was the worst day ever. I dropped three drinks at work this morning, the espresso machine stopped working, Dahlia called in sick so I had to do the morning rush myself and I still don't know the drinks really well. It took me forever to do anything, so the line built up. People got all passive-aggressive and huffy. To make it worse . . . " I sighed. ". . . last night . . . I-I couldn't get any sleep."

The hastily stated final sentence was a lie.

Sort of.

I couldn't get any sleep had always been code between the two of us for *the nightmares are coming back.* Vinita and I always had our own kind of language.

"Again?" she asked softly.

Tears filled my eyes, but I blinked them back. "Yeah, but it's fine." My voice sounded hoarse for just a moment, so I cleared my throat. "Really."

"Katelyyyyn!"

The sharp edges of her reprimand made me laugh—she sounded just like her mother, Vanhi.

"I'm fine, really." A sniffle punctuated my insistence. I pulled off the side of the road, chest heavy. "I just . . . I don't know what triggered the nightmares this time, but I'll figure it out and work through it. It's been a year or more . . . I kind of thought I was over this already."

"You always do."

I snorted. "Maybe healing never ends?"

"Of course it does. It's been five years," she said softly. "Look how far you've come. You've worked so hard in therapy, Kate, but that doesn't mean healing is absolute. You'll slip back into memories every now and then and you'll fight your way back to the light. I'm here for you."

Having a Marriage and Family Therapist as a best friend had been a lifesaver for *so* many reasons.

I swallowed again. "I know. Thank you for the reminder. So, what's up?"

Sighing, she said, "I had a favor to ask, but now I realize it may not be the best time."

"No! Give me the favor." My hands flapped with my insistence. "Give me something that I can do to help you. I can't be in New York with you and your babies and it's *killing me* to be this far apart."

"I know!" she wailed. "I've missed you so much. Once the babies are born, Zayne will fly you out to visit. Amma will be back in Bangalore after then anyway, so I'll need the help. Within a week, you'll be so tired of living with me and the babes, you'll wish to be back there."

"Never!"

"I love hearing that," she cried. "Anyway, something is wrong with Vikram and we need your help. Amma is a mess."

My wrung-out heart twisted at the sound of her older brother's name. It resounded like a dull echo in my brain.

Vikram.

"Vikram?" I whispered.

"We can't get a hold of him."

Vikram, the hero of my childhood. The ruggedly dashing young man that became a wild adult. Vikram, the love of my life. The light in my dark childhood sky. The lover of women and carelessness and impulsivity. My breath came fast just thinking about him, the man I intentionally hadn't thought of in almost five years.

The man I'd never have.

"Tell me more," I said quickly, because more than that would have been a gasp. When the mention of his name set my heart to racing, I already knew I was in big trouble.

"He was supposed to have a surgery a few days ago. Amma spoke to him right before, and he seemed fine. Said that Bastian was going to drive him home afterward. We haven't heard from him since then."

"You think he's okay?"

"I hope so, but he's not answering calls, emails, or text messages. Bastian hasn't answered his phone, either. Awhile ago, Vikram said something about Bastian getting a new job as a fire supervisor, or something. I can't remember."

Stress tugged at her voice, making the vowels slightly longer than usual. I'd do anything that Vinita asked of me. We were sisters from the past. Our childhood had combined in all ways as we grew up next door to each other, intertwining like fate meant to braid us together.

Without Vinita and the safety of her family, there would be no Katelyn today.

"Do you want me to go to his apartment?" I asked.

Her voice elevated slightly. "Would you mind?" Although still bright, I read the hesitation there. Vinita, of anyone, would understand my hesitation, my rules for men. I had three of them.

1. Never alone.

2. Never stranded.

3. Never unaware.

In the last five years, my rules never failed to keep me safe. I'd applied them to every unattached man that I'd met and had never strayed once from the boundary lines.

So far, safe.

Going to Vikram's apartment meant I'd need to go alone. Sure, I could bring a friend, but Vikram wouldn't open up.

Although I hadn't seen him in over five years, even I knew that. Vikram of the past few years was . . . lost.

If any man were safe enough to break one of my iron-clad rules, Vikram would be the *only* one.

"I wouldn't mind checking on him at all," I said, and managed to mean it.

"Really?" she drawled.

"Really."

"Listen," her voice softened, "you know you're safe with Vik, right? That he wouldn't . . . I mean you grew up with him. He thinks of you like a little sister. At least, he used to. You know, when he came home more often and didn't try to shut the world out all the time."

A heavy lump rose in my throat, but I swallowed it back. "Yes, I know."

"Still, if you don't—"

"It's fine, Vinita. Really. I'm happy to help however I can, especially with you so far away. Being near your brother will be the next-best thing to being close to you."

"I miss you," Vinita said. "I wish you could be here for the babies."

"Me too."

I smiled, warmed by the amusement in her voice. Vinita and Vikram had been raised in the US, but kept ties with their family members in South India all their life. Now, Vinita lived in upper New York State with her husband Zayne in an adorable house with a white-picket fence nestled in a neighborhood. She would have her babies without me there to welcome them to the world.

It stung, but what could be done?

"I'll go check on him now," I said. "Text me his address? I just got off work and . . . don't really have anything filling the rest of my day."

"You are the best!" she cried, and the relief in her voice

made everything worth it. "Thank you, Kate. I'll text you as soon as I hang up. Let me know what happens okay?"

I'll fall in love with him all over again, I thought. *That's what will happen. I'll fall in love for a second time with the one man that I love, hate, and can't have.*

"Of course," I said instead. "Talk to you soon."

I ended the call and stared straight ahead with the sinking feeling that I'd just altered the course of the rest of my life.

What had I just gotten myself into?

* * *

Ready for more? Please visit www.katiecrossbooks.com to grab your paperback copy today.

Also by Katie Cross

The Health and Happiness Society

Bon Bons to Yoga Pants (Lexie)

I Am Girl Power (Megan)

You'll Never Know (Rachelle)

Hear Me Roar (Bitsy)

What Was Lost (Mira)

The Health and Happiness Society Collection

Finding Anna

Coffee Shop Series

Coffee Shop Girl

Lovesick

Runaway

Fighter

Shy Girl

Wild Child

Smoke and Fire

Clean Sweep

Protect Me